THE
NAVIGATOR'S
DAUGHTER

THE
NAVIGATOR'S
DAUGHTER

A Kat Lawson Mystery

Nancy Cole Silverman

First edition

ISBN: 978-1-68512-090-0

Cover art by Level Best Designs

This book was professionally typeset on Reedsy.
Find out more at reedsy.com

To Dad
Forever my navigator

Praise for The Navigator's Daughter

"Silverman spins a spellbinding tale of intrigue, family, and the complexities of war. Seeped in historical detail and set against the backdrop of post-war Hungary, *The Navigator's Daughter* takes the reader on a journey that's as much about self-discovery and the bonds of love and loyalty as it is about the past."—Wendy Tyson, author of *A Dark Homage*

"Investigative journalist Kat Lawson is on a mission to fulfill her father's dying wish, but when the secrets she uncovers take a dangerous turn, Kat worries if she'll make it home in time to tell her father 'Mission accomplished.' Silverman's *The Navigator's Daughter*, packed with emotion and intrigue, promises to keep readers turning pages."—Lynn Chandler Willis, award-winning author of the Ava Logan Series, and the Shamus Award finalist, *Wink of an Eye*

"Silverman's tale of a daughter's journey to discover her father's past held me totally captivated and unable to put this riveting novel down. Kat Lawson is equal parts wounded, loyal, and brave, with a healthy dose of skepticism—the kind of heroine I would love to meet in person."—Annette Dashofy, *USA Today* bestselling author of the Zoe Chambers mystery series.

Chapter One

Tuesday, July 16, 1996

Phoenix, Arizona

My father called before ten a.m. I remember because he said he had just been to the mailbox, and mail at the senior center comes early. Before the summer sun has a chance to sear the dusty, desert floor and the July temperatures begin to climb into triple digits. Today's forecast was for a hundred-and-thirteen, but Phoenicians say it's a dry heat, and the locals don't seem to mind.

"They found my plane!" Dad sounded like a kid at Christmas. Not unusual for him, he was always upbeat, at least before cancer had zapped him of his strength and left him living with an oxygen tank—and as a former shell of himself.

"The B-24?" I was skeptical. "The one you bailed out of more than fifty years ago?" My Dad and I are close, and I've always had a kind of sixth sense about him. Growing up, I had heard the story at least a dozen times of how he had jumped out of his plane or the PG version of it anyway. I couldn't imagine any other aircraft that would have had him so excited.

"I have a letter. You need to see it, Kat. Your mom's gone out to get her hair done, and there's something I want to show you. Come by. I'll make coffee."

"Dad, I—"

"Don't give me any crap about chasing some story, Kat. It's not like you're working for the newspaper anymore. And if you're planning to meet up with that ex-husband of yours, that's a waste of time."

"He's not my ex, Dad. At least, not yet, anyway." I bristled at the thought. Difficult as things had been with Josh, I still hated to admit failure. My folks had been married fifty-five years, and I had barely managed three.

"Just get yourself over here, will you? No excuses. You'll understand when I show you why. It's important. Something you're going need to see to believe."

I had a dozen reasons why I didn't have time to stop by my parent's condo that morning. The very least was that I had an appointment with both the pool man and gardener that Josh had forgotten to pay. And I had a call-back for a job interview that afternoon with a small start-up newspaper that I knew wouldn't amount to anything. Not once they learned I had been let go from my previous position for what the paper had called an *inappropriate* workplace relationship with a colleague. In my opinion, the only thing inappropriate about my relationship was that the paper had fired me, and not my boss. He was Teflon, a name they needed to keep, and me…not so much. Even worse, *The Phoenix Gazette,* where I had worked, was owned by the only other paper in town, *The Arizona Republic.* And with my now sullied reputation, I had little hope anyone in the city would hire me.

But for whatever it was worth, I still needed to make an effort and follow through with the interview. My personal life had fallen apart. Dad was dying. My mother was in a deep state of denial and had become a shopaholic. Dad had asked me to take both the credit cards and car keys away from her, and since I was the only child, taking care of my parents was up to me.

* * *

My folks lived across town, about thirty minutes from me. The Roadrunner was a planned retirement community with both assisted and independent living facilities. Years ago, Dad had bought a small two-bedroom patio villa that faced out onto a desert-scaped arroyo with Palo Verde trees and lots of blooming cactus. And so far—despite his advancing cancer—he and Mom had maintained a relatively independent lifestyle.

Dad was sitting on the patio when I arrived. I could see his rounded shoulders with his head bowed from above the low wall that faced the walkway. He looked up and waved as I approached.

"Don't get up." I went around to the front door and let myself in—the smell of burnt coffee permeated their small apartment. I immediately unplugged the coffee pot, poured myself a half cup, and filled the remainder with water. "Want any?" I hollered.

"Already had some. Don't need no more." Dad stood in the patio doorway, shaky, a portable oxygen tank at his side and a large mailing envelope in his hand. "Getting too hot out there."

I nodded to the dining room. "How about we sit inside at the table? It's a lot cooler."

I waited while Dad shuffled across the room and folded his thin, frail frame into one of the cane back chairs at the table.

"You're not going to believe this, Kat. Look what I got in the mail today." Dad took out a thin weathered strip of aluminum from within the mailer and handed it to me. "Know what this is?"

I had no idea.

"Piece of skin from my plane. The old girl must have glided on after we bailed out. Letter here's from a fellow who says he found her in Tomasai, Hungary."

"Who?" I asked.

"I don't know. Some guy named Sandor Zselnegeller. Says he's a researcher. Been looking into the remains of old, downed warplanes since he was a kid. Seems my plane landed in pretty good shape. He was able to give the tail numbers to the DOD, and they matched it up with their records and put him in touch with our group's historian."

"What group historian?" The whole idea some stranger was writing to my dad, trying to convince him that after fifty years, he had found the remains of a B-24—the very same bomber my dad had jumped out of—seemed more than a little far-fetched.

"The historian for our Bomb Group. We keep up, you know. Reunions. Christmas cards. They have a roster of us all."

"I see. And you think this Sandor fellow got your name and address from them?"

"Says he did. Why would he lie?"

My reporter's mind kicked in, and I suspected a scam. My last couple of assignments with the *Gazette* had dealt with seniors who had been ripped off by grifters, con artists who didn't care if they took a senior's last dollar. To my mind—whatever this was—it smacked of the same and likely was some flimflam artist's attempt to get into my dad's pocket. I wasn't about to sit back and watch my father be a victim.

"I don't know, Dad. This all feels a little sketchy, don't you think?"

"I knew you'd say that, but look at this." From within the envelope, my father took out two pieces of paper. The first was a typed letter from Sandor, and the second, a yellowed piece of newsprint, dated March 3, 1945. "This is from a local paper in Tamasi, the day after we bailed."

I couldn't read the headline or the paper's story since they were written in Hungarian. But, a black and white photo of a downed and partially demolished B-24 included with the article had caught my father's eye. He was convinced that the bomber that lay belly-flopped in a field was the same plane he and his crew had bailed out of that fateful day.

In addition to introducing himself, Sandor's letter included a translation of the article. The plane had crashed into the field on March 2, 1945, and later caught fire when a young man, desperate for heating fuel, tried to siphon gas from the wing and was severely burned. The paper had run the article the following day as a warning to others.

I picked up the metal strip my father believed to be part of his plane. For all I knew, the scarred piece of metal I held in my hand could have been cut from a can of lima beans the week before and doctored to look distressed with dark scrapings and what looked like it might have been a bullet hole. But my father didn't think so.

I took a sip of coffee and put the mug down. The taste was cold and bitter. "Okay, let's say this is real—"

"Of course, it's real, Kat." Dad slammed his hand on the table, an unusual reaction for a man who seldom raised his voice. "Why else do you think I'd call you? There's a story here, and I need you to go and find out what happened."

"What do you mean, go and find out? Find out what?"

"I'm home." Mom walked in the door before Dad could answer, a bag of groceries in one hand, a wheelie cart with more behind her, and her hair perfectly coiffed in a grey French twist.

"Ahh, the forever beautiful silver fox has returned." Dad smiled. After all these years, he still grinned like a schoolboy when my mother walked into a room.

Lynn Lawson had that effect on men, she always had, and Dad loved it. Tall and stately with a sense of grace about her. Growing up, I used to wish I was more like her, but I've never been a girly girl. I'm slim like my dad, and at forty-five, my hair is salt-and-pepper like his and boyishly short. Easy to keep.

"You here for lunch, Kat? Or because your dad wants you to listen to his story?" Mom kissed my father on the top of his head then sashayed into the kitchen, where she placed the bag on the counter.

"You know about this?" I waved the scrap of metal mockingly above my head.

"Your father showed it to me before I went out this morning. It's not the first time we've heard rumblings about his plane."

I got up from the table to help Mom put away the groceries. "What have you heard before? And why haven't you mentioned anything?"

"The DOD gave us a heads-up awhile back. They said ever since the Iron Curtain went down five years ago, there've been several organizations who've reached out to them with information about downed planes. I suppose if the DOD thinks the letter's legit, it must be."

"Maybe so, but I'm not so sure. This Sandor fellow, has he asked Dad for anything? Money, maybe?"

"I can hear you," Dad yelled at me from his seat at the table. "And no, he didn't ask for money."

5

I glanced back at my father. He refused to look at me and stared at the letter. My skepticism was unappreciated.

"How's he doing?" I whispered to my mom. The living, dining, and kitchen were all one big open area, but Dad couldn't hear if I kept my voice low.

"He's fine," Mom said. "And he's going to be just fine. Right now, he's fascinated with this letter that came in the mail this morning. Next week he won't remember it, but for the time being, he thinks someone's found his plane, and he's all excited."

"Seems strange, that's all. I mean, why now? After all these years. You need to be careful. There's been a lot of seniors ripped off lately with some pretty cagey schemes. Whatever you do, do *not* let him send any money."

"I wouldn't worry." My mother pulled a bottle of white wine from the bag, then paused in front of the refrigerator.

"He wants me to go," I said.

"Will you?" Mom put the wine in the refrigerator and shut the door.

I was stunned.

"What? Go to Hungary? Are you serious?"

"Steve?" Mom leaned against the refrigerator door. "I think you need to explain to Kat why this is so important to you that she goes."

Chapter Two

O f all my dad's stories, the story about what happened to him *after* he bailed out of his plane was one I had never heard. He had simply brushed over those few weeks when he had been missing in action and never mentioned it. Instead, if asked, he talked about his crew, his buddies, who, even fifty years later, he felt were like brothers.

Growing up, I knew some of my dad's *brothers*. There were reunions with Dad's squadron at the Air Force Academy in Colorado every couple of years. And as the only child of only-onlys—as neither of my parents had siblings—my extended family included the kids from my father's crew who, for a time, became like cousins. We would gather as families for formal functions, followed by picnics in the Rockies and lots of games and storytelling.

The stories were never about the war or any serious scrapes they had experienced. If the men had those conversations, they had them alone at the bar and away from the women and children. But there were a lot of humorous stories I remembered. Particularly those they'd tell while we kids sat around a campfire and toasted marshmallows for smores while the men roasted each other for our entertainment. Like when my dad and Nick Farkas, his tail gunner, were in Italy and tried to bargain with a local farmer and his daughter for some fresh figs and nearly ended up getting shot.

Nick, forever the ladies' man, had spotted a farmer's daughter riding her horse through a field of fig trees. He thought the young woman with long blonde hair flowing about her shoulders looked like Lady Godiva and instantly fell in love. Which, according to my father, Nick did as frequently as the sun rose. Nick convinced my dad that they should approach the girl. But the girl's father, who didn't speak a word of English, wasn't at all happy when he saw his daughter talking to two young American airmen, and even less so when Nick tried to negotiate with the farmer for some of his figs.

Nick's Italian wasn't much beyond a few hand gestures, and he thought the word for fig was figlia. He even kissed the tips of his fingers while talking about the fruit. The farmer, of course, was insulted. He believed Nick was talking about his daughter and threatened to shoot both Nick and my dad and turned his dogs loose on them. My dad said he and Nick never ran so fast in their lives. It wasn't until Nick and my dad returned to the airbase and recounted their adventure with Frank Rizzo, another member of their crew, that Nick realized his mistake. Rizzo spoke fluent Italian and couldn't stop laughing. Figlia meant daughter, and the farmer had had enough of airmen ogling his daughter. After the war, Nick bought a small grocery store in Pennsylvania, and whenever he and Dad would get together at reunions, they would still talk about what a close call that was.

As far as whatever happened to my father's plane or what happened to him after he bailed out, Dad never said. And my mother didn't want to talk about it. She didn't think it wise to fill a young girl's head with war stories. She preferred to talk about how my dad's graduation from flight school in Texas had left them with just enough time to get married before he left for Italy. How all the town's people in Port Orchard, Washington, came together and decorated the church with flowers from their gardens and how beautiful their wedding was.

"Sit down, Kat." Dad tapped the table softly. "And, Lynn, if there's another bottle of wine in the fridge that's chilled, get it."

Mom put three wine glasses on the table and sat down. I asked if he should be drinking, and Dad put his hand up and shushed me. Didn't matter. He had a story to tell.

"The day we were shot down, we had been assigned to bomb the rail lines in Linz, Austria. Our mission was to destroy Hitler's supply line. There must have been a hundred of our planes in the sky that morning. We all knew this wasn't going to be any milk run, and some of us wouldn't be coming home. It was our thirteenth mission, and we jokingly called it our Lucky 13th. Most crews didn't make it beyond eleven or twelve, and believe me when I say, not one of us aboard that day wasn't calculating the risks." Dad paused and took a sip of his wine. "We came in over the Alps, and as we approached the target, the Germans began firing their anti-aircraft guns. Our group swooped in low, and we got hit coming in. Lost one engine, but we were still able to drop our bombs on the rail yard. Took out a whole lot of rail and a few cars, too. Then as we were trying to climb away, we took a second hit. Lost our number two engine on the same wing. We were in trouble. Couldn't get altitude and had to pull out of formation."

I took a sip of my wine and swallowed hard.

"Our pilot, Bob Rupert, was struggling to keep us level. And Mark, our co-pilot, was yelling for us to throw everything out that wasn't bolted down. Alarm bells were going off, and the wind was ripping through the fuselage. Sounded like a hurricane and threatened to pull you out of the plane if you weren't strapped in. Even so, we started tossing everything we could out the bomb bay doors. Then Rupert got on the intercom and told me to find a way out. Either that, or we were going down right in the middle of that nest of Nazis beneath us. I plotted a course toward Pecs, Hungary, behind the Russian lines, about three hundred miles south of us."

"And you thought you could get there?"

"On a wing and a prayer." Dad clicked his wine glass to mine and took a drink. "Earlier that morning, we had been briefed that the Russians had control of everything south of Lake Balaton. I knew there was an airfield in Pecs, and if we could make it that far, the Russians would see us back home. Beyond that—we prayed."

I looked at my mother. "Did you know all this?"

"We didn't talk about it in those days. And when your dad came home, there was too much to do. But lately, since the Air Force first notified your father that a letter was coming about his plane, he's shared some of what happened with me." Mom played with the stem of her glass. "Go on, Steve, tell Kat what happened after you bailed out."

Dad took another long sip of his wine and then began the second half of his story—the part I had never heard.

"Looking back, it's a miracle we made it as far as we did. We were flying low, maybe five-thousand feet, and we had absolutely no cloud cover. I remember looking down at an airfield with German fighters at the ready. They could have come up and taken us out, but I think they could see we were doomed and didn't want to waste the fuel. As it was, we limped into Hungary. Cleared the Kőszeg Mountains by maybe five hundred feet. It felt like you could reach out and touch them. And then we started to have engine trouble. The outside engine on our right wing died, and the inside engine looked like she was about to go. We were just north of Lake Balaton. Bob sounded the alarm and told us to prepare to jump. He didn't think he could keep her in the air. We knew the Germans were below, and I was afraid we'd spin out of control if we didn't jump." Dad drained his glass and signaled my mother for another.

"So you jumped? Into the middle of German-occupied territory?" I asked.

"Didn't have much choice, and I wasn't alone. I was in the bombardier's seat, the nose cone, so I got out first. Nick Farkas, our tail gunner, and Bill Brandley, our engineer, followed. We were close to the lake, and when I didn't see any other chutes, we figured Bob had been able to feather the plane's engines long enough to get the plane across the lake. Can't say I was surprised. He may have been the youngest of our crew, but he was some hotshot pilot. Before the war, Rupert used to wrestle steers for some Texas rodeo circuit. He used to say the controls of that old bird were tougher than the steers he'd hogtied. Lucky for him and the other seven members of our crew, they made it across the lake and bailed out behind the Russian lines and not into German-held territory like Bill, and Nick, and me. Let me tell you, the three of us were scared. If the Germans had seen us, they would have shot us in our chutes. Sometimes you just get plain lucky, Kat."

My mother filled my father's wine glass and sat back down.

"Worst part of it was Nick broke his leg and couldn't walk. The three of us together were sitting ducks, but neither Bill nor I were about to leave him. We took out our forty-fives and huddled together. If the Germans found us, they weren't going to take us alive. Strange as it may sound, before that day, I'd never fired my gun. I had qualified alright, but up until I bailed out, I hadn't needed to shoot anyone or anything."

"Steve," Mom interrupted, "get to the point. You're going into too much detail. Kat doesn't need to know all that." My mother was always the orchestrator of conversation. If my father started to talk about the war, she would inevitably find a way to turn the conversation into something she deemed more pleasant. "Tell her about Adolph."

"Adolph?" I asked. "You mean Hitler?"

"No." Dad coughed and cleared his throat. "Adolph was a boy, maybe six or seven years old. It was a popular name back then. He was the first person we saw after we bailed out. He was pulling this little wooden cart, and he rescued us."

"A boy?" How could a child rescue three grown men, much less hide them in the middle of a warzone?

"Actually, it was Adolph and his mother who rescued us. They lived in a small farmhouse and spotted our chutes. Fortunately, they got to us before the Germans did. You have to understand, there were no men in those villages back then. The men had all been sent to the Russian front when the war started. Hungary had aligned itself with Germany in an attempt to recreate the Austro-Hungarian Empire. Only things didn't work out so well. Hungary lost more than eighty percent of its second army at the Battle of Stalingrad."

"Steve—" My mother circled her hand like she was whipping cream, signaling dad to move on with his story.

"Hold on, Lynn, she needs to understand what happened." Dad paused and took another sip of his wine. He explained the Hungarians were fearful they would lose the war, and the year before he had been shot down, they had secretly signed an agreement with the Allies and switched sides. "Most of us flyers had no idea about the politicking going on. All we knew back then was Germans bad, Russians good. And it was our job to drop bombs on Germans no matter where they were and put an end to it all. What we didn't know was that there was a partisan movement going on in Hungary, and some of them wanted nothing to do with the Germans or the Russians.

They wanted their independence and for the Americans to liberate their country. Among those patriots were people willing to risk their lives like Adolph and his mother, Katarina—"

"Wait a minute? Katarina?" I put my hand to my head. Was I hearing this correctly? My full name was—or is—Katarina Lynn Lawson. I had no idea why my folks had named me Katarina. Lynn's my middle name for my mother, but I never cared for Katarina and had shortened it to Kat. I always thought Katarina was too fancy. It reminded me of a ballerina, and that certainly didn't suit me. I was never the frilly type. I was always a tomboy and more at home on a basketball court. "Was I named for this Katarina woman?"

My father and mother exchanged a look.

"At the time, your father didn't tell me why he liked the name, and I didn't care. I had two miscarriages before you were born, and by then, it didn't matter what we called you. I wasn't even sure you'd live, but your dad liked the name, so I agreed."

"Her name was Katarina Nemeth. Her husband had been sent to the Russian front at the beginning of the war, and he was killed. She was a widow and very courageous. Like you, Kat. What she did was dangerous, and if she and Adolph hadn't done it, I wouldn't be here."

I never thought of myself as courageous. Although my job—or former job—as an investigative reporter for the local paper had put me in some dicey situations. I had recently posed as a temp for a secretarial service that provided call girls for men who got off on chasing their secretaries around their desks. When the paper got wind of the story from a young woman who wanted out and said she was afraid to go to the police for fear of arrest, I convinced my assignment editor to let me go undercover. My father had worried for my safety until he realized my punch after years of self-defense classes was as sharp as my pen, and he needn't worry. When the story came out, a lot of people went to jail, and my father's estimation of my abilities soared.

"The thing is, Kat, I never knew what happened to Adolph or his mother. They risked their lives to hide us in this old Roman fortress. The Germans thought it wasn't much more than a pile of rocks, so we managed. But I never got to say goodbye. It haunts me that I don't know what happened to them."

I was beginning to see why my father wanted me to go. Since he was in no condition to travel, he expected me to be the investigative reporter I had been at the newspaper and find out what had happened to Adolph and Katarina.

"Yes, but—"

"There are no buts, Kat. I need you to do this. Your mother and I don't have much money, but we have enough. I need you to find Adolph and Katarina, and if they need help, I have a little set aside. I'd like for you to offer it to them."

"Dad." I shook my head.

"Look, I know what you're going to say, the war's been over for better than fifty years, and Katarina could be dead for all I know. But Adolph would only be in his late fifties, and you might find him."

"In Hungary? A country I know nothing about?" Now was not the time. Everything I had worked for had fallen apart, including my self-confidence. I could barely navigate my way across town without getting lost. How could I go to a foreign country to find two people I didn't know and who might not even be alive?

"Why not? It's sweltering hot here. You hate the heat, and it's not like you have a job or a husband waiting for you at home."

I rolled my eyes. I didn't need to be reminded my husband Josh had walked out on me after learning about my affair.

"Do it for me, Kat. If you're worried about money, I'll pay for the ticket." I shook my head.

I didn't want dad to pay for the ticket. I had always been thrifty, and the paper had paid me a severance. I was fixed for the next six months, and after that, I'd figure it out.

"Please, Kat, I need you to do this for me." Dad looked at me pleadingly.

I didn't want to disappoint my father, but how could I leave? His health was failing, my mother was in denial, plus I had never been abroad.

"You realize how easily I get lost? How do you expect me to find my way around in a foreign country?"

Dad tapped his heart. "I've faith in you, girl. And don't you worry about me. I'm not going anywhere. Not until I know what happened to Katarina and Adolph. Besides, from the sound of this letter, Sandor would be happy to show you around."

Chapter Three

Thursday, July 18, 1996

Somewhere over the Atlantic

I had never been out of the country before, but I did have a passport. Josh and I had planned to go to Paris to celebrate our anniversary in June, but then the newspaper fired me, and when Josh learned of my betrayal, he walked out, and my world fell apart. And now, newly separated and less than forty-eight hours after hearing my father's story, I had agreed to spend a week in Hungary and was on a plane to Budapest—by myself.

I'm a nervous flyer, and as the flight attendant went through her pre-flight checklist, I fingered a silver locket I wore around my neck. When I graduated from college, my father had given me a small compass to wear. He told me as long as I could find my true north, I'd never get lost. I hoped he was right. I wasn't feeling very confident these days, and my stomach was already upset, thinking about the flight ahead. Seventeen hours from Los Angeles, with a stopover in Chicago and London and then on to Ferihegy International Airport in Budapest.

Soon as we left Chicago, I popped a Dramamine. I hadn't slept much the night before, and I had worn a lightweight black sweatsuit so that I could curl up and sleep on the plane. None of this would have been an issue, except I had been up late the night before packing and watching *Satantango*, a marathon black and white video about the Hungarian revolution. I thought

I should know something about Hungary's recent history before my trip, and I was three-and-a-half hours into it when I realized Dad had forgotten to give me Sandor's letter. Which meant I would have to set my alarm extra early to beat the morning traffic across town, get the letter from my dad, and still be on time for an early morning departure. When my mother noticed my black joggers, I thought she would faint.

In her defense, mom was from a generation that believed one should dress for every occasion. Never once had I ever seen her leave the house without her hair in place and lipstick. When I was small, she made everything I wore. Frilly, lacey little dresses that made me look like Princess Anne. To this day, I think her biggest disappointment with me is that I have absolutely no interest in fashion. Her fear was that I would become one of those bra-burning, Birkenstock-wearing feminists.

She needn't have worried. I hated Birkenstock—as for being a bra-burning feminist—it was a little late for that. I didn't much need a bra, and feminism was what got me up in the morning. It was also what I suspected put a smile on my father's face. He was supportive of my decisions and thought there wasn't anything I couldn't do and shouldn't try. As for my mother and our disagreement over my choice of fashion, it was a constant source of friction. My last-minute dispute with her over whether it was appropriate for me to arrive—as she put it—looking like some fifties beatnik hadn't helped my nerves. Every time I tried to close my eyes, my life and what a mess I had made of it ran like an old black and white newsreel in my head.

I kept replaying the most recent and worst scenes of my life; my affair, losing my job, and Josh. I couldn't remember when I had ever been at such a low point. I tried to tell myself the split with Josh wasn't all my fault. Josh wasn't the most attentive of mates. In hindsight, I had rushed into a mid-life marriage, my second actually, but then at forty-two, why not? What was I waiting for? Prince Charming? Josh was everything I thought I wanted. Smart. Successful. And nice looking.

Our relationship began innocently enough. I wasn't looking for romance. I had been assigned to cover a story about a new Meet Your Match ad section that ran in the paper's classified section. Singles would place ads like; Leggy

Blonde wants to meet Smart Athletic Dude for Sunset Walks or Handsome Batchelor Looking for Fun. My editor wanted interviews and photos for a story about finding love to run in the society section for Valentine's Day. Josh was one of my first interviews. He was new to town, an investment banker with big plans for the city, and easy to talk to. And he certainly knew how to romance a girl. I had never had a man be so attentive. For my birthday, two weeks after we met, he hired a helicopter for a ride to the Grand Canyon, followed by dinner at El Tovar, where the only thing more expensive on the menu is the view. There were countless dinners at fancy restaurants, flowers, and gifts. Every time I turned around, he surprised me with something.

And then, there was the ultimate distraction. Josh bought a house. Not just any house, but a big beautiful mansion on the top of Camelback Mountain overlooking the city. Forty-five hundred square feet of glass and marble with four bedrooms, a huge dine-in kitchen, a formal dining room, and a sunken living room. And the most incredible backyard that I had ever seen with an infinity pool that appeared to just drop off into the city lights. When he showed it to me, I couldn't believe it—and when I didn't think my jaw could drop any lower—he got down on one knee and proposed.

I was stunned—speechless—which for me, was a surprise. I remember Josh asking me, why wait? We weren't kids anymore. We knew what we wanted, and we could take all the time we needed to get to know one another once we were legally wed. He said he couldn't imagine spending the rest of his life without me. In a blur, I accepted.

I should have seen the warning signs.

Finally, somewhere over the Atlantic, after I had drifted off into a fitful sleep, the sharp ring of the cabin's bell woke me. The fasten-your-seatbelt sign lit up, and the plane began to shake. I grabbed the armrest, white-knuckled, convinced we were going to crash. A few minutes later, the captain's voice came on over the intercom and apologized for the rough flight. He announced we had permission to climb to thirty-six-thousand feet, where he expected things would smooth out. Quick as I could, I took my backpack from beneath my seat and held it against my stomach.

My father hated to fly. When I was little, he told me he made a point of avoiding airplanes. He said he had had to jump out of one during the war, which was the first time I had ever heard about his jump, and the thought made me laugh. No wonder my father wanted me to make this trip. Even if he weren't sick, he wouldn't have put himself back inside an airplane. Not for a transatlantic flight. The memories must have been too vivid. The plane jerked again, and I closed my eyes and leaned against the window, my fingers on the pane. It was cold and black outside, and I wondered how my dad and his crew ever survived those bombing runs. Turbulence was one thing, but compared to the flak and the bullets that threatened to bring their plane down—I could only imagine how frightening that must have been. Dad had told me that he wore a heated flight suit, but it didn't always work, and the bombers weren't pressurized. Temperatures could drop as low as forty-five below Celsius. If any one of the crew touched anything without gloves, their skin would have frozen to it.

As the flight started to smooth out, I opened my backpack and settled back into my seat. If we weren't going to fall out of the sky, at least I could study. My mother had slipped a travel guide for Budapest into my bag when she said goodbye—if I wasn't going to be fashionable, at least I could be knowledgeable. I flipped on the overhead light and stared at the cover with a picture of parliament. Its huge Gothic dome overlooking the Danube River, or the Duna as Hungarians called it, the second-longest river in Europe.

I opened the book, and Sandor's letter with his contact information highlighted in yellow fell out, along with a charcoal sketch of a young boy and his mother. I recognized my father's hand right away and knew this had to be Adolph and Katarina. Dad had always been a pretty good artist, and I used to think he could have earned his living as a painter, although he would have disagreed with me. When he came home from the war, he got a job as a salesman—no starving artist for him. Dad had a wife and plans for the future, and while his art became more of a hobby, my father made numerous sketches of me as I grew. He had an eye like a portrait photographer, and despite his age and frailties, I knew that the picture I held in my hand he would have drawn from memory. The boy was blond and dressed in short pants, and the woman wore a long skirt and hat, set rakishly on her head, not so much for fashion as to hide a patch she wore over one eye. On the back was written Adolph and Katarina, 1945 Lake Balaton, Hungary. Attached was a note.

Kat,

I have no idea if you can find Adolph and Katarina, but in my heart, they will forever be the people I have drawn in this picture and the reason I came home. They saved my life, but there is more to this story than I've told you. Hopefully, you'll find them, or at least Adolph, and when you do, you'll understand why it was so important to me you find them. I was never able to say goodbye. In the end, things happened too quickly. Please, if you find them, tell them I remember and remain forever thankful.

Love always,

Dad

I studied the picture in my hand. What had I agreed to do? Was I running away from my own problems and chasing after a memory my father may have confused with any number of movies or books he had read? My father loved old war movies. Maybe he had substituted the theme of one for his own. His doctors said his medication might cause hallucinations or affect his ability to think clearly. Perhaps Sandor's letter had prompted him to manufacture a story about Adolph and Katarina, and he had convinced my mother of their existence. If it weren't for the DOD letter and Sandor's claim about my father's plane, I might have dismissed my father's claim entirely.

And yet, my father had named me for Katarina. Whoever she was, she had to have been real. My fingers traced the outline of her face on the paper. I wasn't sure what it was about her that my dad had captured in his work, but there was something. Grit? Determination? Anger maybe? From deep within me, I felt a kinship. A life interrupted. A war that had left her a young widow. Like me.

Chapter Four

Friday, July 19, 1996

Budapest, Hungary

We had a rocky descent into Ferihegy International. I gripped the armrest until my knuckles turned white. But once we got below the clouds, things smoothed out, and I was happy that I had a window seat. Aside from feeling cramped in the back of the plane, I had a bird's eye view of Budapest, and coming from the dry Arizona desert couldn't help but notice how green the countryside was and how the Danube River divided the city. Buda, the hillier side on the west, and Pest, with its taller buildings on the east. It was 9:30 in the morning—12:30 a.m. Phoenix time—but I wasn't tired. After traveling for nearly twenty-four hours, I was high on caffeine and pumped to get off the plane.

Before I left Phoenix, I arranged with my cell service to allow me to use my phone internationally and then called Sandor. I explained my father had received his letter, but he could not make the trip due to health issues. Instead, I would come in his place and hoped that Sandor would make himself available to me as a guide. While I tried to sound excited, I was convinced that Sandor was nothing more than some self-appointed travel guide who made his living targeting retired American flyers and their families. Everything from his letter to his invitation to my father to visit felt like a scam. I had reported on enough grifters to know, and while Sandor sounded disappointed that my father wouldn't be joining us, I wasn't about to be taken in. However, since I had promised my dad I would go in his place, and I was trying to put together this trip last minute, I accepted Sandor's offer to make arrangements for my visit and pick me up at the airport. I gave Sandor my cell and flight number, and we agreed to meet outside the terminal upon my arrival.

I had no idea what to expect once I cleared passport control. Despite this being an international trip, I was determined to travel light and had only my duffle and backpack with me. I had heard enough horror stories from friends who had lost luggage on international flights, and I wasn't about to check anything or carry on an expensive bag. Everything I needed for a week in Hungary I had managed to pack in my duffle, and what didn't fit there, I had squeezed into my backpack.

I shuffled behind a group of exhausted passengers and followed signs in Hungarian and English through baggage claim and finally outside to the curb where I expected to meet Sandor. Instead, I found myself shoulder to shoulder with Hungarians anxiously hailing cabs, then, suddenly—pandemonium.

One of the policemen who had been standing guard outside the airport doors began yelling, pushing carts and people out of the way, clearing the sidewalk. I grabbed my duffle and stepped back. In front of me, a blue and white police van with lights flashing pulled to the curb. Two uniformed officers and their dogs pushed past me and raced inside. I must have stood there, with my arms wrapped around myself for a good ten minutes before I heard someone yell my name.

"Kat Lawson? Americanski. Over here." A dark-haired, middle-aged man rushed up to me. He was dressed in grey trousers and a plaid collared shirt. The shirt stretched so tight across his middle that the buttons looked as though they might pop. "Kat?"

"Yes," I said, "Are you—"

"Sandor Zselnegeller." From his back pocket, Sandor took a handkerchief and mopped his brow. The morning temperatures were already climbing uncomfortably high. "You Lieutenant Steve Lawson's daughter?"

I had never heard anyone refer to my father as Lieutenant Lawson, but—
"Yes," I said.

"Velcome." Sandor shook my hand. His accent was thick but understandable. "Dis yours?"

Sandor pointed to my duffle bag at my feet.

"Yes."

"Anything else?" Sandor looked around like he was expecting more.

"No. That's it. But—" I pointed over my shoulder toward the door, "what was all that about...with the police?"

Sandor shrugged. "Don't know. But you here now. No worry." Sandor leaned down and picked up my duffle. "Follow me."

Without further explanation, Sandor led the way to his car, a small, rusty-red sedan with balding tires he had parked at the curb. I had no idea of the make or model, but it looked at least twenty years old, and the frame definitely sprung, more lopsided than square.

Sandor stuffed my duffle in the car's tiny trunk.

"Russian made. Piece of crap, but she run good. Sometimes."

I took one look at the car and wondered how safe it was, much less dependable. If I hadn't promised my father I'd come and search for Adolph and Katarina, I would have turned around right then and booked the next flight home. But I had promised, and at that moment, there was nothing I could do.

Sandor opened the car door for me.

"Small joke," he said. "No worry. I make arrangements for you to stay at gasthouse." Sandor shut the door and walked around the car, and got in. "You know gasthouse?"

"Like a pension?" I asked. My guidebook had said there were many small hotels in the city. Some pensions were a step above a boarding house with a few amenities. Some included a room with private baths and some without. I was beginning to wish I had made my own arrangements.

"This better. Hotel too busy now. July is tourist season. But I find room in nice Hungarian home with breakfast. Like gasthouse, but much better price. Not expensive. My friends own. But room not ready 'til noon."

"How much?" I asked.

"For you, twenty dollar. That okay?"

I wanted to kick myself. I had expected a hotel, not a room in someone's home. But now, what was I going to do? Say no? The price was reasonable, and if the room was clean and safe, I figured I'd make do.

"That's fine," I said.

"Good, then if like, I give you nickel-dime tour. That how Americans say, right? Nickel-dime?"

"That's the term," I said. I cradled my backpack in my lap and wondered what I had gotten myself into.

"You no worry. My English get better more we talk. You see."

"It's definitely better than my Hungarian," I said.

"Ez igaz," Sandor said. "This is truth. Perhaps we teach each other." Sandor adjusted the rearview mirror, and we pulled away from the curb.

I doubted I would have much luck learning any Hungarian. What little of the language I had heard sounded very foreign to my ear. And from the signs I had seen in the airport, even more of a challenge to read. But what concerned me more than the language was how easily Sandor had picked me out of the crowd and seemed to know who I was.

"How did you find me so quickly?"

"Was easy." Sandor pointed to my feet. "Americans, you wear ugly tennis shoes." He patted my thigh and laughed. A familiar gesture, but one I quickly dismissed as nothing more than him trying to be friendly. "More small joke. You learn. I make many."

"Ha." I laughed politely. Not only was I convinced the man was a con artist, even worse, he thought he was a comedian.

"You have good flight?" he asked.

"Uneventful," I said.

"First time Budapest?"

"First time out of the country."

"Ahh, then this is good." Sandor gestured out the open window to the city. "The weather's warm, the sun is shining, and my city—the Queen of the Danube—I will show you, and if you like, we stop for chocolate or liqueur. I know best place."

Despite the fact I didn't believe Sandor to be a real tour guide, he was a likable enough fellow. A pleasant-looking man with a round face, deep tan, and a quick smile. And judging from the extra pounds he carried around his middle and the way he dodged in and out of traffic—not only knew the city but her restaurants as well.

We started on the eastern side of the Danube in Pest in front of the Parliament Building. Sandor said the architect, Imre Steindl, has been inspired by England's Palace of Westminster and designed the building in a neo-Gothic style. But in Sandor's opinion, the parliament building, with its red dome and white Gothic spires, was more dramatic—and its spires much taller. From there, we took a quick walk through Martyrs Square. Sandor pointed out the statue of Imre Nagy, who was Prime Minister when Hungary fought to rid the nation of Soviet influence and was later tried for treason and executed. Then on to Saint Stephen's Basilica, a neoclassical cathedral dedicated to Hungary's first king, St. Stephen, and from there to the Jewish Quarter, where we stopped in front of the Dohany Street Synagogue, the largest in Europe. During the war, Budapest had been the last surviving city in Europe with Jews, many of whom thought they had escaped the worst of the war.

"But then, in March 1944, Hitler sends troops to city. Half-a-million Jews are forced into ghettos. And in two months, they disappear. Sent on train to Auschwitz."

Grifter or otherwise, Sandor knew his city and her history, and while appreciative, I was beginning to feel the effects of jet lag. I glanced at my watch. It was four a.m. my time. I wasn't sure if I was hungry or just tired. The long flight was starting to catch up with me.

I covered a yawn.

"You like we get something to eat?" Sandor asked.

My stomach growled at the thought of food. "Yes, that sounds perfect."

"Good, if you want, we come back later and finish tour. But now I think maybe trip is catching up with you. Come. I take you to Gresham Palace. Roosevelt Square. We have nice lunch with a view of the river and famous bridge that ties cities of Buda and Pest together. The Chain Bridge. You like."

I had never seen such a café. Outside, the window display, with its tiered-layered cakes with cream and caramel fillings and chocolate soufflés, was like a work of art. Sandor found a table in the corner and ordered before I had a chance to see a menu.

"You need try dorbos torte. Is traditional here. Trust me, you like."

Trusting Sandor wasn't a matter of taste. My trust issues went much deeper than that of the creamed torte, which I knew I'd like. The delicate tiered cream vanilla cake was six layers high and light, like lemon custard, with chocolate drizzled on top in an intricate pattern that made it look almost too pretty to eat.

"You like?" Sandor took a sip of his coffee.

"Very much," I said.

"Tomorrow, we meet again, and I will show you more. But now I take you to your room. Is this okay?"

"About tomorrow," I said. I pushed back from the table. I was tired, but not so tired I didn't feel it necessary to settle a few business issues before we continued. If Sandor expected to be paid, I needed to know what he intended to show me and how much this private tour would cost. "We need to discuss your fee."

"You don't know?"

"No," I said. "I've no idea."

Sandor waved his hand in front of his face. "For Steve's daughter, there is no charge. Your father is hero. For others, I charge. But for you, for your father, never."

"A hero?" I blinked. Had I heard him correctly? "I don't understand."

"I am, how do you say? A student of history. I have no degree, but I study, and what I know, I keep it here." Sandor tapped the side of his head. "The Soviets, when they were here, would not like what I know or what I find. If they think anyone has anything American, they will destroy it. But I knew one day, our Russian oppressors would leave, and when they did, I hope the Americans would come back. I earn my living contacting flyers and their families whose planes crashed in my country and areas around it. I have maps and pictures, and I offer tours. I tell those who return the history they not know. For them, what I do is a job. But for you, Kat, I do not charge. For you, it is my pleasure."

"I'm sorry, I don't understand. You're not going to charge me?" I asked.

"How could I charge the daughter of a hero?"

"My father never mentioned anything about being a hero."

"There are many things that happened during the war people do not talk about. Perhaps that is why your father wanted you to come. So you would know."

If this was a con, it was a good one. Everything, starting with the letter my father had received to the personalized tour that now wasn't going to cost me a penny, felt like a setup. But I wasn't about to be a victim of a scam. I paused and considered my options. Either Sandor was an excellent actor and spinning a lie, or he was exactly as he presented himself—a history buff, curious about downed World War 2 aircraft, and in the business of shuttling retired airmen and their families around and sharing with them the history of his country. Obviously, the man knew Budapest, and I would be lost without his help. While I wasn't a hundred percent comfortable with him, I reminded myself that while grifters usually made their living off their wits, they were seldom physically violent.

"Alright," I said. "But, let's get something straight, shall we? The reason I'm here is that my father can't be, and while he wants me to visit the site of his crash—which you seem to have convinced him you've found—the real purpose of my visit is because he wants me to find someone. And for whatever reason, he seems to think maybe you can help."

Sandor put his coffee cup down. "I'm listening."

"Look, I can't do this on my own. And looking for anyone my father may have known during the war is probably impossible if not a waste of time. But if you can help me, I'll be happy to pay for your expenses, provided they're—"

I was about to say reasonable. I had figured twenty-five dollars a day wouldn't break me when Sandor held his hand up.

"Please, save your money. I not want. Things are tough here, many Hungarian have a hand out, but I do not need your money. I want to know story of Lieutenant Lawson and what happens to him. Like you, I was born after war. My grandmother lived in the same small farm town where your father and two airmen hide. I know this because she tells me. He was famous. We all knew about Lieutenant Lawson."

Sandor paused and took a cigarette from his pocket.

"I've never heard any of this," I said. "Please, tell me."

"I was maybe seven when my grandmother brings me to the village near where your father hid. I remember sitting with her and looking up at the sky. She tells me stories about the brave American airmen who jump from big bombers. She calls them heroes, and I never forget." Sandor stirred his coffee. "Years later, when I start to search crash sites I see in fields, I get lucky. I find one plane with a tail number I can read. This does me no good with Russians here, and I must wait. But after Russians leave, I make contact with your DOD." Sandor explained how the DOD ultimately connected him with my dad. "When I see your father's name on list for survivors, I get very excited. I tell myself I know this name, and I wonder if it is the same Lieutenant Steve Lawson my grandmother told me about. He was famous hero for her town."

My father was never one to brag. He had a closet full of trophies from golf and tennis tournaments but never displayed them. Bragging was one of the issues my dad had with Josh. He thought my husband had a big mouth, and the more he got to know him, the less my dad had to say about him. Dad didn't talk about other people. I guess he thought I'd figure it out. He always said the praise you give yourself isn't worth having. If you have to remind people about how great you are, maybe you aren't. My father had lived a modest life, and if he had been a war hero, he wasn't about to tell me, and consequently, if there were a medal or two in the closet from the war, I never knew about it. But I wanted to know.

"Does the name Adolph and Katarina Nemeth mean anything to you? My father said they rescued him, and he wants me to try to find out what happened to them." I was tempted to take my father's charcoal sketch from my backpack and show it to him but decided against it.

Sandor lit his cigarette, took a puff, and then began to tell me a story.

"Katarina was one of the old ladies who would visit with my grandmother when I was little. But is she is alive today?" Sandor shrugged. "I don't know. Katarina had a hard life. They all did back then. My grandmother died before the Russians left. Six years now. She never lived to see them go. Maybe Katarina is dead, too. But Adolph?" The corners of Sandor's mouth turned down. "I am sorry. I only know his name and that he is Katarina's son. I know nothing about him. The people in that area, they were Swabians, German Hungarians. Things were not good for them after the war. The Russians were not kind."

"Did they kill them?" If the Russians had done their own ethnic cleansing after the war, it wasn't public knowledge among those in the western world. Not immediately after the war anyway. Whatever happened behind the Iron Curtain stayed behind the Iron Curtain. It was only now that much of what had happened here was being uncovered.

"Many died. Some were taken away to camps. There is much to tell. And tomorrow when I take you to see your father's plane, I will tell you more. And later, I will take you to town where your father hid. Maybe we find Adolph and Katarina. If we do, it will make me happy too."

I yawned and covered my mouth. My eyes felt as though they had weights on them. All I could think about was how much I wanted to lay down.

Sandor took several Hungarian bills, Forint, from his pocket and put them on the table. "Come. You're tired. I take you to my friend's house now. Tomorrow we start our visit."

Chapter Five

The apartment where Sandor arranged for me to stay was a three-story walk-up above a small bakery on the Pest side of the Danube with a view of the river. Sandwiched between a complex of neo-classical prewar buildings, the entrance was accessible by a narrow door painted bright red. I couldn't have asked for a better location.

Sandor carried my bag up the stairs, a long narrow hallway painted black, to the apartment's first floor and rang the bell. His friends, Miklos and Nora Nabor, answered with their infant son, Márkó, who I figured to be about six months old. The baby looked a lot like his father with dark curly hair and brown eyes but with a big toothless grin.

Nora greeted me with an enthusiastic handshake while balancing the baby on her hip.

"Velcome," she said. Her accent was even thicker than Sandor's.

I mumbled a thank you, and Nora invited us in.

The apartment's accommodations were modest but quaint. The living room was sparsely furnished with a couch, rocking chair, coffee table, and television. I noticed a few pictures on the wall and a newspaper on the table. In the corner of the room was a wrought-iron circular staircase. Nora gestured for us to follow.

The five of us, Miklos, Nora, with the baby on her hip, me, and Sandor with my bag, squeezed up a narrow staircase. Nora stopped on the landing for the second floor, pointed in the direction of two closed doors, said something in Hungarian, which I gathered meant those were their bedrooms, and then continued up the stairs. I ducked as we came to the top of the

29

stairway, nearly hitting my head on the slanted ceiling. Miklos flicked on a wall switch, illuminating a small alcove or attic area crammed with old furnishings, paintings, and a couple of battered-looking suitcases, which had been pushed aside for the addition of the guest quarters.

Nora opened the guestroom door, and the first thing I noticed was the scent of fresh paint and yellow sunlight as it streamed into the room through a pair of windowed French doors. A double bed with a small wooden side table and lamp was in the center of the room. Centered above the bed was a single piece of artwork, a framed poster that I immediately recognized from my college art classes as *Painter on the Road* by one of my favorite impressionists, Vincent Van Gogh. The room appeared so untouched and pristine, I wondered if I might be its first resident.

"Bath here." Nora opened a slim door to a closet-sized bath, complete with a pull-chain toilet and shower. "And coffee here," she pointed to a coffeemaker on the dresser, "You make or come downstairs. Your choice."

Sandor explained that neither Nora nor Miklos spoke much English, but he didn't think it'd be a problem.

I yawned. Then apologized. All I wanted to do was lie down. I tossed my backpack on the bed. My body was aching for a nap.

"But first, come see." Sandor went to the French doors and opened them with both hands on the handles. "Voila!"

I joined Sandor on the balcony. Below us was the river walk and an unobstructed view of the Danube River and the Chain Bridge.

"You like?" he asked.

"Yes. Very much. It's lovely." I hadn't expected anything so perfect, and I was beginning to think perhaps I'd been too harsh of a judge. At least as far as Sandor's ability to find me suitable lodgings. The room was more than I anticipated and for much less than I thought I'd have to pay. "It's perfect."

"Good, then until tomorrow, I say goodbye. If you like dinner, I suggest you try restaurant on the riverwalk. All good."

Sandor nodded to me, turned to leave, and then stopped at the door. He spoke briefly to Miklos, his voice barely above a whisper as he reached into his pocket and pressed a couple of bills into his friend's hand. Sandor left with Miklos close behind. Nora nodded to me as she snuggled Márkó on her hip, and the baby waved as she quietly closed the door behind her.

Alone in the room, I was too exhausted to unpack and lay down on the bed for what I thought would be a short nap. I checked my watch. It was two-thirty in the afternoon, five-thirty a.m. Phoenix time. Dad was an early riser, but not that early, and while I was tempted to call and let him know I had arrived, my eyes felt heavy. I could barely keep them open. I promised myself I would take a short twenty-minute power nap, then explore the riverwalk. But by the time I woke, the sun had set, and it was eight-thirty p.m., and I had slept for nearly six hours.

The noise outside my open balcony doors had gone from the muffled sounds of afternoon strollers along the riverfront to the jazzy strumming of fiddlers playing at sidewalk cafes. I took my camera from my backpack and went to the balcony to get a couple of pictures. The light was perfect. Photographers call it the golden hour when the light is softer and almost magical. If I had been on assignment for a news story, I would have snapped a few more shots. Instead, I rustled through my backpack for my phone and dialed the number for the international operator. I waited for the signal to input my folk's number, then listened as a series of beeps connected me. I wanted to share the moment with my dad.

He answered right away.

"Greetings from Budapest," I said.

"How is it?" he asked.

I wandered back out to the balcony. "Here. Take a listen. I'm about to take a walk along the Danube." I held the phone up so that my father might hear the sound of violins in the background.

"Is it blue?"

"Looks gray," I said. "but it's beautiful just the same."

"And did Sandor meet you at the airport?"

"He did."

"I assume he's okay? That all your suspicions were unfounded."

"I'm not so sure about that. He set me up in a friend's home. He said July is tourist season, and because I came in last minute, all the hotels were booked.

But, I have to say, the room's nice, and the apartment's right on the river. As for Sandor, he appears to be quite the entrepreneur. Says he makes his living giving tours, but he doesn't want money from me for some reason. He said his grandmother was from the same small town near Lake Balaton, where you hid. He seems to know a lot about you. He said you were a hero, Dad."

The line went quiet, and for a moment, I thought we had been disconnected.

"Dad?"

"I wasn't a hero, Kat. Adolph and Katarina, they were the heroes. If Sandor's grandmother was from around the lake area, she might have known them. Did you ask him?"

"He said his grandmother knew Katarina, but he doesn't hold out much hope. A lot of time's past." My father started to cough, and I waited until the spasm cleared. "Dad, are you okay?"

"I'm fine. Maybe it's Sandor's letter or because you're there. I don't know, but a lot of things are starting to come back to me. Things that keep an old man up at night."

My father explained he had a nightmare last night and woke up in a cold sweat. He said he was back inside his plane. Right before he had to bail.

"You want to talk about it?"

"I don't know that talking about it does any good. And I don't want your mom to know. She worries."

I wondered if the medication my father was taking had caused him to hallucinate, and being so far away, I felt helpless to do anything about it.

"But don't you worry, in the light of day, my memories aren't all bad. Some of them are almost funny. 'Least looking back, they are. Did I ever tell you I got stuck the first time I tried to bail out? Took me three tries. Finally, pulled my knees up into my chest, prayed to God the Germans on the ground wouldn't shoot me, and rolled out through the nose cone. All I could feel was this rush of cold air pushing past me and the sound of my heart beating in my ears. Believe me, it was pretty damn loud. Didn't have any sense of falling, though. Felt more like I was floating—pretty nice as I think back on it. I remember looking down at the countryside and seeing this tall white church steeple, and I figured it was a sign everything was going to be okay."

Dad was the preacher's son and had grown up in a parsonage next to the church. If anything were going to bring him comfort in those frightening moments, it would have been a church steeple.

"Only thing is, in my dream, it wasn't that way. I didn't see the steeple. I was in my chute, fumbling with my ripcord, and I couldn't get the damn thing to open. Suddenly, it opened, and I was hanging like a target with the Germans below me. They started shooting. Rat-tat-tat. Rat-tat-tat. I woke up in a cold sweat. And I realized it wasn't shooting at all but the water sprinklers against the window. Guess I'm a bit jumpy these days."

"I'm sorry, Dad. I wish there was something I could do."

"Find Katarina and Adolph. I need to know what happened to them. Those two haven't crossed my mind in years, and now I can't sleep without knowing."

I changed the subject.

"I found the sketch you did of Katarina and Adolph. It's good. You still got it, Dad. It almost looks like a black and white photograph. Mom put it in the back of the guidebook."

"I wanted you to see them as I saw them—innocents, caught up in a war they hadn't caused and could do nothing about."

I thought back to the drawing, Adolph in short pants, standing with his mother, her hand on his shoulder, a hat on her head, and a patch on her left eye.

"Was Katarina blind in one eye?" I asked.

"She was, but if you're going to ask me how, she never talked about it. And I didn't ask."

"She spoke enough English that you were able to communicate?"

"Katarina spoke several languages. She learned English from her father. He had been a banker. Before the war, England had made loans to Hungary, and the family had traveled enough that she picked up a lot. She was a smart woman and physically strong. She may have been blind in one eye, but it never slowed her down. It was her that spotted our chutes and sent Adolph ahead to find us."

"I'm surprised you trusted him," I said.

"Eh, we didn't know what to think at first. Adolph didn't speak much English, but none of us wanted to shoot a kid. Fortunately, Nick's family was from Hungary, and Nick understood enough to know that Adolph wanted us to follow him and that he was there to help. Together we managed to get Nick into Adolph's cart, and by the time Katarina caught up with us, she made it clear we needed to go with her before the Germans could find us."

"But the Germans, they must have seen the chutes."

"If they did, Katarina took care of it. She took two of our chutes, tore them up, and threw them in the river. Mine, I helped her to stuff beneath Nick in the cart. The idea was to make the Germans think we had drowned. The woman risked her life for us, Kat. You have to find her."

"I'll do my best, but it might be that the best I can do is get pictures of where you hid, and maybe your plane, too."

"Listen to you. Don't tell me what you can't do. You don't know until you try." Dad had seldom scolded me, but I could hear the disappointment in his voice. "You're beginning to sound like that no-good husband of yours. Since when did you start doubting yourself?"

That stung, and I let it sink in. I had been questioning myself and everyone else around me ever since I'd lost my job—and Josh. But there was no point in hashing it out on an international call. I would need to work those trust issues out myself.

"Maybe I'll get lucky. Sandor volunteered to take me to your hide-out tomorrow. Who knows, could be I'll find something when I'm there."

My father started to cough again. Mom took the phone and said Dad needed to rest, then started in with questions about what I'd seen, everything from the food to what people were wearing.

"And, Kat, I know you're not much for fashion, but if you get a chance, check out some of the knit shops. Harriett was there last year and brought back a beautiful sweater made from pigs' wool. Can you believe it? Wooly pigs? Evidently, they're rare but quite the thing in Europe. See what you can find. And paprika. You have to bring some home—Hungary's known for its spices. We'll cook up some goulash when you're back. Your dad will love it."

If I had let my mother go on, I worried I would never be able to pay for the call. I promised I'd check in again and hung up.

Chapter Six

I felt refreshed after my nap and couldn't wait to stroll along the river and explore. From my balcony, I could see young couples walking hand in hand. Their voices, along with the sound of sidewalk musicians, floated in the air while the smell of fresh-baked bread wafted from the riverside restaurants.

After Sandor's snip about my tennis shoes, I took a pair of walking sandals from my duffle. I didn't want to look too obviously American, and slipped into a simple, sleeveless, black cotton dress, then donned my fanny pack, making sure I had my wallet, passport, and few Hungarian forints. My guidebook said most restaurants preferred cash but warned of pickpockets, particularly along the riverfront. Despite the fact my mother would have disapproved of my choice of accessories—a fanny pack was not a handbag—I wasn't about to carry a purse. It wasn't my style, and with my small, moon-shaped bag strapped securely around my waist, I felt safe.

Sandor hadn't mentioned anything to me about house rules or if I needed to let Miklos and Nora know if I was going out. I decided to ask for a key, but I heard arguing in the kitchen when I reached the first floor and changed my mind.

I didn't imagine I'd be too late. The sky was just getting dark, and the river, now inky black, was mixed with the reflection of dancing lights from the bridge and passing boats. I walked briskly along the riverwalk.

My guidebook defined the sights and sounds of Budapest as one of incredible beauty yet a soulful sadness. Its people of mixed ethnicities. Hungarians, or Finno-Ugric Magyars, Turks, Slavs, various Germanic tribes, and Romas or gypsies. All of whom shared a past as gray as the river. I stopped and snapped several photos of the Chain Bridge and the Buda Castle, both illuminated with yellow lights that made them almost fanciful, then spotted a small café with an empty table facing the water.

In the past, I wouldn't have been comfortable sitting in a restaurant and dining alone. I seldom went out to eat by myself at home, not unless it was to grab a quick burger and return to work or maybe to pick something up if Josh was out of town. I was always on a deadline. But now, in a foreign country, I felt free to people-watch and gather my thoughts without interruption. And the twinkling lights that framed the restaurant's edifice and the white linen tablecloths added a touch of elegance and felt oddly welcoming.

"American?" A waiter with a white apron tied about his waist appeared at my table. More efficient than friendly, he held a pencil and notepad in hand.

"Do you speak English?" I looked at the menu, all in Hungarian. Words with lots of double vowels, consonants, and accent marks. None of which made sense to me.

"Some," he said. "You want, I suggest something?"

"Yes, please."

"Fish soup. Cabbage rolls. How you say…stuffed pepper?" He tapped the eraser end of his pencil on my menu and pointed to several items. "All good here."

"Your favorite?"

"The chicken paprikash. You like it. I bring." He scribbled a note on his pad. "Wine?"

I looked to a neighboring table where a group of older men, who must have been at least my father's age, sat with shot glasses.

"What's that?" I pointed to a small, round-shaped bottle with a gold cross on a red background.

"Unikum, Hungary's national drink. They celebrate tonight. Two brothers, separated by the war, have found each other again."

"After all this time?" I wondered if this might be some kind of omen, a sign of good things to come.

"It happens. People come back. They search. Sometimes they find each other. It's nice to see."

"I'll try the Unikum," I said. Maybe it would bring me luck in my own search for Katarina and Adolph.

What it did was make me gag. The stuff was foul-tasting. I was happy the waiter had thought to bring me a beer, which I had to drink to chase it down. As for the chicken? Dinner was delicious, moist, and spicy.

When the waiter brought the bill, I vowed I'd never try Unikum again. He laughed and said he wasn't surprised. Few foreigners liked the drink. It had been a favorite with Hungarians until the Russians took control of the country after the war. The communists forced the company to nationalize and changed the original recipe. After the Russians left, the company returned to making Unikum the old-fashioned way, and the drink once again became a national favorite.

"No offense," I said, "But I think the Russians may have been on to something."

"Very funny. You come back, I take care of you, no more Unikum. You ask for Dion." He pointed to a name tag on her shirt. "I am named for Dionysus, the God of wines. I find you good wine to drink with dinner. We have many."

I settled the bill, surprised by how inexpensive it was. Including the tip, dinner was six US dollars or about twelve hundred Hungarian forints. An American could live well in Hungary. Even better, one could sit at a table all night and not be disturbed. Dion was in no rush to clear my table. So, I sat, and people watched as couples strolled the boardwalk, their eyes mysteriously slipping past my own and never engaging. I wondered who they were and how they managed? Were they close or drifting apart, like Josh and me? How many secrets did they hide from each other?

Disgusted that I had allowed Josh to enter my thoughts, I got up from the table and determined I needed to walk. Even if Josh had been here, we wouldn't have been one of those couples walking hand-in-hand. We would have argued. Lately, we had grown so distant from one another we seldom talked, and when I pushed him to tell me what was going on, he'd get mad at me.

I started walking toward the Chain Bridge. My body had yet to adjust to the time zone, and I was too keyed up, my thoughts of Josh too jumbled to return to my room. And now that the sun had set and the weather cooled, I was curious to explore the riverwalk. I was about to take the pedestrian walk across the bridge when a young man approached me with a stack of postcards.

"Lady, you like private tour of river? I have nice boat. Take you anywhere you like. Tell good stories." The boy pointed across the street to the river, where a small motorboat was tied to the shore. "You like. I promise."

If I hadn't worked as an investigative reporter at the newspaper, I might not have considered the boy's offer. But after years of following leads and talking with dubious sources, I had a pretty good sense of people. And this scrappy-looking boy, with his dark hair in his eyes, looked about as menacing as a firefly. I was feeling adventurous.

"How much?" I asked.

"Ten US dollars," he said.

My guidebook had been very explicit about not rewarding Gypsies. They called them Romas and said they couldn't be trusted and would hound tourists begging for money. But this boy wasn't begging. He was selling. Negotiating.

"Five," I countered. "But only to the castle and back. It's getting late." I pointed to the Buda Castle across the river on the hill.

"Plus one dollar for tram to top of hill." The boy held up one finger. "Too dark to walk now. You will thank me. I can show you best spot for photograph."

"Fine," I said. I handed the boy another bill. My tour of Pest that morning with Sandor had been quick, and with the few days I had to see the city, I didn't imagine I'd have a lot of free time to sightsee.

"Follow me." The boy skipped ahead and pointed to an overhead pedestrian crosswalk that led from the riverwalk to where half a dozen cruise boats were docked. "I take you fast. The castle closes one hour. We hurry. Come."

The boat was small but fast. A single outboard, that when gunned, was noisy and wet, splashing me and the sides of the vessel with the Danube's black waters.

"What's your name?" I hollered

"Adrian," he shouted back. "You?"

"Kat," I said.

"You tourist or business lady?"

"Tourist," I said.

"I think you lucky lady," he said. "First-time visit, I can tell. But not last. You have big adventure here."

I would have bet money he told everybody the same thing. "And you're a gypsy with a fortune to sell."

"If you like, I can read. Five-dollar."

"No, thanks," I said. "But may I take your picture?"

"One dollar." Adrian raised his index finger above his head.

"I've already paid you six," I said. "Five for the ride to the castle and one for the tram. Seems like that's enough."

"You like to bargain, I can tell." Adrian crossed his arms and leaned back against the boat's motor.

"Come on, smile." I took the camera from around my neck and pointed in Adrian's direction, hoping for an artsy shot with the Chain Bridge's yellow lights in the background. It was only then that I took note of the young man's face, the glint of a gold tooth, and the distant nomadic look in his pale, green eyes, reflective of a thousand generations before him.

"Your English is pretty good," I said.

"I have good ear and learn enough to survive. I speak six languages. Romanian. Russian, Hungarian, German, some Yiddish, and English. Including language of love." He leaned forward and touched his heart. "You have good fortune. You like, I can tell."

"No," I said. The last thing I needed was another romantic complication in my life.

"But you are searching for someone. I know."

"Isn't everyone?" I wasn't about to tell Adrian the purpose of my visit. I was already dealing with Sandor. One flimflam man was more than enough.

"Yes, but you different. You smart and very lucky lady. I think you find everything you come for and more. Much more. Some good. Some maybe not so good, even dangerous. You should be careful."

I wasn't about to be intimidated by Adrian's implication that trouble might await me. As far as I was concerned, the gypsy was over-selling and hoping I'd acquiesce and ask for him to read my fortune. I snapped a couple more shots of the river.

Adrian slowed the boat as we passed a river cruise ship and pointed to the top of the mountainside on our left.

"You see the white statue...woman on top of Gilbert Hill? Look like your American Statue of Liberty with palm leaf above her head?" I snapped another quick picture. "This is gift from Russians. They give her to us to celebrate liberation from Nazis. But inside we laugh. Russians are not our liberators. They no better than Germans. Before here, in Budapest, they kill many Jews. And when they come here, many more, some like me, disappear."

I reloaded my camera. Thankful I had thought to bring extra film in my fanny pack.

"And beneath the Buda Castle where I take you now. Is secret hospital hidden in rock, like cave. It is built before war as bomb shelter and hospital for Hungarian people. Later, Russians use for research. Is closed now. Not for tourists, but one day maybe it will open again, and I will show you. You have questions, you find me here on river. I know many stories, things no one else will tell."

We pulled up to the riverbank below the castle, and Adrian jumped ashore and offered me his hand. "Come. You hurry, we catch ride to top."

I followed Adrian to the funicular and found a seat where I could see the river as we rode to the top while he paid for our tickets. The ride was slow and bumpy, but the view of Pest, with its city lights and Parliament, directly beneath a full moon and reflected in the river, looked like something out of a fairytale.

"You won't have time for castle tour, but I take you quick to best place for photo. Adrian pulled me ahead to a lookout along the castle's stone wall, where I had a hundred-and-eighty-degree view of the river and city below. "You like?"

I snapped off a half dozen shots. The yellow lights on the bridge and the riverboats reflected in the river's water created an almost magical look.

"Beautiful," I said.

"Good, you come back. I give you better tour in daylight."

"Thank you, Adrian, but—"

"You think you are here for short visit and not see me again. But I know better. You will be back. You have many questions. And you can trust me."

Chapter Seven

It was past eleven p.m. by the time Adrian dropped me back where he docked his boat. The riverwalk was still packed with people strolling and enjoying the late-night views of the city. Cafes were beginning to close, and musicians were packing up their instruments. I hurried in the direction of Miklos and Nora's apartment. I was worried I might not find the bakery or the red door that led up to their residence, and if I did, the door would be locked.

Luckily, I needn't have worried. The bakery had a small illuminated sign above an outdoor counter, and the door leading up the stairwell to the apartment was unlocked. I didn't know whether my hosts had anticipated my late arrival or if it was customary. All the same, the last thing I wanted to do was to disturb anyone. Quietly, I tip-toed up the dark staircase to the apartment. From inside, I could hear the baby crying. I tried the front door, and it was unlocked.

Nora and her husband were in the living room. Miklos was pacing the floor with Márkó in his arms. Nora had an open bottle of brandy in her hand, and with her index finger in the infant's mouth, was trying to massage the baby's gums. I didn't have to speak Hungarian to know the baby was teething.

Nora nodded to the bottle in her hand. *Did I want a glass?*

I shook my head, tried to give a sympathetic smile, and headed up the staircase to my room.

When I had left to go to dinner, I had yet to unpack. But from the looks of things, someone had come in and put my things away for me. The clothes in my duffle bag now hung neatly in the closet, with my shoes on the floor. The few cosmetics I had packed in my backpack—cleanser, moisturizer, and lips sticks—had been placed on a small stool next to the bathroom sink, along with a small vase and a single flower. The bedsheets had been turned down, my pillow fluffed, and a square of chocolate on top of it. On the nightstand next to the bed was my journal. And on top of it, two small black-and-white photos that I had stuffed inside. One was of my dad, looking very 1944, in his Army Air Corp uniform and wheel hat, with a pipe in his hand. The other was of his crew, ten young men standing and smiling in front of a B-24.

Maybe it was because I was in a foreign country or that I had been suspicious of Sandor from the get-go, but something didn't feel right. Whether Miklos and Nora considered unpacking my things as part of their service, I wasn't used to it, and I didn't like it. It felt more like a violation. As though somebody had been snooping through my things.

Listen to you, Kat. I could hear the disappointment in my father's voice in my head, and it frustrated me.

Why couldn't I just accept that Nora and Miklos were Sandor's friends and doing their best to make me comfortable? Or that Sandor was who he said he was, a World War Two war buff who had found my father's plane and believed my father to be a war hero?

I'll accept that working for a newspaper had made me more skeptical of strangers and maybe even a little hard to deal with. Dad thought I was jaded, and Josh refused to even talk to me about my work. He thought reporters were like ambulance chasers, which hadn't helped the growing chasm between us.

Living in Arizona, I had reported on enough snowbirds who had been the victim of such swindles. All of them had been loosely based on facts and associated with credible sources—like my father's plane crash and the DOD. Around which, an engaging chiseler, like Sandor, might weave a clever tale. Elderly couples received bogus calls from scam artists posing as their grandchildren and claiming to be in trouble and needing financial help. Fake calls from banks targeted seniors, telling them they needed to update their personal information because the bank had found a dormant account with their name on it and wanted to make them a refund. In each case, the mark or the elderly targeted senior was encouraged to meet with a charming middle man—the equivalent of a masked bandit—who would assure them they were in good hands, only to have their life savings or considerable sums disappear.

But, despite the fact both my personal and professional life were on the skids, I wasn't about to be anybody's fool—not when it came to protecting my father. Sandor may have been a war buff, but he hadn't met the likes of me. I didn't doubt that growing up in Hungary after the war, Sandor had heard many stories about downed airmen and their aircraft. As for whether or not he had a grandmother who had told him about American airmen hidden in her village and that she knew about Katarina, I had no idea. He could have made the whole thing up based on the stories he had heard. But what Sandor couldn't have counted on was my father remembering Adolph and Katarina. Or that my dad would want Sandor to help me find them. In fact, thinking back on Sandor's reaction and how surprised he was when I asked him about them caused me to wonder. *Had my request troubled him?* And if so—game on, buddy. Whatever Sandor Zselnegeller was up to, he wasn't going to outsmart me.

I grabbed the chocolate off my pillow and let it melt in my mouth. Sweet as it was, it left a bitter taste. I slipped my father's pictures back inside my journal. If Nora had searched my room, what was she looking for? Had Sandor arranged for me to stay here because it was convenient, or was it something else? I looked around the room, convinced Nora had deliberately gone through my things. But why?

Chapter Eight

I went through everything. I couldn't sleep until I had searched every pair of pants and every top I had brought with me. My shoes. My cosmetics. Even my underwear. Everything. Not so much to take inventory and assure myself nothing had been taken, but to ensure nothing had been added. I checked pockets, even the lining in my duffle and backpack. Plus, the insides of my shoes.

I had heard enough stories about tourists accused of drug smuggling in foreign countries to be concerned. The airport had been papered with posters warning travelers not to accept packages and never let their bags out of sight. Unwitting tourists made an easy mule for a crafty drug cartel. The idea that something might have been planted inside one of my bags was chilling. And then I remembered the scene at the airport when I had arrived. The police sirens, the cops with their drug-sniffing dogs that pushed past me and raced inside. Had some unsuspecting tourists like me been found with drugs?

I was frantic and convinced that in my exhausted state, Sandor was dealing drugs and intended to set me up or at least blackmail me. Coming from a border state like Arizona, I had seen dozens of drug smugglers prosecuted and all kinds of scams. I once reported on a couple of college students who had tried to blackmail an exchange student to finance their plans for a spring break to Cancun. Turned out the romantic duo had planted what looked like cocaine in the student's suitcase and then offered to drop him off at the airport. On the way there, the student's friends revealed the drugs and threatened to report him to the authorities if he didn't pay his friends to make the situation disappear. They might have gotten away with it, too, were it not for the fact this wasn't the first time the darling duo had tried to blackmail a foreign student. But, the student's family was concerned that their son had withdrawn so much money from his bank account before his return flight home and called the police. The police, alerted to the possibility of such a scam, were ready and waiting for the young couple when they arrived to drop their friend at the airport. Then, just as the exchange—money for powdered sugar—was in process, the police swooped in and made an arrest. It was all very dramatic and made for a great story. But for me, in a foreign country, and suddenly feeling as though I was about to be somebody's mule, I had no idea who I could trust or what I should do. No wonder Sandor wasn't going to charge me for his tour. He could blackmail me for thousands more. All Sandor had to do was show me what had been planted in my bags, then threaten to go to the authorities. We both knew if drugs were found, the police would throw me in jail—but, for a price, Sandor could help.

I re-checked, checked again, then triple-checked every pocket, including the hems in every piece of clothing I had—anywhere someone might have hidden something. When I didn't find anything, I sat down on the bed, exhausted. *Dammit, maybe I was overthinking this. Maybe Nora was just trying to be helpful.*

I tossed my backpack on the bed. It was late, my room was a mess, and my clothes were scattered everywhere. I had done everything but turn the mattress over. All I wanted was a hot shower and sleep. By the time my head hit the pillow, all I could think about was how tired I was. Whatever Sandor was up to, I'd figure it out tomorrow.

* * *

I was in a fog when my cell phone rang the following morning. So startled by the sound that when I opened my eyes, I had forgotten where I was.

"Good morning, Kat. Sander here."

"Who?" I struggled to clear my head.

"This is your wake-up call. I hope you slept well."

47

"What time is it?" I felt as though I had just put my head down. Was it morning already?

"Nine o'clock, my American friend." Sandor sounded a little too chipper. "I thought I should call. Make sure you didn't oversleep. Some clients do their first day. We need to get early start. How you say, chop-chop?"

I reached for my watch on the bedside table. I had reset it to the local time before I went to bed, but my eyes refused to focus. I wasn't sure I was ready for Sandor's chop-chop morning.

"Oh, and wear something comfortable. We're going to the lake. We'll be hiking, and it'll be hot. See you in thirty. I have big surprise."

I forced myself out of bed, my legs like rubber, and into the small bathroom, where I splashed cold water on my face. Thirty minutes later, dressed in shorts, a t-shirt, and—what I now feared everyone in Hungary would think of as my ugly white tennis shoes—I was downstairs in front of the bakery.

"Good morning, Kat. You look rested. I hope you had a good night and slept well." Sandor motioned for me to follow him toward the Elizabeth Bridge, where we had parked the day before.

"I did, thank you."

"And your room? Everything okay?"

Now would have been the time to say something about Nora's search through my personal belongings. But I liked the room, and after a good night's sleep, I wasn't so sure I hadn't over-reacted to Nora's good housekeeping skills. However, my suspicion of Sandor hadn't changed.

"Everything is fine," I said. "And might I say your English is much better today." All part of the ruse, I thought. It certainly wasn't as broken as yesterday.

"It helps to practice." Sandor lit another cigarette and walked ahead.

"Aw, and I thought perhaps that might be your surprise." My mumbled response was a tad sarcastic and probably wasted on him since he was nearly out of earshot.

To my surprise, he stopped. "Pardon me?"

"I said. I'm looking forward to your surprise."

"Good. I have big surprise for you." Sandor kept walking.

I hoped Sandor's big surprise might be that he had rented a car for our day trip to Lake Balaton. I wasn't looking forward to sitting in the bucket of bolts he had picked me up in the day before.

"I invite my wife to join us." Sandor gestured to his sorry-looking car. "She loves Americans, and her English is better than mine. I hope this okay?"

Standing next to Sandor's two-door rusty-red bomb was a pale-skinned, pretty brunette with a pageboy cut, wearing a short frilly, cotton shift, and a welcome smile.

I immediately felt underdressed.

"Oh, and I thought the surprise might be your car."

"You no like my car?" Sandor shrugged, hands in the air.

I matched him with the same gesture, hands up, and looked up at the sky. "Small joke," I said.

Sandor grinned then introduced us. "Kat, meet my wife, Aanika."

Aanika kissed me once on each cheek, first left, then right—what I assumed must be the Hungarian way—then held my hands and squeezed them like we were old friends.

"I hope you like Hungarian sandwich, black bread with cream cheese and black cherry jam. You know about Hungarian cherries? Best in the world."

"And she make Túróstáska for dessert. You see, is excellent." Sandor patted his wife's behind, then opened the car door for me to squeeze into the backseat.

Aanika settled herself in the front passenger seat and turned to look at me. "If you'd like something to drink, there's hot coffee in the thermos and paper cups in the hamper. And if you're hungry, I make croissants." She pointed to a small wicker basket next to me. "The drive to the lake is long, even the way Sandor drives." Aanika winked at her husband.

I poured myself a cup of coffee while Sandor explained his wife worked as a secretary for her uncle's trucking firm. He sometimes picked up odd jobs from her uncle, but whenever he had Americans in town and Aanika could take time off, she liked to join him to practice her English. Which, unlike what Sandor said, was noticeably better and with less of a heavy Hungarian accent.

"I love America," she said. "It is such a big country."

"Have you ever been?" I asked.

"No, but maybe one day we come and visit you." Aanika looked at her husband and raised a brow.

"You have to pardon my wife." Sandor put his hand on Aanika's knee. "Under the Soviets, it was difficult for us to travel. And we haven't done as much as we'd like. But Aanika and I spent our honeymoon in Keszthely. It's not too far from where your father was hidden. When she heard you wanted to visit the lake, she asked to come."

"Keszthely is the largest city on lake," Aanika said. "You ever hear of it?"

I shook my head.

"It is very popular with tourists. There are many shops, and the palace is beautiful, but Sandor says we have no time to see today—maybe later."

"Sorry, Kat." Sandor checked the rearview mirror, caught my image, and continued to talk with his eyes on me. "If you come back, I show you, I promise. But today, we take the scenic route by the lake. Longer drive but less traffic than highway, and you see countryside. Very green and pretty. I know a good spot by the lake where we stop for lunch. You get lots of pictures for your father, I promise."

Nervous Sandor's eyes were on me and not on the road, and that the traffic around us appeared to have no regard for any speed limit or particular lane, I pointed ahead to a row of grey concrete buildings. Like sentries, they stood, one after the other, void of any style beyond their flat block walls and narrow windows.

"Russian?" I asked.

"Panelház." Sandor continued to stare in the rearview mirror. "Russians build after the war. Ugly, no?"

I nodded. I wished Sandor would keep his eyes on the road.

"Made too fast." Sandor continued to stare at me and took one hand off the wheel. Then like some crazed orchestra conductor, gestured in the direction of the towers. "Precast concrete and poor construction. Cold and dark inside. No one want to live there. But cheap." Then turning and looking at me over his shoulder, he asked. "What do you think?"

"Cloooooooose!" I curled in almost prenatal position as a car—little more than a rollerskate on wheels—zipped unexpectedly in front of us.

Sandor swerved around the car whose backseat we had nearly joined and continued to talk as though nothing unusual had happened. With one hand, I grabbed the back of Sandor's seat while I steadied a sloshing cup of coffee that threatened to spill down the front of me.

"Too close," he said. "No room for privacy. Aanika and I have apartment near the old Jewish Quarter with courtyard for visit with friends. Very nice. But when the Russians come, they not like such design and build towers like block walls. No space for people to gather. The Russians worry people might use such space for talk of politics or to organize."

Sandor reached across Aanika's lap, and with one hand on the wheel, took a map from the glove box and handed it to me.

"Here, you like, you can follow along on map. We go west from city on north side of lake, past Szigliget where we see old castle ruin on top of the mountain."

I stared at the map, thankful to have something to take my mind off the traffic and Sandor's driving. Budapest to Szigliget was about a hundred and ten miles or what should be a two-hour drive depending on how heavy Sandor's foot was on the accelerator.

Aanika reached over the seat and pulled a croissant from the wicker basket next to me. "So, what is it you do? Sandor didn't say, but I told him, I think you must have a very important job."

I wasn't quite sure how I wanted to answer. I didn't feel the need to explain my unemployed status. Instead, I said, "I'm a reporter. I work for a newspaper."

"A reporter?" Aanika slapped Sandor's shoulder with the back of her hand and said something in Hungarian—the equivalent I felt of an *I told you so*—then took a bite of her croissant. "Do you cover stories about murder and robbery?"

I hadn't expected such a question. "Sometimes," I said. Of all the things Aanika could have asked me, particularly after last night and my frantic search through my room, the topic of murder sent a chill down my back.

"But usually nothing so serious. I prefer more human interest stories. Travel features and such."

I didn't want to let on that I had worked as an investigative journalist or give Sandor any idea I might be suspicious of him.

Aanika brushed a crumb from the side of her mouth. "Will you write about your trip here and your search for your father's plane?"

"Perhaps."

Sandor looked back up into the rearview mirror. "When you do, you'll include me too, right? When people read, I become big famous Hungarian tour guide." Sandor winked.

I smiled. If I was still working for the newspaper, I might have pitched my editor the idea of a daughter coming to Hungary to search for her father's downed aircraft. But now that I didn't have a job and couldn't be sure this trip wasn't just some kind of hoax designed to separate me or my father from his life's savings, I didn't know what I might do. If it turned out Sandor planned to blackmail me or, even worse, use me as a mule to smuggle drugs into the country, I'd be lucky if I wasn't arrested and ended up writing my tale of woe from the inside of some lonely Hungarian jail cell. But, if I was wrong about my suspicions and Sandor wanted nothing more than to show me my father's plane and his hiding place, then maybe this might make a good story. That is if it turned out to be true. If not, the idea of a story about a woman traveling to Hungary to find her father's downed aircraft, only to be taken in by some grifter who had manufactured a story like that of a lot of former WW2 airmen, probably wouldn't amount to anything more than a paragraph's warning in any newspaper's travel section. My former colleagues would laugh—a good investigative reporter would have known better. No wonder they fired her!

Aanika continued with her questions. "Did your father talk about Lake Balaton?"

"Very little," I said. "The only time my dad mentioned the lake was when he jumped out of his plane. He said he remembered seeing a church steeple and figured everything would be okay."

"Is your father religious?" Aanika stirred her coffee and looked at Sandor.

Their eyes met, and Sandor clenched his jaw. I sensed he was uncomfortable with Aanika asking so many personal questions.

"His father was a minister," I said. "He grew up believing in a higher power."

"Enough talk about past," Sandor said. "I tell you now about Lake Balaton. We call it the Hungarian Sea…"

Aanika's eyes glossed over. Her interest in the area's geography wasn't much greater than my own, and I sensed we had both tuned a lot of what Sandor said out. At least I had until I heard him say, "…the day your dad tried to fly over it, there were Nazi troops everywhere, like ants."

It felt strange to be driving into an area where my father had hidden a half-century earlier, knowing the forest had been full of German soldiers, foraging for food and burning villages to the ground. If the Germans suspected anyone had sympathies with the Allies or might be hiding Jews or downed American airmen, they would have been shot.

"Everyone was suspect," Sandor said. "No one was safe."

Chapter Nine

We had driven for almost two hours, and the traffic had increased as we got closer to Keszthely. I was ready for a break, looking forward to lunch and the chance to stretch my legs. Ahead of us, a blinking yellow light indicated we had come to a crossroads on the outskirts of the city. The area was clamoring with tourists.

Sandor looked up into the hills. "There it is. You see it?"

I leaned forward, my hands on the back of Aanika's seat, and stared out the open window. Sandor pointed to what looked like little more than a pile of dark rock surrounding the remains of a single tower. Not much different from several other ruins we had passed that morning. Perhaps that was his plan, show me a long-forgotten pile of rocks, claim this was where my father had hidden, and take a few pictures.

We drove about a hundred yards further before Sandor stopped the car, then, without a word, got out and paced the side of the road.

"What's he looking for?" I asked Aanika.

"The road up to the fortress. He hasn't been here in years. It's not marked." Aanika looked anxiously out the window while Sandor walked the roadside, then stopped and stooped down to clear some weeds.

"Found it!" Sandor gave a thumbs-up, raced back to the car, put the red beast in reverse, and slammed on the brakes.

I gripped the back of Aanika's seat to keep from falling forward.

"Hang on!" Sandor took a sharp turn, and the red beast groaned like a wild boar as we bounced up over the road's berm and onto what once might have been a narrow-rutted trail, now overgrown with weeds and wildflowers.

I held tight to the handgrip in the backseat while Aanika put one hand on Sandor's shoulder and, with the other, hugged the open window as we bounced along, hitting our heads on the beast's roof until we came to an empty field surrounded by tall trees.

Sandor continued to moderate as he drove around tree stumps and rocks that threatened to end our drive. "When I was little, this was where my grandmother would bring me to hike. Before the war, it was all farmland, rich vineyards, and small farmhouses. They're gone now. What the war didn't destroy, time and politics did. All that remains is the land."

"I'm surprised you can still find your way." I had seen no roadside markers, and the field ahead of us was a mass of wild poppies. Any remnants of the past had long since disappeared. All that remained of the vineyard were a few zealous vines that crept like spider webs up tree trunks.

"I'm good with directions," Sandor pointed to the lake. "Lake Balaton is south, Keszethely is east. And the Carpathian Mountains your father flew over to the north."

I checked my compass locket from around my neck. The directions matched exactly.

"Before the war," Aanika said, "Sandor's grandparents owned a small farm near the lake and would come for vacation. They were quite wealthy. They had a caretaker who looked after the place when they were in the city, but when the war broke out—"

"Things changed." Sandor interrupted abruptly. Almost as if he wanted to stop Aanika from talking before she might say too much.

I wrestled the conversation back. I wanted to know more about the area and asked Aanika if she had ever been here before. "No. I've asked, but Sandor said it was too long ago, and there was no point."

Sandor put his hand on Aanika's knee while describing the area. "It wasn't until after the war that my grandmother came back, and I came with her. That's when she told me the story about the people who lived here and why I knew who Katarina and Adolph were. Back then, everyone around this area knew about Katarina and the fortress. But no one talked about it until after the war." Sandor stopped the car. "I think we stop here for lunch. I hope you're hungry?"

My stomach growled at the thought of food, I hadn't eaten since last night, and I was starving.

Sandor told Aanika to get the picnic basket from the back seat while he got a blanket from the trunk.

I had to admit if this tour was some game Sandor was playing, he was better at it than I had credited him for—and Aanika, if she knew anything at all, hid it beautifully. Together they were as close to the perfect couple as I could imagine. But I wasn't about to be fooled. Sandor undoubtedly intended to show me some probable location where my father *might* have hidden, and then his downed B-24. But how would I know if it was real? All I knew for sure was that I wouldn't be at all surprised if Sandor were to suddenly turn around and pleaded some hardship for which he would expect me to pay money, and that wasn't going to happen. At least not before lunch, not with the warm smell of freshly baked bread wafting from the picnic basket next to me.

Sandor found a place to spread the blanket beneath a tree while Aanika unpacked the picnic basket. In addition to the black bread sandwiches with cream cheese and black cherry jam, Aanika had included an assortment of cold cuts, nuts, and various regional cheeses. We finished them with a bottle of white wine while Sandor pointed to the stone tower and explained that both it and several of the other ruined remains in the area had all been part of an early Roman occupation.

"Nika, where is your Túróstáska?" Sandor reached for the picnic basket.

Aanika slapped Sandor's hand and took a plate from within the basket with several puffed pastries she had prepared for dessert. Then teased it beneath her husband's nose and pulled it away. "You want?"

Sandor swiped at the plate.

"Say, please."

"Pleeeeease, kedvesem." Sandor grabbed her wrist playfully.

Then taking one of the pastries from the plate, Aanika stuffed it into Sandor's mouth and made a gooey mess on his face. Then kissed him on the cheek and licked her fingers.

I enjoyed how the two of them played together like newlyweds, so fun-loving and convincing. *Was this all an act for my benefit?* The playfulness had died out for Josh and me after our first year of marriage, and then the loneliness hit. Josh was seldom home, and when he was, he didn't want to talk. The isolation I felt living in that big house all alone on the hill was suffocating. It was no wonder I had an affair.

Sandor stretched out on the blanket, put his head in his wife's lap, then reached into his pocket and pulled out a joint.

"You like?" He took a puff, then offered it to me.

My heart stopped. In some countries, the mere possession of marijuana could result in prison or even a death sentence. I wasn't sure about Hungary, but I didn't want to find out.

"No," I said. "I don't smoke."

"Of course not." Sandor shrugged and took a puff. Then extinguished the smoke and put it back in the basket. "So, are you ready to hike?"

Chapter Ten

S andor led the way through the forest until we came to a clearing, then stopped to catch our breath. Ahead of us, a field of bright orange poppies surrounded the remains of a barn and a split rail fence. In the center lay various pieces of farm machinery, rusted and long since forgotten.

"Was this Katarina's place?" I asked.

"I don't know. Maybe. But that's not what I'm looking for. Listen." Sandor put his finger to his mouth. "You hear that?"

"What?" Was it the sound of birds, the wild geese we had seen flying low over the lake, or the breeze as it rustled through the trees he wanted me to notice?

"The river," he said. "It runs from the mountains to the lake. If we follow it, it should lead us to a trail beneath the fortress where Katarina and Adolph hid your father. The river is the only way I know how to find our way."

Sandor quickened his pace toward the sound of the rushing water. By the time Aanika and I caught up with him, he was standing on a rock at the river's edge. Aanika put her hand on my shoulder to balance herself while she caught her breath.

Sandor tossed a rock in the river, then offered Aanika his hand. Together they rock-hopped across the river. Once on the other side, Sandor paused and did a visual check of the mountain. Then announced he had found the trail that led up to the top of the fortress.

When we got to the top of the mountain, I was thankful that a section of wall surrounding the fortress had crumbled. It was easy to climb over some of the fallen rocks and into the courtyard. Several small, stone roofless dwellings of various sizes lined the fortress walls and opened onto the interior courtyard facing a well's remains. From where we stood to the tower directly across from us, the entire complex was no larger than the size of a football field and eerily quiet.

I took my camera and immediately began snapping pictures of the ancient rock wall, the tower, and the well in the courtyard. Sandor warned me not to get too close to the well, but I couldn't help myself. I got several artsy shots then focused my lens on the well's black hallow. "Anyone there?"

The sound of my voice echoed back.

Sandor grabbed my arm and pulled me back from the ledge. "You don't want to fall. You could get hurt."

"How deep is it?" I asked.

"I don't know. A hundred feet maybe? The Romans dug down to pull water from an underground stream."

"What about when my father was here, was there water? And what about food? And the hike up the mountain? That couldn't have been easy. How could they have made it without being seen? Or, for that matter, how had Katarina and Adolph managed to bring them supplies?" I was beginning to doubt the logistics of the location. How could anyone survive here? Did Sandor really expect me to believe him without some proof?

"You ask questions I have no answers for. I can only tell you what my grandmother told me when I visit with her in Keszthely after the war."

"Did your grandmother know Katarina?" I asked.

"Like I said, everybody back then knew about Katarina. But, during the war, my grandmother tells me nobody talks. It was too dangerous. If the Germans found out what Katarina hid, they would shoot everyone. Other villages hid Americans, and when the Germans found out, those that helped hide them were marched into the streets and shot, and the villages burned. After the war, there are only sad stories."

"Did you ever meet Katarina?"

"Once, when my grandmother takes me to the marketplace, she buys me something sweet to eat, and we see her there. I remember she is tall, and I am frightened because I see a patch on her eye."

"She had a patch?" I looked down at the setting on my camera. I didn't want Sandor to see the surprise in my eyes. My father's sketch had shown Katarina wearing a patch, but the fact Sandor appeared to know didn't mean he had really met her. With Sandor's love for history, he might just have known the famous partisan was blind in one eye.

"Yes. Katarina comes to our table, and she talks to my grandmother. Katarina tells her she has returned from Russia, and I hear them talk about the fortress and the things she has hidden there. It is the first time I hear about your father and the men with him."

I walked across the courtyard and stooped down to look inside one of the small stone structures. The Romans might have used it for storage, but hiding three airmen for any time would have been difficult.

"What else did Katarina hide here?" I asked.

"There were things from the church in Keszthely. I remember Katarina telling my grandmother about them. A priest from the church had approached her. He was worried the Germans would steal statues and artwork and send it back to Germany. Some things could be hidden in the church cellar, but not all. Those pieces of artwork the church could not hide, Katarina hide for them." Sandor crushed out his cigarette. "Come, I have more to show you."

I followed Sandor up a stone stairway to the top of one of the remaining walls and snapped a few more photos, including one of Sandor and Aanika with the lake Balaton behind them. Pictures to verify that this was the same scene my father had seen while in hiding. The view was spectacular—the water blue as the sky—and with the mountains behind me, a perfect marker of our location. I wanted as many shots as I could take to share with my father.

Sandor pointed in the direction of the lake. "From here, you can see how close your father was to the lake. If he had crossed Lake Balaton, he would have bailed out behind the Russian lines, and you and I, we never would have met."

How convenient for Sandor's story. The location of the fortress. His admission there had been other American flyers hidden in the area. And

Katarina—a war widow everyone knew, but none spoke openly about. It all made for a nice story, yet, I had seen nothing that would convince me what Sandor told me was unique to my father's experience.

"Yes. There would have been no need for us to meet," I said.

"Follow me." Sandor turned back to the stairs. "There is something more you need to see inside the tower. It may help to convince you."

Was it that obvious?

I followed behind him. At the bottom of the stairway, Sandor pointed to a square opening at the tower's base. If there had ever been a door to cover it, it was long since gone. I ducked and followed Sandor inside.

Despite the tower having no roof, it was dark and dank. A few weeds had taken root and grew up inside and clung to the stones.

"Look, here." Sandor pointed to an inside wall. "When I first see this, I think it must be graffiti. And then I see names."

On the wall, I recognized my father's name, Lt. Steve Lawson, and Sergeants Nick Farkas and William Bradley. Beneath the names, a series of numbers had been scratched into the rock. 781 02 03 45.

"What do the numbers mean?"

"I believe they represent your father's squadron and the date they were shot down. I think they put them here so the world would know they were here."

I pressed my fingers against the scratches. The names and numbers almost looked like hieroglyphics. They had obviously been there for some time.

"Excuse me." I walked outside. I needed a moment to process everything I had just seen. Unless Sandor had come back and marked the wall inside the tower with my father's name and that of Nick and Bill, then this fortress, this crumbling old ruin, had to have been where my father hid.

"Are you okay?" Aanika put her hand on my shoulder.

"I can't imagine what it must have been like. Or how Katarina and Adolph were able to fool the Germans. My dad and his men would have been right in the middle of it all. It's hard to believe the Germans didn't know they were here."

"It may not have been as difficult as you imagine," Sandor said. "Adolph and his mother were German-Hungarians. To survive, Katarina had to convince the Germans she was loyal to their cause. And that may not have been hard for her to do. Her husband had been sent to fight with the Germans on the Russian front, and with a son named Adolph—a very German name—I'm sure they believed her. My grandmother tells me Adolph had a small cart, and the Germans asked him to collect radios from the town's people. The Nazis didn't want anyone to know what was going on with the war, and when Adolph would bring the Germans the radios, they would reward him with chocolate."

"Katarina was smart," Aanika said. "She hid eggs, apples, and cheese, beneath the blankets in Adolph's cart, and when she thinks it safe, she brings them to the fortress."

"But, I do remember Katarina telling my grandmother about a close call. She said she was terrified." Sandor explained that Katrina and Adolph were in their barn, filling Adolph's cart with food, blankets, and a radio to take to my father when she noticed their goat had gotten out of the pasture. She looks and sees a German soldier with the bleating goat coming toward them. Sandor acted the scene out.

"Grüß Gott ," the soldier said, "Ist das deine Ziege?" Is this your goat, he asks? Then quickly, before the soldier could enter the barn, Katrina took the food and the radio hidden beneath the blanket and put them on top so they can be seen. She knows if the soldier comes into barn and starts to look around and finds radio hidden beneath blanket, he might find other hiding places, too. She tell him she has gifts for the soldiers. Blankets and goat cheese to give them, plus a radio Adolph has found. But the soldier is desperate for food and takes blanket and goat cheese for himself and tells Adolph to take the radio to the Germans like always. After that," Sandor said, "Katarina and Adolph, they only make the trip in the dark when they think Germans wouldn't see them."

"I wish I could have met her. You don't think there's any chance she's still alive. Maybe living in Keszthely?"

"I don't think so. Towards the end of my grandmother's life, she didn't go out much. I doubt they saw each other, and I can't imagine Katarina's life was much different."

"What about Adolph?" I asked. "Did you ever meet him?"

"No, Adolph was older than me. He wasn't around when I was growing up. After the war, the Russians took many Swabians and sent them off to camps. Adolph and his mother were separated. The Russians sent the kids to special schools. My grandmother tells me she never sees Adolph with Katarina after the war. But later, Katarina tells my grandmother, she is very proud. Adolph has done well with school and is studying hard to be a doctor."

"But," Aanika tapped me on the shoulder and clapped her hands. "If Katarina is alive, there's a chance she might still visit the marketplace in Keszthely. All the old women visit the marketplace there every Saturday. They come, dressed in black, for the flowers and a few groceries, then go to the cemetery to visit the graves. If you like, Kat, we could come back to Keszthely on Saturday and look around."

"There's not an easier way?" I asked. "Like a telephone directory or something?"

Sandor put his arm around Aanika's shoulder. "There is, but it is not so easy here, Kat. Many people don't have a home phone, not like in American. A phone is expensive. And even if Katarina was alive, she could be living in a spare room in someone's home, and we'd never know. Plus, with all she's been through, you have to consider, Katarina may not want to be found. I really hate to see you get your hopes up."

Aanika put her hand on Sandor's chest. "Yes, but the shopping's great there, and it so pretty this time of year. It's worth the trip even if we don't find Katarina."

Sandor touched the tips of Aanika's fingers. I could see he didn't think a trip to Keszthely was worth our while, but what Aanika wanted, Aanika got. Sandor caved.

"Whatever you want. I know you would love to show Kat around Keszthely, and you should go. Get ice cream in front of Festetics Palace and go to the marketplace. I doubt you will find Katarina, but it will be fun for you. Unfortunately, I can't come with you, the two of you will have to go alone. I have a client to meet on Saturday, but tomorrow, Kat, you and I will go to see your father's plane."

Chapter Eleven

It was nearly seven p.m. by the time Sandor and Aanika dropped me back at the apartment, and other than Sandor's offering me a joint, I was feeling pretty good about the day. It wasn't like I had never smoked a little marijuana. Although, I wasn't about to touch the stuff—not in a foreign country. In hindsight, Sandor's offer seemed innocent enough. And, after seeing my father's name and that of Bill and Nick on the tower's wall, I was inclined to think that Sandor was telling me the truth. The more I got to know him and watch him interact with his wife, the more I began to think that maybe my suspicions regarding Sandor were unfounded. That being in a foreign country, with my own insecurities surrounding my current situation with Josh and my job—or lack thereof—had caused me to misjudge him. In fact, my mood was so buoyed as I said goodbye that I found myself hugging them like family and telling Aanika how much I was looking forward to returning to Keszthely with her on Saturday. As for my concerns about Nora and her search of my room, I put it behind me and decided Nora was nothing more than a busybody trying to be overly efficient to impress her first American guest.

Rather than go directly up to my room, I returned to the same small restaurant I had visited the night before. Dion, my waiter, stood out front, his white apron tied neatly about his waist, staring at the river.

"Can I get a table?" I pointed to the empty table where I had sat before. "Same as yesterday?"

"Yesterday?" Dion paused, looked at me as though he were trying to place my face, then smiled. "Ah, my American friend. Come." He nodded for me to follow and led me to my table, where someone had left a newspaper.

The front-page story had a three-inch banner headline above a black-and-white photo of a young woman. She was handcuffed and standing between two police officers in front of the airport curb exactly where I had been the day before. My throat tightened as I stared at the shocked expression on her face.

"What's that all about? I pointed to the newspaper.

"Drugs." Dion looked over my shoulder at the paper. "She was caught trying to smuggle cocaine in her luggage. The police busted a ring. She said she was set up, but the laws here are very strict." Dion swept the paper from the table and handed me a menu. "You have good day?"

My stomach knotted. In my head, I had a vision of Sandor offering me a joint and Nora searching through my room. Like an iceberg, my doubts about the two resurfaced, and I felt a chill down my back. I swallowed hard. No matter how friendly Sandor and Aanika had been to me, I needed to stay vigilant. I was in a foreign country. I didn't know the laws, and I didn't speak the language.

"Yes, I did, thank you. I went to Lake Balaton. It's beautiful there."

"You go for spa, or maybe wine tasting?"

"Neither," I said. "I went to see the lake and some of the ruins, one in particular, just past Szigilget Castle."

"And you not stop for wine tasting?" Dion pulled the chair out for me to sit.

"No."

"Big mistake. Best vineyards in the area. I bring you my favorite." Dion disappeared back into the restaurant's kitchen and returned with an empty glass and a bottle of Pinot Gris, or as he called it, *Olaszrizling*, a white wine. He filled the bottom of my glass and waited while I tasted it. "You like?"

I swirled the glass like I had seen wine enthusiasts do and held it up to the light. Anything to take my mind off the vision of Sandor and the joint he had attempted to hand me. Thankfully, I had recently interviewed a sommelier for the paper, and I knew the basics; a swirl of the glass to release the aroma, then the glass to the light to check for the wine's legs or tears that slipped down the side of the glass. The more tears, the higher the alcohol content. And finally, the smell test, a deep inhale of the wine's fragrant bouquet to prepare the taste buds.

I took a small sip and held it in my mouth for a moment, then swallowed. "Very light. Flowery, with a slightly bitter almond after note."

"You know your wines." Dion filled my glass. "Here, we say Olaszrizling is the taste of Hungary. Sweet but melancholy. Next time you go to Lake Balaton, you must buy and bring home."

Dion suggested I pair my wine with a bowl of Halászlé, a hot spicy paprika-based fish soup with potatoes and peppers, which I might have done under different circumstances. But after seeing the front page of the paper, I decided to order a second glass of wine and sat back to enjoy the scene in front of me. But all I could think about was Sandor and the joint he had offered me. Was it a test?

Sandor was looking for a quick way to make a buck, but drugs? It just didn't feel right. As for my fears about Nora searching my room and maybe hiding drugs, I had no proof. Looking at the river, I knew Dad was right. I had needed to get away from home and clear my head. I took a sip of my wine and wished my father had been able to come with me. He would have loved to sit and watch the riverboats as they cruised up and down the river and the couples as they idly strolled the riverwalk, stopping long enough to read the menu in front of the small outdoor cafes.

I took my camera, shot a couple of pictures of the river, and then signaled Dion to bring my bill. I wanted to get back to my room and call Dad. I had a lot to talk to him about, and I knew he would be waiting for my call. He would be anxious to know if Sandor had taken me to see where my father had hidden and what I thought. I took a final sip of my wine and got up from the table.

"Kat! My American friend. Is that you?" Coming down the riverwalk was the young gypsy who had driven me in his motorboat the night before. He stopped, just feet from my table, and with his hands in the air and a big smile on his face, said. "Is me, Adrian. I have been thinking of you."

I looked away, wishing I were anywhere but where I was and that the young man would go away. I didn't want to create a scene. Whether Adrian had been thinking of me or not, I suspected upon spotting me, his first thought was that I might be a soft touch for a couple of bucks. I immediately regretted that I hadn't heeded the warning in my guidebook regarding gypsies to not engage them.

Dion waved Adrian off like some homeless dog or cat. To avoid any further incident, I took a couple of Hungarian bills from my fanny pack—enough to cover the cost of my wine—and left them on the table. Then got up, and with my head down to avoid any chance of eye contact, started back in the direction of Nora and Miklos's apartment.

Adrian chased after me.

"I think you have a good day. Am I right?"

"It was very nice," I said. I didn't want to appear rude, nor did I want to encourage the boy. I kept my head down and quickened my step.

Adrian wasn't about to be dissuaded and skipped alongside me.

"You visit somewhere special. Maybe find what you come for. But not all, I can tell."

I stopped abruptly. I needed to put an end to this. Politely, but firmly I said. "I visited Lake Balaton. It was beautiful, and now, I'm sorry, but it's getting late, and I need to go."

Adrian pulled an accordion file of postcards from inside his jacket, allowing them to cascade from his hand to the sidewalk.

"You see Lake Balaton, but I bet you do not see caves. I have pictures. Many tourists miss." He pointed to a picture on one of the cards of a beautiful blue grotto with an iridescent blue light. "You should see. Very beautiful. Very mysterious."

I kept walking. I wasn't going to be bothered.

"Natural wonder inside mountain with many secret tunnels. Not everyone see, but I show you. Romans use years ago. You lucky lady, I make you very good price."

"No, thank you," I said.

"You not want card?"

"No," I said, this time more adamantly, and kept walking.

Adrian tore a card from the strip and chased after me. "Here, you take. You change mind, I show you."

"Good night, Adrian."

Chapter Twelve

When I got back to the apartment, the front door was unlocked like it was the night before, but this time, neither Miklos nor Nora were in the living room. I could hear them in the kitchen with the baby, their voices low and muffled. I figured they didn't want to be disturbed and had left the door unlocked for me. Rather than announce my return, I hurried up the circular staircase, threw my fanny pack and the postcard Adian had given me on the bed, and called home.

While I waited for the call to go through, I paced the room with the phone against my ear.

"Hello?" Dad answered right away. It was almost noon his time, and he sounded tired.

"Hey there, Dad, good news." I tried to sound upbeat and told him about my trip with Sandor and his wife to the ruined fortress where he had hidden.

Dad's response was slow, and his voice raspy. "So, Sandor found it."

"He did. He said his grandmother had taken him there when he was a small boy. Although I don't think he had been there in years. It wasn't easy to find, but what a view! We crawled around. Went up on the wall and inside the tower. Sandor even showed me where you scratched your name and the date you crashed. That was you, right?"

Dad coughed. The coughing jags sounded worse than when I had left. I waited for him to clear his throat.

"Yea, that was us. Didn't want anyone to forget we were there."

"You okay, Dad?"

"I'm fine, Kat. Don't you worry about me. Doc's got me on some new meds. Don't much care for 'em, but what can I do? Die?"

"Dad!"

"Come on, Kat, give me a break. Talk to me about what you saw. Tell me, you got some good pictures."

I forced myself to focus on my visit with Sandor and Aanika, not on my father's failing health. I needed to keep his spirits up.

"You bet," I said. "I got lots. Wasn't an easy climb up that mountain, though. I can't imagine how you got up there. Nick with a broken leg, and the Germans all around you? It's a miracle you weren't seen?"

"Whadda, you mean, seen? We didn't climb up any damn mountain. There was a cave."

"What?"

"A grotto, by the riverfront. Had a whole maze of tunnels connected to it. Didn't Sandor show you?"

"No, he didn't." I picked the postcard up off the bed and flipped it over. On the back was a history of the area—once an active volcano, lava flows had formed tunnel tubes or fissures that went on for miles beneath the mountain's surface. Strange Sandor hadn't mentioned anything about a cave.

"Lucky for us, Katarina and her son knew about the fortress. The Germans thought it was just some century-old ruin. Nothing but a pile of rocks, not much use to them. They didn't know about the grotto or the tunnels that led up inside to the fortress' well."

"The well?" I remembered Sandor had pulled me away from what must have been the well in the courtyard's center.

"The Romans used the grotto and those tunnels hundreds of years before. Dug down through the fortress's center courtyard and the volcano's crusty tunnels to create a well. And off of it, a hiding place that served as an escape route. Pretty ingenious, huh?"

"And that's how you got in and out of the fortress, through the well?"

"It was perfect. Unless you knew about the tunnels, you wouldn't know it was there." Dad started to cough again.

My mother picked up the phone.

"What well are you two talking about?" she asked.

"Dad said there was a cave leading to the inside of the fortress where he hid." I explained Sandor had taken me there today. But he never mentioned a cave, much less a tunnel, leading to the inside of the well. "I don't think Sandor even knew about it."

"Oh, come on, Kat. There you go, being all suspicious again."

"Strange though, don't you think?"

"Maybe he did and didn't want to risk getting lost underground with you." Dad sounded adamant. "It's not like those tunnels are mapped, and things could get pretty scary down there. Could be a lot of reasons why he didn't mention it. The important thing was that Katarina knew about it, and the Germans didn't."

"Yeah, while I still think it's odd Sandor didn't say anything. He told me everybody in the village knew about Katarina and what she was doing—and hiding. Sandor's too much of a historian not to know about the caves in the area. How could he not know?"

My mother butted in. "Yes, well, I'm just thankful the cave was there and that Katarina knew about it. And that the Germans didn't find your Dad before she did."

My father coughed again, then struggled to talk. "I'd say it was a pretty close call. We had just taken off our chutes and were looking for somewhere to hide when Katarina found us. She told us to follow her, and at that point, seeing a woman who spoke English and wasn't pointing a gun at us seemed like a pretty good idea. We packed Nick in the cart, Katarina said something about a cave, and we followed."

I looked at the picture of the cave in my hand, the shadowed, craggy-looking walls low over a pool of turquoise water. Dad was claustrophobic and hated tight spaces. "I can't believe you hid inside a cave. You hate things like that."

"I also didn't like getting shot at and jumping out of planes. But at the time, there wasn't much choice."

"I suppose not."

"Sometimes you gotta kick fear in the butt and go with it. Faith over fear,

Kat, it's what got me through."

"How long were you there?"

"In the grotto? Not long. Once we got Nick out of the cart, Bill and I were able to help him through the tunnel. Some of those passageways go on for miles, and there were room-sized caverns inside big enough to hide a small army. Fortunately for us, Adolph knew where he was going, and we hid in a cavern right below the fortress. And when we wanted, we could climb up through the well to the courtyard."

"But how?"

"The wall's notched with cuts in the rock, so it was an easy enough climb—that is, if you didn't look down. Don't know if we would have figured it out ourselves or not, but Adolph did. That kid could climb up and down inside that well like it was a ladder."

"What about water? Was there water in the well?"

"Oh, yeah. Probably still is, but you got to have a bucket to get it. Katarina brought us one, and she and Bill, our flight engineer, fashioned a kinda pulley over a tree branch so we could haul it up. Later, we used it to get Nick up inside the courtyard, although he spent most of his time in the cave. Bill and I would climb out and enjoy the sunshine."

"And you didn't worry about the Germans?"

"We could see them and hear them. But the Germans didn't know we were there, and they weren't about to climb up some mountain top for the joy of it."

"And you hid there, inside that cave for the entire time?"

"We did. We were there for about a week, week-and-a-half. I don't remember exactly. Time goes by differently when you're hiding. One day melds into another. I know Nick was in a lot of pain and having a tough time. Katarina was a nurse. She fashioned a splint for his leg and brought him some tea she had made from the bark of a willow tree to help with the pain. Maybe it did, I don't know."

"Well, it never slowed him down. That's for sure." My mother laughed. "Kat, you must remember Nick. He was the fabulous dancer who would dance with all the ladies at the reunions. I think your father has always been

73

a little jealous."

"I wasn't jealous, Lynn. I just didn't like the way he held you."

"Oh, you silly man. He was just having fun."

I remembered the reunions and the dances. I was barely thirteen. Dad always loved to dance, but one time he wasn't in the mood, and Nick pulled my mom out onto the dance floor. I think Nick was a little drunk, but Mom was light on her feet, and they looked like Fred Astaire and Ginger Rogers in my mind. Only, Dad wasn't happy about it. It was maybe the only time I ever saw my father get upset with my mother. Soon as the dance ended, Dad took my mom by the hand and went outside. I don't know what was said. We never talked about it, and the few reunions we attended after that, I sensed my father's relationship with Nick was strained. I don't think I ever saw them chatting together again.

Dad dismissed my mother's musings with a tsk and continued to talk about what they did while hidden in the fortress. Nick spent most of his day trying to recuperate and learning to walk with a splint, while Bill used Nick's knife to carve small animals from the scraps of bark he found in the fortress courtyard.

"And what about you, Dad? What did you do to pass the time?"

"Katarina brought me a sketch pad, and I drew pictures of the area."

I took the picture my father had drawn of Katarina and Adolph from my backpack and stared at it. "And with all of Katarina's comings and goings, the Germans were never suspicious of her?"

"I didn't say that. But I suspect Katarina might have been untouchable. She never said exactly, but I got the idea the soldiers didn't bother her because she was friendly with the Oberfuhrer."

"The Oberfuher?"

"The top-ranking German officer in the area. Adolph would show up sometimes without his mother. He would tell us the Oberfuher was visiting and that Katarina had asked him to leave. It didn't take much to figure Katarina was doing what she needed to do. She was no fool, and I doubt we were the first American airmen she had hid or what else she might have hidden in those tunnels. It could have been gun powder for all I know. That's what the partisans did. They helped downed airmen get back from behind enemy lines, blew things up when they could, and disrupted the German's plans."

Whoever Katarina was, I liked her. She was no longer just a name and a face my father had drawn on a blank piece of paper. She was someone I wanted to know.

"Kat, promise me you'll try to find them."

"I'll do my best, Dad." I closed my eyes and hoped that was possible. "I'm going to see your plane tomorrow. Sandor's taking me to Tamasi, where he says he found it. Then Saturday, I'm going to Keszthely with Sandor's wife, Aanika. That's where Sandor's grandmother lived and where he thinks Katarina last lived. If she's still there, I'll find her."

"And Adolph, too."

"And Adolph, too. I promise."

* * *

I took my journal from beneath my pillow where I had left it and began to make notes. I wanted to annotate my thoughts on the day before I closed my eyes. I started with my trip to Lake Balaton, the fortress, the wall, the well, and the fact Sandor hadn't mentioned anything to me about it. With as much history as Sandor knew, I couldn't believe Sandor didn't know anything about the caves in the area or the secret tunnel beneath the fortress we had hiked to that day.

I drew a line beneath the section about the fortress, then wrote Sandor's name, followed by a series of question marks. Just because Sandor smoked a joint didn't mean he was into smuggling drugs. Illegal or otherwise, I figured pot was something those who could and wanted to did—like bootleg liquor back in the days of prohibition. And as a part-time trucker, Sandor probably had no trouble getting what he wanted for recreational use when he wanted it.

On a second line, I wrote both Sandor's and Annika's names, followed by my observations on how comfortable they were with each other and how much I enjoyed my time with them. In some respects, their playful ways reminded me of my relationship with my first husband, Eric. I leaned back against the pillow with the pad on my knees and stared at my notes. If Eric hadn't died, I wondered if we might be the same. I missed the way we teased one another, the way I felt in his arms. When Eric left for Vietnam, he had prepaid for a long-stemmed single red rose to be delivered every Friday. The deliveries continued for a year, even though his jet had crashed his first week there. I wrote his name and drew a heart next to it. *If only.* After Eric, life got more complicated. I finished college, started working at the newspaper, and then, twenty years later, I met Josh. I penned Josh's name beneath Eric's and, following it, put another large question mark.

Chapter Thirteen

I forgot to set my alarm and overslept the next morning. If it hadn't been for the sunlight streaming through the window, I might not have woken until much later. I glanced at the bedside clock. It was almost nine-thirty, and I had promised to meet Sandor at the Elizabeth Bridge at ten. I showered, dressed, and was just about out the door when I remembered I had left my favorite lip gloss next to the bathroom sink. I had forgotten it yesterday when I went to the lake and wished I had had it. But when I returned to the bathroom, it was nowhere to be found. The cosmetics on the small glass stand next to the sink had been rearranged, and my favorite cherry-tinted lip gloss was missing.

My first thought was that I had misplaced it. Or that Nora, when cleaning the bathroom, had knocked it off the shelf and into the trash. Whatever, I decided it was no big deal. It wasn't like lip gloss was expensive or something I couldn't pick up at any drug store in Budapest. But after talking with my father last night and learning about the cave beneath the old fortress and that Sandor had failed to mention anything about it, my suspicions regarding Sandor and Nora had once again tilted out of favor. The thought that Nora might have been looking through my things sent me to the closet to double-check that my passport was still stuffed inside my oversized leather bag. Finding it, I dismissed my concern, at least as far as Nora was concerned, and hurried down the stairs.

Nora was vacuuming the living room. She turned the machine off when she saw me and reached into her apron.

"'Dis yours?" In her hand, she held my lip gloss. "I find on floor." She handed me the small tube and smiled. Her lips were cherry-red.

"Why don't you keep it." I tossed the lip gloss back to her and went out the door.

Sandor and I needed to have a talk.

* * *

I met with Sandor by Elizabeth Bridge, exactly as we had planned. According to my guidebook, the drive to Tamasi was about an hour-and-a-half, and if the early morning temperature was any indication, we were in for another hot day.

"You have a good night? I hope Miklos and Nora take good care of you." Sandor opened the beast's door for me, and I ducked and folded myself into the small passenger seat.

"Couldn't be better hosts," I said. I had no plans to say anything about my suspicions. Certainly not about Sandor's pot-smoking, and definitely not about Nora and Miklos until I understood just how close Sandor was to them. "Nice people. Have you known them long?"

"Forever." Sandor lit a cigarette and hung his arm out the beast's open window. "Miklos works at the Copy Center next to Saint Stephen's. Funny story about his job."

Here we go again, another long story. I crossed my arms and settled back against the beast's hard, cowhide seat.

"Do you believe, before Russians leave, there is only one copy machine in all of Budapest? The Russians had it locked away in a jail cell. Not because they feared it would be stolen, but because they didn't want anyone to use it. Copies were illegal, and back then, nobody understood why anyone would want to make them. It is a foreign idea to us. But after Russians leave, we find this copy machine and learn maybe this is a good business idea. Miklos is smart and a good salesman, and he opens the first copy store here, and today he runs The Copy Center, next to Saint Stephen's—the biggest in all of Budapest. I am very proud of him." Sandor took a puff of his cigarette, blew a circle of smoke out the window, and continued with his story. "But things have not always been good for Miklos. His first wife ran off with a Russian when the Soviets leave, and Miklos is sad for a long time. I worry about him. Then he meets Nora. She is young and pretty. No?"

"Yes, very," I said. I appreciated the story as much as I did the insights it offered me about Sandor's relationship with Miklos and Nora. "And they seem very happy."

"She saves his life. Puts him back together again. The guestroom, it is her idea. They just finish. I think it is very nice, best in all of Budapest."

"So, I must be their first guest," I said. "Everything in the room looks brand new."

"They just finished last week. Perfect timing for your visit."

"Yes, how convenient." A little too opportune, I thought.

"They give you breakfast? Nora makes good muffins. Not as good as Aanika make, but please, don't tell her I told you so. Nora will be very mad at me." Sandor winked.

I explained I hadn't had breakfast, and Sandor nodded to the backseat where Aanika had prepared a thermos of hot coffee along with a small basket of Hungarian sweet rolls. The rolls looked like croissants but were sweet and salty. Exactly what I needed to wake me up while Sandor launched into another story about the history of Tamasi.

Tamasi was named for Saint Thomas and built on a Roman settlement. The town had three catholic churches and was once popular with the Russians who visited—not because of the churches—but because of the wild animal preserve, one of the best in Europe. The lodge, of which there were several, and the preserve Sandor wanted us to visit had once belonged to the Estherházy family, Hungarian nobles whose roots dated back to the middle-ages and were part of the Hapsburg Monarchy and Austro-Hungarian empire. Today, the park hosted the world's largest population of fallow deer and water birds.

"You don't know venison 'til you had red deer stew with Hungarian Noodles." Sandor patted his stomach. "I know special lodge. They make best in the world."

The thought of a heavy meal so early in the day didn't excite me. Not to mention the idea I would be dining beneath the heads of what was on the menu and possibly eating Bambi.

"Best in the world, huh?"

"Good place to stop for lunch," he said.

I suspected Sandor hoped he had whet my appetite with his meaty descriptions and that I would offer to pay for lunch. Partial payment, no doubt for his services, which he had insisted, were free, but that I had begun to feel had strings attached with dollar signs that were about to pop up like an old fashion cash register. Still, we did have to eat.

"Tell you what," I said. "Since you're driving, lunch is on me."

"You pay for?"

I nodded. So far, Hungarian food appeared to be a bargain. How expensive could lunch be?

"You will like it. It is expensive for a Hungarian like me, but I think it is a fair price for you. I have only one question."

"What's that?" I asked.

"You want we have lunch first or after we see your father's plane?"

"How about after," I said.

"Good." Sandor flicked his cigarette out the window and pressed his foot to the floorboard.

As we picked up speed, Sandor continued with his history of the area. The Russians had done nothing to clear the landscape of downed aircraft. There had been many, but few where the wreckage had remained intact. However, the B-24 my father had flown that fateful day had belly-flopped into an empty field, and its tail number was clearly identifiable. Consequently, Sandor had been able to contact the DOD, and via their records, piece together my dad's flight that day, and ultimately the names and members of his crew.

"Your father was lucky," Sandor said. "His crew made it out alive, but the young man who found the plane later tried to siphon gas from wing and is badly hurt. People here needed fuel. It was very cold. When he tries to get gas from plane, the wing catch fire. Farmers put the flames out, but the boy was burned. I find story in paper and send your father. You see it?"

I told him I had.

"Bombshell Betty, she is like a ghost in the field. I wish your father could see her."

"Bombshell Betty?" The name meant nothing to me. I had never heard it before, nor even thought about what the plane's name had been.

"Your father not tell you name? Big picture of sexy lady in red swimsuit with blonde hair on the fuselage. Maybe your father name her?"

"I don't think so." From the various reunions my family attended with the crew, I knew it was the pilots who had naming rights. I didn't recall ever hearing any specific name for any one plane. But I did know the nose art was painted onto the big bomber's side by the crew. Unlike in the movie *Memphis Belle* I had watched before coming, Dad said crews seldom flew the same plane twice in a row. Often, planes returning from a mission were so shot up that they needed to be repaired before they were ready to fly again. Squadrons had additional planes at the ready, and the crews flew whatever bomber they were next assigned. I doubted even if I were to tell my father the plane's name that he would remember.

"There she is." Sandor pulled the rusty red Russian beast to the side of the road and got out.

I grabbed my camera and began taking pictures. Like a downed bird, Bombshell Betty lay silent. Her head—the cockpit—twisted and broken from her body, her wings spread-eagled, her mighty double tail with its gun turrets pitched at an awkward angle was several feet above the ground. I took the compass-locket from around my neck and checked the plane's position. My father's last-minute calculations to head south-east of Linz, Austria, to Pecs, Hungary, had worked. Another fifty miles, and she might have made it.

I snapped several more shots and wondered if Dad would recognize her? The left wing was broken, and her engines were embedded in the dirt. The right-wing, blackened from the fire, was still intact. I walked to the area between the cockpit and fuselage where I could see inside the plane and snapped a photo of the pilot and copilot's seats.

Sandor went to the nose cone.

"You see there?" Sandor pointed to the remains of the navigator seat on top of the plane in front of where the pilots sat. Then to the nose cone where the bombardier would have sat, now buried in the dirt.

Despite the fact the Bombshell Betty was in relatively good shape, there was no way if Dad had been sitting in the bombardier's seat, he would have survived the crash.

"She was an amazing plane." Sandor pointed to her engines. "Four air-cooled radial engines. Big boxlike fuselage beneath high wings. A twin tail. And a tricycle landing gear." Sandor had done his homework. He knew the plane as well as he knew his history. He walked around the old bomber and pointed out her specifics; a wingspan a hundred-and-ten-feet, and when fully loaded with eight-thousand pounds of bombs, she weighed fifty-six-thousand pounds and cruised at about twenty-five thousand feet. "Your Army Air Force called her the Liberator. Her crews called her a flying coffin."

I shook my head.

"You know a lot about her," I said. I moved back between the nose cone and the fuselage and refocused my camera lens to get a better shot of the plane's interior. "How did anyone get into one of these things?"

"Wasn't easy. She didn't have a door like on a passenger plane. The crew got in through the bomb bay. Pilot, copilot, bombardier, and navigator, through the nose."

I took a couple more photos of the interior. From what I could see, there not only wasn't a door, there was no insulation. Only the plane's thin metal alloy walls. "It had to be noisy and cold inside."

"Flyers wore gloves and electric flight suits, but they didn't always work. At twenty-thousand feet, temperatures were below zero. She was colder than a witch's tit."

"Funny," I said. "That's exactly how my dad described it."

"I hear from other flyers," Sandor said. "Come, look here." Sandor pointed to the jagged edges of a big hole beneath the plane's right wing and another just below the pilot's seats. "A rocket ripped through the fuselage. It took a good pilot to keep her in the air. Amazing she didn't do a nose dive and take everybody with her."

I shared with Sandor that I remembered meeting Bob, my dad's pilot, at the Air Force Academy at one of the family reunions. Even years later, Bob was still a scrappy fellow. Slim, like he was in the picture of him with his crew in front of their plane. Despite being the pilot, Bob was the youngest member of their crew. Barely eighteen.

"Funny story," I said. "After the war, when Bob returned home, he was too young to get his driver's license. His father had to drive him to the DMV so he could take the test."

"They were brave men, and she was a good plane." Sandor hit the side of the plane with the palm of his hand. "And after your dad and rest of the crew bail out, Bombshell Betty sailed on like a glider until she belly-flop right here in this field."

I asked Sandor to stand in front of the plane and took a couple more shots, then suggested we head to the lodge for lunch. I was getting hungry, and with what I had seen of the plane, I had more questions, including a few about the grotto beneath the old fortress. Lunch, I figured, was going to be interesting.

Chapter Fourteen

I was surprised to learn the Gyulaj forest surrounding Tamasi had six hunting lodges. Each with a restaurant and a specialty—deer, fallow deer, or roe deer. I had no idea there were so many types of deer, but Sandor knew them all. He described their differences and their preparation in mouthwatering detail, right down to the spices and the savory blend of the mixed meats and vegetables included in each dish. Listening to him, I had no doubt that while Sandor may have been knowledgeable of his country's history and culture, he was equally as versed in her epicurean specialties and eager to share it with his American clientele. And I quickly determined, since Tamasi and Bombshell Betty was less than an hour-and-a-half drive from Budapest, that my father's plane was a popular show-and-tell destination, frequently included in his tours either as a pre-or post-lunch option.

As for the lodge Sandor had chosen for our lunch, I didn't know what to expect. My father wasn't a hunter, he disliked guns, and coming from Arizona, the closest I'd ever been to any type of lodge was a dude ranch where I had gone as a Girl Scout to learn to fish and horseback ride. I liked to fish, but the idea I had to kill what I caught—much less chop off their heads—didn't appeal to me. As a result, I spent most of my time learning to ride, and I was a pretty good equestrian. So when we pulled up in front of Esterházy Hunting Lodge, nestled behind a wrought iron fence decorated with gold-tipped spears, and I could see it wasn't some rough-hewn wooden hunter's camp, I was awed. I felt as though I had been immediately transported back into the eighteenth century. The lodge was an elegant baroque manor house—more like something I might have expected to find in Disneyland than in the middle of the forest. A sign posted outside the gate indicated the lodge had been built in 1770, with stones from the Count's Castle in Tamasi.

Once inside the gates and beyond the lodge's handsomely carved double doors, we were greeted by the maître d' dressed in black tuxedo pants, white shirt, and red jacket. While it appeared tourists didn't need to be dressed to impress, I felt intimidated in my crop pants and ugly white tennis shoes as we were led through the dining room, beneath heads of wild boar and deer mounted on the walls above us. The entire room with heavy, wood-carved high-back chairs and tables with white linen cloths, silver, and crystal goblets felt very formal.

Sandor waited for me to be seated. "If you like, I order for you. Or perhaps I make a suggestion."

I glanced at the menu, all in Hungarian but with pictures. Determined to try one of their specialties, I pointed to the roasted pheasant. At least its mother wasn't hanging on the wall above me. Sandor looked pleased and ordered the red deer stew for himself.

"Wine or beer?" His eyes never left the menu.

"Beer," I said.

"Jó választás. Good choice for a hot day." Sandor indicated to the waiter he wanted two beers, then spread his napkin on his lap. "You have good visit, I think."

"Yes," I said. "I think so, too. And I appreciate you bringing me here and showing me my father's plane."

The waiter returned with our drinks, and I was about to raise my glass and offer a toast, but Sandor stopped me.

"Is bad luck to clink glasses. You know why?"

"No. But I'm sure you have a story. "

"Is very important that you know." I held my glass while Sandor explained that in 1848 when the Habsburgs defeated the Hungarian army, the Austrians celebrated in Vienna by clinking glass. "So loud we hear in Hungary and vow never to clink glasses again."

"That was almost two hundred years ago, Sandor. It's been a while."

"We have long memory. Today we say, egészségedre." Which sounded something like eggie-a-shay, and I didn't even try to repeat it. Instead, Sandor raised his glass and said, "To your health."

I did the same.

We had a few more sips of beer, and I was prepared to ask him about the cave beneath the old fortress when Sandor put his glass down.

"Kat, I feel as though we have become friends, no?" Sandor gestured with an open hand.

"Yes, I think so. I've enjoyed meeting you and Aanika very much. You've both been very kind to me."

"Then, you mind I ask personal question?"

I had no idea where Sandor might be going with this and braced myself for the unexpected.

"Why you come to Hungary alone? I see gold band on right hand and empty ring finger on left, with tan line. Is there not a Mr. Kat at home?"

I glanced down at the simple gold band from my first marriage on my right hand. I'd never taken it off. Seven years after Eric was shot down, and the Air Force had declared him dead, I had moved it from my left to my right ring finger. And even though it had been better than twenty years, I still couldn't bring myself to take it off. As for the absence of the ring Josh had given me, I assumed it was still on the kitchen table next to the note Josh had left for me when he walked out.

"It's complicated," I said. I wasn't about to tell Sandor I was separated. I wasn't even sure if I was—at least not officially. In the back of my mind, I hadn't come to terms that Josh and I might be over. I still felt obligated to resurrect whatever was left of our marriage.

"All love is complicated," Sandor said.

Now I was uncomfortable. I felt as though Sandor was prodding.

"Yes, well, some of us are luckier than others," I said.

"And you have no brothers or sisters?"

I shook my head. "Nope, just me. I'm an only child."

"This is not what I expect. When my grandmother tells me about Lieutenant Lawson, I think when he goes back to America, he has a big family and is very successful."

"Sorry to disappoint you. I come from neither a big family nor one with a lot of money. Dad was a salesman, and my mother's a housewife. They've been married for fifty-five years, and they're not rich. In fact, they're very middle class."

"We not have such middle class here. Under Russians everyone is the same. No one have money. I think America middle-class have much more, and those that come find good opportunity for investment."

"Ah, is that what this is all about?" Finally, Sandor was about to reveal the real reason for offering me this exclusive, no-charge tour. "And I suppose you have an idea for such an investment?"

"My country like your wild west. We have many opportunities here now that Russians leave. Good investment, if you want, I can suggest—"

"Sandor, stop." I put my hand up. "I appreciate that you've helped me. You and Aanika have been hospitable, and I'm looking forward to going back to Keszthely with her tomorrow. Maybe I'll find Katarina, who knows. But I'm not interested in any foreign investment. If that makes a difference to you, then I'm afraid we're done here. I'm strictly here because my father wants me to find Adolph and Katarina. And if I can't, well—."

"To Adolph and Katarina." Sandor raised his glass. "May you find them."

"But you don't think there's much of a chance, do you?"

Sandor put his drink down.

"You are not first to come back," he said.

"Has someone else come back looking for Adolph and Katarina?" My father said neither Bill nor Nick had returned. "Were there other fliers that Katarina hid? Before my father or after?"

"I don't know who comes to look for Katarina, but she was not alone. Other partisans like her risked their lives. Last year, I did a tour for two Americans. Like your father's, their plane was shot down, but in Yugoslavia. Partisans there hide them in villages and build secret airstrip in the middle of woods. The Americans land big C-47 in the middle of the night and rescue hundreds. The Germans never knew. These Americans, sometimes they come back to see and pay respects."

I blinked. Did I hear Sandor correctly?

"Hundreds of airmen? How could the Germans not know?"

"The partisans hide them like Katarina hid your father. They bring them to secret camps in forest, where together they work with their bare hands and shovels to clear make runway."

"And then in the middle of the night, the Air Force flew in a C-47 and landed it in the woods?" It seemed like an impossibility. If Sandor's understanding of history hadn't been so thorough, I might have doubted him. "How did I not know this?"

"Even now, there are many secrets. Back then, like here, Yugoslavia had different partisan groups, each with their own loyalty. Some to Russia. Some for their own independence. Siding with the wrong side if discovered today could send someone to jail or worse."

"So it's political. Even now," I said.

Sandor nodded. "It is, but Americans have good pilots back then, and mission is big success. Many Americans, including some spies, return to help us." Sandor said.

"You mind if I ask you a question?"

"You want to know if I have a brother?" Sandor winked. "Small joke."

Before I could laugh out loud, the waiter interrupted and placed a silver domed serving plate in front of me. Then, with the kind of presentation I had only seen in old black-and-white movies, lifted the dome with one gloved hand while the aroma wafted from the plate to my nose. The waiter then repeated the same performance and placed Sandor's venison stew in front of him, and with equal efficiency and style, offered him a large silver spoon for tasting purposes.

Sandor took a healthy spoonful of the stew's juices and smacked his lips. The waiter bowed and backed away from our table, and Sandor dabbed his mouth with his napkin.

"I'm sorry to say, I have no brother. Like you, I'm an only child. What you want to know?"

I took another sip of my beer. I was going to need a little courage.

"My father said there was a tunnel inside the mountain. The entrance was from a grotto by the river. He said it led up inside the mountain to a well behind the fortress wall. The tunnel was where they hid. I'm curious if you knew about it? And if you did, why didn't you show me?"

"This is two questions. But I am not surprised you ask. The mountains are full of tunnels."

"Then you did know about it."

"No." Sandor took another taste of his venison.

"I don't understand."

"I knew about the cave, but I never go inside. It is very dangerous. And when I am little, my grandmother warns me not to go." Sandor put his spoon down and explained that a small boy had been lost while playing inside the caves one summer. The locals put together big search party, but the water level had risen, and by the time they found the boy, he had drowned. "It is very sad, and I promised my grandmother I would never go inside the caves. And to this day, I have not. Is not something I like to talk about."

Sandor's answer was smooth. In fact, I thought it might be a little too smooth. Josh would have given me the same type of answer when he didn't want to talk about something. But I wasn't done, and I wasn't about to be put off. I decided I'd play along.

"I get it. I don't like caves either, and tight places make me nervous. In fact, last fall, the newspaper wanted me to cover the Kartchner Caverns outside of Tucson." I explained that the caves were probably similar to those beneath the old fortress—two-and-a-half miles of passageways with giant cavernous rooms beneath the desert floor, and if you didn't know about them, you wouldn't suspect they were there. "It should have been an easy assignment, but just the idea of getting trapped underground gives me the creeps."

"Then you understand. We are both, how you say, claustrophobic?"

"I suppose we are," I said. I took a taste of the pheasant. "You mind if I ask one more question?"

"Another question? Kat, I think you are more curious than hungry." Sandor took a knife and fork to a large piece of venison and began to saw it.

"I need to know why you think my father is a hero? He won't tell me. All he would say is that the real heroes were Adolph and Katarina. And I need to know. What did he do?"

Sandor put his knife and fork down. "Your father killed a man."

"What?" Sandor must have misunderstood me. "You mean because he was a bombardier and he—"

"No." Sandor put his elbows on the table, his hands fisted, one over the other, and sighed heavily. "Your father is a hero because he risked his life to save Katarina and Adolph. Katarina tells my grandmother Lieutenant Lawson killed a German soldier to save her. If he didn't, Katarina's secret hiding place is no more, and many people in the village would die. That is why your father is a hero to us."

I stared down at my food, my appetite suddenly gone. I had never questioned whether my father had killed anyone. He had been a flyer, and he and his crew were responsible for dropping bombs. That's what they did to win the war. But hand-to-hand combat was something totally different. No wonder Dad never wanted to talk about what had happened to him when he was missing. When I was in grade school and studied the war, I remember asking him about it. After Pearl Harbor was attacked, Dad volunteered. He applied to be a navigator because he didn't like guns and had always been good with maps and geography. Ironically, the only day he'd ever sat in the bombardier's seat was the day they were shot down.

"How did it happen?"

"One night, a German soldier spotted Adolph and Katarina with their cart on the trail as they headed back to their small farm from the fortress. Perhaps this soldier was lonely and hoped to share a smoke with Katarina beneath a full moon. Or maybe he was suspicious and wanted to see what she hid beneath the cart's blanket. Whatever, it didn't matter. Katarina had broken curfew. Everyone in German-occupied territory needed to be home by eight o'clock."

I folded my hands beneath my chin and listened as Sandor explained what had happened.

"When the soldier realized Katarina didn't want to share a smoke, he got angry and threw back the blanket on the cart, and when he finds it empty, he asks what she is doing? Why wasn't this hausfrau home and her son in bed? Then Katarina grabs the blanket. She tries to throw it over the soldier's head and begins to hit him. Your father is watching all this from the tower, and he jumps from the wall and races to Katarina's rescue."

"And he killed him?"

"He did. But not with a gun. Everyone in your dad's crew carried a forty-five, but if your father fired a gun, it would signal other troops in the area. So they fight, and your father used a knife to slit the soldier's throat. Once this Nazi is dead, your father and Katarina hid the body in the cave so it would never be found."

"Your grandmother told you this?"

"Not for many years. After Katarina returns from the Russian camp and the Russians leave, and she tells my grandmother her story. It is only then that my grandmother tells me. She wants that I never forget."

I covered my mouth. My appetite was gone. No wonder my father never wanted to talk about what happened here.

Chapter Fifteen

I had mixed feelings about calling home and talking to my father that night. Part of me couldn't wait to tell my father I had seen his plane, and the other half of me worried I might say too much and end up talking about the German soldier my father had killed outside the fortress walls.

I felt like I had stepped into a minefield. I didn't want to say something that might unearth some suppressed memory and trigger another nightmarish episode. I worried too much talk about my father's plane or the war would upset him. The last couple of calls home, I could hear him struggling to breathe, and I knew—despite his saying differently—he wasn't getting any better. But we had agreed I would call, and I knew he would be waiting by the phone.

It was almost eight p.m. my time—eleven a.m. in Phoenix. I sat down on the bed and promised myself I'd offer only as much information about the plane as I felt would make him happy. I planned to keep my conversation light and steer clear of anything even close to traumatic.

Dad answered before I even heard the phone ring.

"Hey there, Kat, did you see my plane?" Despite his raspy voice, Dad sounded surprisingly energetic.

"You mean Bombshell Betty?" I felt we were off to a good start.

"Was that her name?"

"You don't remember?"

"Nah, once you were inside, one plane was pretty much like the other. Cold and boxy. Didn't much matter what plane you were in long as she brought you home. But, come to think of it," Dad coughed, and I waited while he cleared his throat, "I do remember it was Nick who chose her name. Bit unusual, Bob, our pilot, wanted to name her after his mother, Betty. But Betty was a popular name back then, and there was already a Betty Boop. It was Nick who suggested Bombshell Betty, and we all liked the image. How'd she look?"

"As you might imagine. She's pretty beat-up, but she's all there—nose to tail. I did get some pictures, though, and lots of them. The good news is that Tamasi is less than fifty miles from Pecs, where you had set course. You almost made it, Dad."

I could hear the rustle of papers. Dad said he was looking at a map. Even after the war, he had continued to collect maps of all kinds. He had a file cabinet full of them and was convinced they might be helpful one day, old as some were. His assumption wasn't without merit. Before the war, the government had requested anyone with maps of Europe to turn them in. The US had a shortage of good maps, and the government needed all they could get. I pictured him sitting at the kitchen table with a map of Europe in front of him, charting Bombshell Betty's location from Tamasi to Pecs.

"I've been thinking a lot about those old planes, Kat. You remember the time your mother and I took you to the airshow at Davis-Monthon in Tucson so you could see one?"

"You mean when that F-16 strafed the airfield, and you tackled Mom and me?"

When I was in high school, we had been invited to Davis-Monthon, a large airbase, to tour their boneyard of retired military aircraft, including a couple of old B-24s. It was going to be a pleasant trip down memory lane—or so I thought.

After the show, Dad wanted me to see inside the B-24. It was the first time I had ever seen one up close or realized just how big and boxy the plane was. As we approached the old bomber, an F-16 buzzed the field—the sound like rolling thunder. Dad pushed Mom and me down to the ground, face first, and covered us with his body. He said it was a knee-jerk reaction to hearing the jet overhead and laughed it off.

But now, with the war better than fifty years behind him, I wondered if he might be dealing with some type of posttraumatic stress. Since coming to Hungary, I had learned things about my father I didn't know. Things he didn't talk about. Stories he hadn't told me. And after listening to Sandor, situations I suspected my father had hidden from himself that had started to haunt him.

"Ugh," Dad groaned. "I forgot about that."

"Selective memory," I teased.

"Maybe so. What I do remember is what a sturdy plane she was and how much abuse she took. It's a miracle she didn't crash with us all on board. A lot of things that could have gone terribly wrong went right that day."

"Went right?" That seemed like an odd way to put it.

"Yea went right. A lot of guys weren't so lucky and didn't come home. But we did. Sometimes I think it just wasn't our time. If it weren't for Katarina and Adolph rescuing us and that Nick had a knife on him, none of us would be here."

"A knife?" I bit my bottom lip. After hearing Sandor tell the story about how my father had used a knife to kill the German soldier, I wondered if this was a conversation I should steer clear of. Particularly on the phone.

"Didn't I tell you that story?"

"I don't think so. You sure you want to talk about it now?"

Dad went on as though he hadn't heard me.

"Nick's brother sent him a Bowie knife for his birthday. I think his brother had some kind of premonition that Nick might need it. Good thing, too. Nick got it the day before we were hit. If he hadn't had the knife on him, he wouldn't have made it. I remember seeing him bailout right behind me. He was struggling with his chute. Couldn't get the damn thing to open—ripcord was stuck. Fortunately, he had his knife strapped to his leg and cut the cord just in time. The chute released, but still, he hit the ground so hard, he broke his leg."

I sighed. I was relieved Dad hadn't remembered the knife fight with the German soldier. A memory I feared might send him over the edge and with me too far away to comfort him.

"You okay, Kat? You sound tired."

"Jet lag," I said. "I'm still catching up. But you sound good."

"Eh, I'm fine. Sleeping better. But a lot of memories are starting to come back. Maybe 'cause you're there, or it's the new meds the doctor's got me on. Whatever it is, something's messing with my head. But you know what they say. If it don't kill you—"

"Dad—"

"Hey, it's not all bad. I was thinking about Adolph the other day, and I remembered something he said."

"What's that?"

"It was night, and Adolph had come by with some supplies. I think it was one of the nights the German commandant was visiting Katarina. Adolph was upset, and I didn't want the others to hear our conversation, so we snuck up to the courtyard and hid in the tower. The tower didn't have a roof, and I remember looking up at the stars and thinking how bright they were. They looked so close it felt like you could reach out and touch them. Adolph was worried, so I started to tell him stories about the stars, but he didn't want to talk about the stars. He said he was worried the Germans would find us and kill his mother. I told him that wasn't going to happen. That I had a plan, and soon as we could get back to Italy, we were going to come back and bomb the smithereens out of those Nazis. And you know what he said?"

"No, Dad, what did he say?"

"Mind you, the kid's English wasn't too good, but I knew what he meant. He looked up at me and said, 'Lieutenant Steve, you come back...you no boom-boom Adolph.' Poor kid, he was worried we might miss and hit him and his mom. I told him not to worry. He'd know it was us because we'd tip our wings, and those Nazis better watch out."

I laughed. Dad always had a way of making me laugh, no matter how serious things were, and I imagined he must have made Adolph feel safe and laugh, too.

"That's a good story, Dad. And, if I meet Adolph, I'll be sure to remind him."

"Any word yet on those two?"

"Katarina and Adolph? Not yet, but I am going back to Keszthely tomorrow with Sandor's wife. She seems to think that if Katarina's still there, we might find her. That is if she's still alive."

"Steve? Is that Kat?" My mother picked up a second phone and immediately started talking.

"Honey, I've got some news you're going to want to hear." My mother could have run the society section for the newspaper. She always had an ear out for trends and local happenings, and I could tell from the high pitch in her voice she was bursting to tell. "You'll never guess who I ran into last night. I was at a fundraiser for the Phoenix Zoo and—"

"Who, Mom?" Not that I was really interested in local gossip, but I knew I wasn't going to be able to get off the phone until I asked.

"Nina Pulliam, she's—"

"I know who Nina Pulliam is." Nina Mason Pulliam was a journalist in her own right and married into the Pulliam family who owned both the *Arizona Republic* and the *Phoenix Gazette*—in essence, my former employer.

"Well, I'll bet you don't know this. The *Gazette* is closing. I overheard her say so to a friend that they plan to merge the paper with the *Republic*. It sounds to me like you got out at the right time."

It didn't feel like there was a right time. If a merger were in the works, the likelihood of my ever getting a job at the *Republic* had suddenly dropped to zero. As did my stomach.

"I'm not so sure there's ever a right time to be unemployed." I had been out for a month, and already I was beginning to think my path back to any newspaper in town looked pretty slim.

"Well, I wouldn't worry about it, but best not burn up all your money on expensive cell calls. You should reverse the charges next time."

"Ahh, look who's talking money." My father laughed. "Call me if you learn anything about Katarina and Adolph and take lots more pictures. Love you, Kat."

Dad hung up, and I stared out the French doors at the river. I needed a walk and fresh air to clear my head.

I headed down the stairs and heard voices coming from the kitchen. I wanted to let Miklos and Nora know I might be late. It was later than when I had gone out the night before, and I couldn't count on them leaving the door open.

Nora was seated at the kitchen table with an elderly man I hadn't seen before. He was pale and rail-thin and hunched over a bowl of soup. The baby's highchair was empty, and given the hour, I figured Miklos must have taken the baby upstairs to bed. I apologized for the interruption and pantomimed using a key, twisting my wrist as though opening a door. Nora stood up, mumbled something in Hungarian, then took a key from within her apron and pressed it into my hand. The understanding had required no translation. If I were late, I was to let myself in. I thanked her, and with a lot of head-bobbing, wished her goodnight and started off in the direction of the Chain Bridge.

Chapter Sixteen

I t was close to nine p.m., and the sun had just started to set. A gentle breeze had kicked up, causing small waves to form on the river, and the cooler air felt fresh against my face. I slipped the key Nora had given me into my fanny pack and quickened my step. It was good to stretch my legs.

I kept thinking about Sandor and what he had told me about my father—Lieutenant Lawson, the hero. How the young German soldier had stopped Katarina below the fortress' wall, and my father had come to her rescue, slitting the soldier's throat. His quick thinking had saved not only Katarina and Adolph but everybody in the village as well. No wonder Dad never wanted to talk about what had happened when he was missing in action. I wanted to go home and sit with him like I had seen Nora sit with the old man and care for him. Whatever their relationship, I envied her. I wanted to share the pictures of Lake Balaton with my father and tell him how beautiful Budapest was with her nineteenth-century buildings and show him photos of Sandor with his plane.

But I couldn't go. I had to find Katarina and Adolph. Not just because I had promised my father that I would, but because I needed to find Katarina for myself. The more I had learned about the woman who had rescued my father, the more I wanted to know. If she were alive, I wanted to thank her. If I hurried home now, what good would it do? I wouldn't have the answers my father wanted, and what did I have to look forward to?

I didn't have a job. My last interview had ended with a cold, 'we'll call you.' Translated to mean, don't bother to call us. And, if my mother was right, the newspaper I had worked for was about to merge with the city's only other major paper, and there was little chance I'd find a job with my former competitor. Not with my sullied reputation. By now, I was a marked woman who had used her sexuality to seduce her boss and secure the best stories. Nobody cared that he had come on to me or that I was super lonely. I might as well have been emblazoned with a red letter on my chest if not my resume. Every reporter from the *Gazette* would now be interviewing with the *Republic*. I had little hope, and there was nothing I could do about it. I felt as though a door had been slammed in my face. I'd be lucky to find a job writing want ads.

I crossed the Chain Bridge, her yellow lights like a necklace dripping from her beams, as traffic darted from one side of the river to the other. I was about to go north along the river's Buda side when I spotted Adrian's small motorboat idling next to the shoreline.

I wasn't going to stop. I had no reason to, but then I noticed a middle-aged American couple trying to negotiate with the gypsy and felt it was my duty to help my fellow countrymen.

I took the path from the bridge to the shoreline. "Are you looking for a ride?"

Despite my feelings that the gypsy could be a nuisance, I felt somewhat indebted. Adrian had shuttled me to the Buda Castle my first night. And if he hadn't shown me his postcards and pictures of the caves and the tunnels around Lake Balaton, I might not have understood just how massive the tunnel structure was beneath the old fortress. For that, I was thankful. The least I could do was put in a good word. Or perhaps a subtle warning to my fellow travelers that the young gypsy, while knowledgeable, once rewarded, might stick to them like a lost puppy.

"Nah, this punk already took us for a ride." The American, a large, heavyset man, and his wife of equally large proportions brushed me off. "This kid wants a tip. I gave him ten bucks. I'm not giving him one dime more."

"Is not a tip." Adrian stood in the center of his boat, his hand on the motor's handle. "Cost for ride to castle ten dollars. Five dollar each. They want to go to castle, and I buy two tickets for the funicular. That two dollars more.

Twelve dollar total."

"I paid five dollars for the same trip last night," I said. "Plus, a buck for the tram to the top."

"Who asked you?" The man took his wife's hand and started to leave.

I stepped in front of him. I was surprised by my own action. The man was twice my size, but I wasn't about to back down.

"Hey, the kid's just trying to earn a living. Why don't you pay him what you owe him?"

"Screw you, lady." The man tried to push past me.

I put my hand on his arm. "Hey, no need to be rude. Just pay him what you owe."

"Take your hands off me." The man wrested his arm away from me, reached into his pocket, and took out two single dollar bills. Then wadding them up threw them into the boat. "Next time, I'm sticking with an official tour guide. None of this gypsy crap."

I was stunned and embarrassed. I wanted to apologize, but Adrian shook his head no and looked away as though he were checking to see if we had been heard.

It was obvious Adrian didn't want to make a scene. He waited until the couple was out of earshot before he spoke.

"Thank you. If they call police, I have trouble."

"Some people can be real jerks," I said. "I'm sorry."

"You good lady. If you like, I give you ride or do free reading for you." Adrian nodded to the seats where the couple had sat.

"No," I said.

I wasn't interested in a gypsy reading, and I started to move on.

Adrian untied the rope from the dock. "Tell me, why you come here all alone? Pretty lady by herself. You not tourist. I think maybe you come to find love?"

I stopped and bit my lips. *If Adrian only knew how wrong he was.*

"No, Adrian. I'm not looking for love."

"Then you search for something else. Everyone look for something. Maybe you want to find someone or something from past." Adrian coiled the rope and threw it on board the boat. "I help others. If you like, I help you, too."

"Thank you, Adrian, but I don't think so." If Sandor, with all his knowledge of history and stories his grandmother had told him about Katarina, couldn't find my father's rescuer, I doubted a gypsy boy born years after the war would have any ideas. I turned and, with my hand over my head, waved goodbye.

"If you not want my help, is okay with me. But you need good guide. After the war, everything destroyed. All you see—everywhere is bombed. Bridges. Buildings. You need guide to show you. You have?"

"Yes, Adrian, I have a guide."

"Someone you trust?"

I looked up at the night sky. Of all the questions Adrian might have asked, why did he ask about my guide? Had he some inkling I didn't trust Sandor?

"He found my father's plane, and he showed it to me."

"Ah, so it is your father you come for."

"Yes. He was shot down near Lake Balaton during the war. He wants me to find someone for him. Someone who helped him to escape."

"Your father, his is American flyer, right?"

"Was," I said.

"I hear such stories many times. Tell me, this plane your guide shows you, you believe it is your father's?"

"I think so. And he took me to a fortress above Lake Balaton, where he believes my father hid. Everything about it was as my father remembered, and there was a tunnel from the lake to the fortress courtyard inside. Exactly like that on the postcard you gave me. So yeah, I think he knows something."

"Maybe he is okay guide. Some not so honest. Still, if you need my help, I owe you now."

I considered what it might mean if Adrian felt he owed me and could think of no reason why I shouldn't ask him if he knew anything about the partisans. Particularly partisans who had helped American flyers shot down during the war. Sandor had said Katarina's name was well known among them. And if Adrian had helped other Americans there might be a chance he had heard her name before and could help me as well.

"Perhaps you might know," I said, "does the name—"

"Katarina Nemeth?"

"—mean anything to you?" I was stunned. "How do you know?"

"You say you go to Lake Balaton. Everyone knows about Katarina. She helped many people. My people too. And now you want to know if she is still alive."

"Is she?" I asked.

"I think yes. After war, Russians come and send some gypsies and those they not like to camp to reeducate. My godmother is very sick and meets Katarina in such a camp. Katarina is a nurse. She helps my godmother, and later, when they come back, Katarina helps my godmother find my mother."

"Is your godmother still alive?"

"No, but my mother tells me about Katarina. I think she is very old but not dead."

"When was the last time your mother spoke to Katarina?"

"After Russians leave. I know because my mother gives Katarina painting by famous gypsy artist Janos Balazs, as thank you for her help. You know this artist?"

"No."

"He was poet and artist. Very talented. Make colorful portraits, like Picasso. You know him?"

"Picasso? Yes, but Balaz, I'm sorry. I've never heard of him."

"After war, Balazs paint picture of two women, and he gives one to my godmother. Her family is very good to him. He was orphan, and they care for him. She hides painting. If Russians find they steal for sure. Later, after Russians leave and my godmother die, my mother finds this painting, and she gives it to Katarina."

"Do you know where Katarina was when your mother gave her the painting?"

"Keszthely. If you go there, you will find her. She is old, but many people know her."

* * *

I was feeling pretty good by the time I got back to the apartment. The house was quiet, and I used the key Nora had given me to let myself in and tipped-toed up the staircase. The walk had cleared my head, and talking with Adrian left me feeling optimistic I might find Katarina. All-in-all, it had been a good day. I had seen my father's plane, and I felt as though I was making progress on piecing together what had happened to my Dad and his crew. As for Sandor and whatever scam he had up his sleeve, I was tired of feeling whipsawed. One minute I thought he was up to something, and the next, he seemed to explain it all away, leaving me to doubt myself. What I needed was a good night's sleep.

When I opened the door to my room, the first thing I noticed was the chocolate candy on my pillow—and next to it—where it shouldn't be, was my journal.

I threw my fanny pack on the floor.

Damnit, Nora, not again!

I had left my red journal beneath the nightstand, and now it stared back at me from atop the bed. If I gave Nora the benefit of the doubt, she might have discovered my journal beneath the nightstand when she came into my room to turn the sheets down and accidentally kicked it with her foot. Perhaps, she thought I'd misplaced it and put it on my pillow so I would find it. But I didn't believe it. Nora was a snoop, and I was uncomfortable with the idea she had been looking through my things. I snatched the red notebook off the pillow and thumbed through it. Nobody in the house spoke English, not well enough anyway to have read any of my hen-scratching. Why should I worry? My conversations with Miklos and Nora had been little more than a few words, followed by a lot of awkward head bobbing and forced smiles. Certainly, not complete sentences or anything to indicate either Nora or Miklos could read English. The fact my journal was on the pillow meant nothing at all. All the same, I felt violated. Like someone was watching me.

Chapter Seventeen

T he following morning, I woke to the sweet, faint smell of freshly baked blueberry muffins. As I lay in bed, I wondered if Nora was baking or if the warm, buttery scents that had caused my stomach to growl were coming from the bakery below the apartment. I had skipped dinner the night before, and since Sandor had told me breakfast was included with my room, I dressed quickly and hurried down the stairs.

"Good morning." I ventured as far as the doorway between the living room and kitchen and waited until Nora saw me.

The kitchen was bright. Sunlight streamed through the window over the table where Nora was seated. Across from her, the old man I had seen her spoonfeed the night before sat quietly. While at the end of the table, Márkó was in his highchair playing with his food. When the baby saw me, he squealed and began pounding his plastic spoon on his tray.

I smiled and waved. "Good morning, sweet face."

Nora stood up and wiped her hands on her apron.

"Reggeli?" she asked. Which I assumed meant breakfast.

"Yes, please," I said.

Nora pointed to a wooden chair next to the old man, then placed an empty coffee cup on the table. I sat down next to the old man. He made no notice of me. He held a blueberry muffin in his hand and stared at it, his hands shaking, like he didn't know what to do with it.

"Egyél, papa." Nora filled my coffee cup, sat down, and buttered the old man's muffin.

The efficiency and the tenderness of the moment touched me and reminded me of muffins and Sunday mornings growing up. I used to call my dad the Muffin Man because he would rise early to make muffins while mom slept in or tried to anyway. Once the muffins were in the oven, Dad would turn the stereo up full blast, and we'd grab my favorite stuffed animals and parade throughout the house. Then, with the sound of John Philip Sousa playing in the background, we'd march into my parent's room, where mom was still sleeping, and bombard her with my arsenal of stuffed animals.

I would have liked to share the story, but Nora's English wasn't good enough to understand, and I felt certain any attempt on my part to pantomime the bombing of my sleeping mother might be misinterpreted. Instead, I took a muffin from the basket in the center of the table and began to butter it. That's when I noticed the tattoo on the inside of the old man's arm. My eyes caught Nora's. I didn't need words. The old man, her papa, was a survivor.

* * *

After breakfast, I met Aanika next to the Elizabeth Bridge. She said Sandor had a private tour that morning with a group of American investor types who wanted to see the sights, and he had arranged for an air-conditioned bus for them. We got the rusty-red Russian bomb.

"He wanted you to know he's sorry he couldn't come today." Anaika pulled out in traffic as she spoke. Like Sandor, she was an aggressive driver, and I braced myself with one hand on the dashboard as she dodged around the car in front of us.

"It's okay," I said. "Gives us some time for a little girl talk and maybe to shop, too." I still needed to bring something home for my mother. "This will be fun."

I was looking forward to chatting with Aanika alone and learning as much as I could about Sandor, and I wanted to put her at ease. I knew she was interested in America, and with Aanika being a chatty sort, I didn't think it would be too hard to get her talking. After our first meeting, when she had peppered me with questions about what I did for a living, I figured it was time to turn the tables. I planned to ask as much as I could about her and, of course, Sandor. After spending some time alone together, I hoped I would better understand what it was about Sandor that bothered me. Maybe I would even be able to rest those nagging doubts I had about Sandor using me for some illicit drug trafficking deal. Or at least find out what sad story he might be about to propose for which he would want my money.

"I've been looking forward to it." Aanika shifted gears, and the car lurched forward. "You'll have to forgive Sandor. He can get carried away with his stories."

"I'm used to it. My dad never talked a lot about the war, but he could weave a tale that could fill an encyclopedia when it came to maps and history. I'd have to look for excuses to leave the room. He could go on and on, and—"

"And on." Aanika filled in.

I rolled my eyes. "I'm afraid I'm a bit more interested in people. How did you and Sandor meet?"

"At a soccer game with my girlfriends. Sandor was there with some of his friends, and they were cheering for the wrong team." Aanika looked over to me and puffed out her lower lip out. "Poor man."

"Why is it I don't think Sandor would tell that story the same way?"

We both laughed.

"Maybe because he remembers differently, but my team won. And Sandor had to buy us all drinks." Aanika flashed her ring at me, with a nice-sized diamond on her right hand, and smiled. "He's been buying my drinks ever since."

"How long have you been married?"

"Five years now. We got married right after the Russians left." Aanika looked back at the road ahead. "And you? How long have you been married?"

From Aanika's question, it was apparent that Sandor had mentioned to her I was married. An issue I had deliberately avoided talking about at lunch. The stigma and sting of my separation were still fresh and uncomfortable. I didn't want to get into it. But now that it appeared to be out in the open, what could I do? This was, after all, girl-talk.

"Three years," I said.

"Any kids?"

"No. Josh and I got married too late for all that."

"And Josh, he's your first?"

"Husband?" I teased.

"I'm sorry, I only ask because, like you, I married late, and Sandor wasn't my first."

"Oh?"

"It's a long story and not a very pretty one." Aanika looked back at the road and put her foot on the accelerator. "You have to understand I wasn't born until after the war, so much of what I know is only from what I've heard. My family lost everything. Sandor and I live in an apartment building. It was once a grand estate that belonged to my grandfather's family." Aanika's eyes glanced over to me and then back to the road. "He was a nobleman, and my grandmother was very privileged with maids who spoke both English and French. It's why I learned to speak English when I was little. It's always been important in my family. When the Germans came being of noble birth wasn't a problem. But things were very different after the war under Russian occupation. My grandparents, father, and brothers were forced to move into two small rooms and share what had been our big house with persons we didn't know. By the time I was born, I had no idea what it was to grow up any differently. The Russians had stolen anything of value. I never knew about what it was to have riches of any kind, and there was nothing left of my family's estate, only the peeled paint from the walls." Aanika looked at me and tilted her head matter-of-factly.

"I'm sorry."

"Don't be. At least we weren't living in a Russian-built concrete tower like many people were, and we scraped by. Life wasn't easy, and because my family had been part of the aristocracy, the Russians refused to allow me to go to college. I suppose they felt we had had too many breaks in the past, and it was time I realized my privileged life was no more. I had little joy in my life and very little hope for the future. My father died right before my sixteenth birthday, and I went to work for my uncle's trucking company. That's when I met my first husband." Aanika gripped the wheel.

"My grandmother, however, never approved of him. You see, he was a Jew, and when my grandmother found out, she insisted I get a divorce. And because I was underage, there was little I could do. I'm sorry to say, even after the war, my grandmother was on the wrong side of history. She wasn't going to have her granddaughter married to a Jew. By the time I met Sandor, my grandmother had died. My only regret is that we didn't meet earlier. Sandor would have loved to have had a family."

"And you would have liked kids, too?"

"More than anything. Sandor is so good with kids." Aanika brushed her short dark hair behind her ear. "Sandor was an only child. His mother and father died when he was very young, and he lived with his grandmother. My sister's got two kids, though. Daughters. Sandor's great with them, but his favorite is Márkó."

"Márkó? Miklos' baby?"

"They're related, you know." Aanika seemed surprised I didn't know. "They're cousins. Didn't he tell you?"

"No, he didn't mention it." Although I did remember Sandor telling me Miklos and Nora were friends. Had he deliberately omitted that they were family, or did he think it didn't matter? And then, because I didn't want to appear like it was an issue, I added, "Although there is a strong family resemblance."

"Isn't there? Miklos and Sandor used to look a lot more alike. At least, before Sandor and I got married. It's my fault, Sandor's thicker around the middle now. It can't be helped. He loves my cooking, and I spoil him."

"And what about Nora? Have she and Miklos been married long?"

"A couple of years." Aanika glanced over at me, then back to the road. "She's all about the baby. Miklos' last wife, she ran off with some Russian. I don't know what would have happened if Miklos hadn't met Nora. She's younger than Miklos, but she's exactly what he needed. She takes good care of him and his grandfather as well."

"The old man?" I was getting an earful, family dynamics and all.

"His name is Kalman. You must have met him. He lives on the first floor, behind the kitchen. He's quite old, and not well, and he's—"

"Got a tattoo." I point to where I had seen the numbers on the old man's arm.

"I was going to say he's a survivor. But yes, the tattoo is from the war. I think Miklos' first wife got tired of taking care of him, but Nora's wonderful. She cares for Kalman like he was her own."

"So, Kalman is Sandor's grandfather, too?"

"Great uncle. Sandor's grandmother, Margit, was Kalman's sister."

"Than Sandor's Jewish?"

"You didn't know?"

"No," I said.

"Does that make a difference?" Aanika's eyes slid from the road to mine.

"No," I said, "Not at all. I just didn't know."

"Being Jewish still makes a difference here. Anti-semitism didn't end just because the war did. When the Russians came, if you were Jewish, you couldn't be a member of the party, and if you weren't a member of the party, your opportunities were limited. Maybe that's why Sandor didn't tell you. There are some things he likes to keep secret."

I looked out the window at the countryside—the trees like sentries guarding the forest. "Yes," I said. "He is a mystery."

We drove for another thirty minutes before Aanika pulled over to a shaded area beside the lake. "I need coffee. And I made Kiffles, but you can't eat too many. There's lots to eat in the market at Keszthely. You won't be sorry." Aanika nodded to the picnic basket in the backseat. "You like?

I was still full from breakfast, but I wasn't about to say no to anything Aanika had made.

Aanika filled my cup, then reached back over the seat for one of her homemade Kifflers.

"Enough about me. I'd chat all day if you let me. What about you?" Aanika licked her fingers. "You didn't answer my question, were you married before?" Then touching my knee, she apologized. "I don't mean to pry. It's just you're attractive and smart, and I can't imagine you being single all those years."

I took a sip of my coffee. Aanika was easy to talk to, and after she'd shared so much with me about her life, I felt I should share something about myself as well.

"You don't need to apologize. It's okay. Like I told Sandor, it's complicated. The fact is, I'm separated. And Josh isn't my first. I was married when I was very young to my college sweetheart. I don't talk about it much. And I don't think about it much either."

"No?" Aanika tilted her head. "Not ever?"

I looked out at the lake. *Who was I kidding?* "Only when I brush my teeth at night, go to bed, and wake up every morning. He's always there. I sometimes even make a note or two about him in my journal. He was killed in Vietnam."

"I'm sorry. I thought perhaps there was someone." Aanika pointed to the gold band on my right hand. "And was that your wedding band?"

"It was. Eric was MIA—"

"Like your father."

"In a way, yes. But my father came home. For Eric, though, it was seven years before the Air Force officially declared him dead. The war had long since been over. But, you're right, Eric was a lot like my dad, tall and good-looking, and he had a great sense of humor. Maybe if he had come home, life might have been different."

"That had to have been hard."

"It was. Eric hadn't been in Nam but a week when his F-4 crashed. At first, I didn't believe it. I mean, it happened so fast. Who gets shot down on their first mission? I ended up joining a group of MIA wives. Believe me, it's not a club you ever want to belong to. One day, toward the end of the war, several wives got calls from the DOD asking them to come to Hickam Field in Hawaii. The POWs were coming home. A girlfriend of mine called, her husband was MIA like Eric, and he was coming home. I remember sitting and staring at the phone for the longest time, hoping it would ring. But it never did. And then I watched the coverage on TV. Straining to see if maybe Eric was there. That somehow, the DOD had made a mistake, and he was with those the North Vietnamese had released. But he wasn't."

Aanika's eyes filled with tears that long ago would have been mine.

"I can't cry about it anymore. It was a long time ago. But looking back on it, I think it's why I waited so long to get involved again. My mother said I should have picked up and gone on when the war ended, but I couldn't. It's probably why I was never a hundred percent committed to Josh. I think I was gun-shy, and it's probably my fault I wasn't as committed as I should have been."

"Nonsense." Aanika wiped her mouth and threw her napkin down. "Some men just don't deserve a good woman. I'm sure you've done everything you could."

"I like the way you think." I raised my hand, and with an open palm, we high-fived each other and laughed.

Chapter Eighteen

As we got closer to Keszthely, Aanika talked more about the town where she and Sandor had spent their honeymoon and how excited she was to return for a day's outing. She went on about the beauty of the Festetics Palace, the museums, there were several—everything from cars to dolls—the cafes, and the shopping. One day she and Sandor hoped to buy a small piece of property, maybe somewhere close to the lake, and enjoy a simpler life.

Despite my interest in hearing about Keszthely and all it had to offer, I couldn't help but notice that Aanika had stopped talking about her personal life. I felt as though she was trying to lead the conversation in an entirely different direction, and I was uncomfortable with it.

Until that morning, it had never occurred to me to ask where Sandor's family was during the war. Like every other able-bodied, young Hungarian man, I had assumed Sandor's father had been in the Army and that Sandor didn't like to talk about it. Particularly with Americans, since we would have been on opposing sides. But after learning Sandor's family was Jewish, I wanted to know everything about them and how they had survived.

I began with some reasonably simple, straightforward questions. "Was Sandor's family from Keszthely?"

"No," Aanika said. "The Zselnegellers were from Budapest. They were quite well-to-do. Sandor's grandfather was a pharmacist. He owned several pharmacies there and another here in Keszthely, plus a farmhouse for vacations. But toward the end of the war, Sandor's grandfather worried for his family's safety and sent his wife and daughters away."

"And they came here, to Keszthely?"

"By then, Hitler had sent his troops into Hungary, and the German Army had purged the forest and small towns of any Jews hiding there. Many Jews from Poland and those who could escape Germany had tried to sneak across Hungary's borders. They hoped to find refuge in our forest or in Budapest. Of course, they didn't. The Germans were waiting for them. Those that got as far as Budapest were rounded up and exported to concentration camps. Sandor's grandfather thought if he could get his family out of the city and to the small farmhouse outside of Keszthely since it had already been declared Judenfrei that they could hide there and be safe. They didn't have many options."

"Is that how Margit met Katarina?"

"I don't know, I guess." Annika shrugged. "Sandor never mentioned how his grandmother knew Katarina. I suppose if Katarina's alive, you could ask."

Up until that very moment, I had believed Aanika had been as engaged in the hunt to find Katarina as I was. But there was something in Aanika's very lukewarm answer that caused me to wonder if Sandor might have said something to her. He had been adamant we didn't have enough time to visit Keszthely when we went to the fortress. I hadn't questioned it at the time. But now, judging from Aanika's response, I felt like our day trip to Keszthely was about to be nothing more than a shopping trip.

"You don't sound as optimistic as you did two days ago," I said. "Something wrong?"

"No. Not at all. It's just, you have to remember, Kat, it's been more than five years since Sandor's grandmother last saw Katarina. She was old then, and old here isn't like it is your country. Katarina had a hard life. She may have passed."

"That could be," I said. "But I've come too far, and I'm determined to find Katarina and Adolph, too. Dead or alive. I need answers. My father asked me to find them, and somebody in this town must know something about them or at least what became of them."

Aanika sighed. "I just hope you're not disappointed if we come up empty-handed."

"Ha." I scoffed. "I doubt that's going to happen. Didn't you say the shopping was great here?"

"Better than great. That much I can promise." Aanika pointed to a large, gothic church as we approached the city's outskirts. "And if we're lucky, we can park in the church lot. The market's a short walk from there."

As we pulled into the church's parking lot, I noticed several big glass-topped tour buses. The lot was busy, and parking was limited. But Aanika spotted a tiny space between two monster buses parked directly in front of the church. I closed my eyes as she squeezed the red beast between the two buses and put the car in park. A move that would have been totally illegal in the US.

"Perfect," she said.

I opened my eyes, and gasped. There, directly in front of me, was the steeple my father had seen.

I grabbed Aanika's shoulder. "This is it."

"What? What's wrong?"

I pointed to the church directly in front of us with its red-tiled roof and tall cone-shaped steeple that reached several hundred feet into the air.

"The church spire," I said. "It's got to be the one my dad saw when he bailed out. It has to be."

"How can you be so sure?"

I got out of the car and stared up at the bell tower. On top of it was the tall cone-shaped steeple that would have been visible for miles. Aanika came and stood next to me.

"Because it's exactly as my father described." Somewhere at home, I had a picture of my father when he was maybe four or five, sitting on the steps of the parsonage next to his father's church. In the background was the church with a tall white spire. And looking at it now, I felt for sure it must have been the same spire. I remembered my father telling me that he knew everything would be okay when he bailed out and saw that steeple.

I took a couple of quick shots with my camera, then took the compass locket from around my neck to check my position. The coordinates matched perfectly. The lake was to the south of us. The fortress where my father hid was to the west, and the mountains his plane had barely skimmed over were to the north. There were other churches I had seen on the drive along the lake, but the tall, white skinny steeple on this church was exactly like the one my father had described.

"Are you okay?" Aanika looked at me like she thought I might faint. "I've got water in the car if you need any."

"No, I'm fine. Katarina's here. I know it. We're going to find her. You'll see."

I wasn't about to tell Aanika about my conversation with Adrian the night before. Or that in addition to seeing the church's steeple, I had been inspired by a gypsy boy along the banks of the Danube who claimed to know about Katarina. Aanika would have laughed if I had told her. But Adrian had been right about the cave and the tunnels beneath the old fortress, and if he thought Katarina was still alive, then so did I, and I was determined to find her.

"Let's hope." Aanika grabbed my hand and started to pull me down the street. I sensed a lack of enthusiasm.

"What do you mean, let's hope?"

Aanika squeezed my hand. "It's nothing. Come on, there's a sweet shop around the corner. It's on the way to the marketplace. The last time Sandor and I were here, there was a lifesized bridal dress made with icing in the window. It looked like real lace. And over that way," Aanika waved to the right of the church, "is a doll museum. If we hurry, we might even be able to get tickets to the castle."

I dropped Aanika's hand. "What's going on? When we were at the fortress, you couldn't wait to come back here to help me find Katarina. What's happened?"

"It's tourist season, Kat. Look around you. I didn't think about it at the time, but there are so many people here now that even if Katarina was still living here, we'd be lucky to find her. And if she is alive, she very well may be gone on holiday."

"That's sounding like a good excuse. You sure that's all it is?"

Aanika wouldn't look at me. I could feel she was hiding something.

"I'm sorry. I should never have encouraged you. It was silly of me and selfish. I wanted an excuse to come back to Keszthely, and at the time, it seemed like a good idea, but really I don't know what I was thinking."

"Well, stop it. Whatever it is, we're here to find Katarina, and you're going to help me. So, let's go. Show me around."

* * *

I had never seen anything like Keszthely or the open-air marketplace in the center square. Aanika explained that local farmers hauled their fresh produce and meats to the city center every Wednesday and Saturday and set up tables and colorful umbrella stands. Each stacked with vegetables and fresh fruits with row after row of flowers bursting in bloom and hanging racks of fresh garlic and peppers.

The market was crowded. Locals dressed in shorts and t-shirts moved through the crowd as though on a mission, skirting couples with baby buggies and bags stuffed full of groceries, while bigger children chased ahead and darted between the stalls and old ladies that moved like snails dressed in black. And tourists with their cameras clicking sampled the farmers' choices as they hollered back and forth to one another—"Hey, try this one!"

I scanned the marketplace for Katarina while Aanika stopped to talk with locals. Once or twice I heard her use Katarina's name, but speaking in Hungarian, I had no idea what she was saying, and each time, heads shook, and fingers pointed in different directions. Aanika translated that several people remembered hearing about Katarina, but no one had seen her in years.

I refused to give up and searched the crowd, scanning the faces of old ladies. There weren't, but a handful, each of them covered head-to-toe in black and very bent and old-looking. If one of them were Katarina, I wouldn't have recognized her. The only picture I had of the woman who had saved my father's life was a black-and-white charcoal sketch my dad had drawn of a much younger woman.

Finally, after I had chased down and stared into the face of every senior woman in the market, I gave up. I found a table where I could sit and enjoy the warmth of the afternoon sun while I waited for Aanika to finish chatting with an elderly couple.

When Aanika finished, she shook her head and joined me at the table. "I'm sorry. I tried."

"I know you did."

"You want an ice cream? There's a great place around the corner."

"Why not?" I was disappointed. I had been so hopeful I'd find Katarina. But the reality was it was better than fifty years after the war, and despite Adrian's prophesy and hoping I might find her, I wasn't feeling lucky.

"Come," Aanika said. "It's just a short walk, and the Festetics Palace is beautiful with all the flowers in bloom this time of year. You'll love it, I promise."

I got up from the table, and we started off down a narrow side street crammed with stores and tourist stands with trinkets, maps, and small Hungarian flags. Aanika knew the city well, and we dodged shoppers and cyclists as we made our way toward the palace. We had gone about half a block when I noticed an old woman on the other side of the street coming in our direction.

"Wait." I stopped and stared at the old lady. There was something about her that caught my attention. Not that she was dressed any differently than the other old women I had seen in the marketplace. Like them, she wore a long black dress with the hem of her skirt hitting well below her knees, and despite the heat, black stockings and heavy black shoes. Her hair, or what I could see of it beneath her hat, was grey, and she walked with the aid of a cane. But not stiff and crumpled, but tall and with a sense of purpose. "That's her."

"No, it can't be." Aanika grabbed my arm and tried to pull me forward. "Come, let's go."

I refused to move. Across the street, the old woman had stopped and was looking in a window.

"Look," I pointed to the glass where I could see her reflection. "She's got a patch on her eye. Who else could it be?" I let go of Aanika's arm and hollered to the woman as I chased across the street. "Katarina?"

The old lady stared at me blankly. "Do I know you?"

Aanika hurried to join me. "Kat, really we mustn't—"

"Stop!" I lifted my arm above my head so Aanika couldn't grab me and pull me away. With my heart pounding, I looked at the old woman. "Excuse me, but is your name Katarina Nemeth?"

The old lady narrowed her eyes and nodded slowly. "Who wants to know?"

"I do. My name's Kat Lawson. I'm Lieutenant Steve Lawson's daughter."

Katarina rested her hands on her cane and studied my face as though she were trying to rekindle a memory.

"You rescued my father. You hid him—"

"Yes, I remember." Then slowly, with the tips of her gnarled fingers, she touched the side of my head. "You look a lot like him. At least how I remember him."

I brushed my fingers through my short hair. "I'm probably a little more salt and pepper than he was when you knew him. But yes, people say I look like him."

"And this is?" Katarina placed a frail hand on Aanika's arm.

Aanika looked like she was about to freeze. Afraid to say anything.

"This is Aanika Zselnegeller. She's married to Sandor, Margit's grandson?"

"Margit? Yes, she and I were friends for many years. I miss her."

"We've been looking for you," I said. "Is there somewhere we could talk? My father wanted me to come back to find you, and now that I have, I've got so many questions. Could I buy you a drink?"

"Not here. I'd prefer it if you came back to my house. It's not far from here, and my son, Adolph, will be there soon. I'm sure you'll want to meet him as well. I know he'll want to meet you."

Chapter Nineteen

Aanika linked her arm through mine, and we followed Katarina down the street. The old woman was surprisingly spry, and despite a slight limp and the use of a cane, she walked ahead of us at a brisk pace. Aanika pulled back, and I sensed a hesitancy in her step.

"What's going on?"

"Nothing." Aanika rested her hand on top of mine and squeezed it. "I just wish Sandor were here, that's all."

"Do you really?" I pulled her closer to me. "Because I am beginning to think that maybe you didn't believe I'd find Katarina or that Sandor didn't want me to. And now that I have, I can't help but wonder why."

"That's nonsense. Of course, I'm happy you found her, and Sandor will be too. I'm just surprised. Sandor was convinced Katarina had died. We discussed it last night, and he told me so."

"Did he?" I wondered if that might explain why Aanika's formerly enthusiastic attitude to search for Katarina had so suddenly changed? Was Sandor concerned we might uncover some secret he didn't want anyone to know if we found the old woman? And if so, what could it possibly be?

"Ladies?" Katarina stopped in front of a stately looking, two-story residence, similar to those I had seen along Budapest's famous Andrássy Avenue, their Champs-Élysées. Surrounding the home was a tall wrought-iron fence. Katarina nodded to the gate. "Do you mind?"

Aanika rushed forward and unhooked the lock.

We followed Katarina down a narrow footpath that led past the side of the house—or more precisely, what appeared to be a mini-mansion—to the backyard. My guidebook had described the architecture of such buildings as Renaissance Revival. In the mid to late 1800s, the style was inspired by the beauty of Paris and Vienna and had ushered in a golden age of architecture. The mansion was as fancy as any I had seen in the city with its thick white walls, tall, perfectly aligned windows, and a center front door. The only difference was that this front door was covered by a blue and gold Swedish flag. Which I found curious.

The backyard included a vegetable garden and six tiny garden apartments surrounding a courtyard with a bubbling fountain. Based upon the different colored doors and the presence of a rocking chair in front of each, I quickly surmised this was some type of senior living center.

The door leading to Katarina's apartment was painted a warm autumn orange. Inside, the living quarters were small. There was a living room with a tiny fireplace, kitchen galley, bath, and bedroom. The unit was bare-bones but clean and sparsely furnished. I considered it comfortable, but with very little evidence of anything personal, except for a single piece of artwork that hung above the fireplace.

I stepped closer to look at the painting, a colorful abstract of two women. If what Adrian had told me about the picture his godmother had given Katarina was true, then this was it.

"Is that a Janos Balazs?"

"You know him?" Katarina hung her hat on a coat rack by the door. Even with the eye patch and her advanced age, she was still a strong, handsome woman.

"I know he was a gypsy artist. Unfortunately, I don't know much more than that."

"Few people do. But I'm happy you asked. The painting was a gift from a gypsy friend, and I'm quite fond of it. She and I spent some time together in a Russian labor camp after the war. She was very sick, and I nursed her back to health. Balazs had been a friend of her family, and when the war broke out, and he left to serve, he gave it to her for safekeeping. After we were freed, she gave it to me as a thank you."

So, Adrian had been telling me the truth. His godmother had known

Katarina.

"May I get you something to drink?" Katarina asked.

"Please, don't trouble yourself," I said.

"It's not a bother. I made lemonade this morning, fresh from the garden. Did you notice the trees when you came in?"

I glanced out the window at the back of the big house. Several fruit trees shaded the vegetable garden that appeared to be well-tended.

Katarina took three glasses from a cabinet and a pitcher from the refrigerator. "My son Adolph is usually here by two. When it's hot, like it is today, I like to make fresh lemonade for him."

Katarina poured herself a glass, and Aanika took two glasses from the counter and offered me one.

"So, tell me, ladies, how did you find me?" Katarina took a seat in the rocker across from us. "I can't imagine it would be easy. I haven't seen Sandor since he was a boy, and I keep a low profile these days. I doubt anyone knows where I live."

I glanced at Aanika. I wasn't sure where to begin. But clearly, based on the fact Katarina hadn't seen Sandor since he was a child, we had gotten lucky in finding her. Just like Adrian had said, I would. *Lucky.*

Aanika began, "When Kat told me she wanted to find you, I thought maybe I could help. I hoped if you were still in Keszthely, you'd be like many war widows and visit the marketplace on Saturdays."

"You would have made a good spy," Katarina said.

"Yes, well," Aanika laughed nervously, "the fact is, we'd given up, and we were about to go for ice cream, when—"

"You spotted me, walking down the street."

"Actually, it was Kat who spotted you."

"I noticed the patch on your eye." I regretted the words the minute I said them.

Katarina touched her brow. "Yes, it is a little hard to hide, isn't it? And I don't make much effort these days."

"I'm sorry, I didn't mean to—"

"Call attention to it? I'm long past the point of vanity. Scars can be a badge of glory. It's all what you make of them. Besides, I'm glad you found me. And I'm pleased to meet you, Aanika. Margit worried Sandor would never settle down. She thought he was a bit of a playboy. But obviously, looking at you, pretty as you are, he's done quite well. I approve. And now that we've met, I have something I think you should have."

Katarina excused herself, shuffled to the bedroom, returned with a small box, and handed it to Aanika.

"What's this?" Aanika looked surprised.

"Allow me." Katarina opened the box, took out a string of pearls, and put them around Aankia's neck. "They belonged to Margit, Sandor's grandmother, your mother-in-law. She always had such lovely jewelry. She gave them to me long ago for a favor she didn't need to repay. I tried to return them to her many times before she passed, but she wouldn't take them. She insisted I keep them. But, now that we've met, I want to give them to you."

"Me?" Aanika fingered the strand of pearls. Their soft iridescent glow was radiant against her pale white skin and dark hair.

"Yes, you. I've never been one for pearls myself. They don't suit me. But on you, they look elegant, and I'm sure Sandor would agree you should have them." Katarina settled back into the rocker and looked at me. "And you, Kat. I didn't even know you existed. I could only hope that our Lieutenant Lawson had made it back to America." Katarina paused and took a sip of her lemonade. "I was very fond of your father. He was a good man. He kept our spirits up, and we believed if anyone could make it out behind enemy lines, he could. But all we could do was hope. After he left, every time I'd hear the bombers overhead, I'd look up in the sky and wonder, is that him? Did the lieutenant make it? We had no way of knowing. How is he?"

"He has cancer," I said. "Mentally, he's sharp as a tack. But he's not well enough to travel, and he asked me to come instead." I explained how Sandor had found my father's plane and contacted him through the DOD. "Dad was anxious for me to find you and see where he had hidden."

"So you've been to the fortress?"

"I have, and I don't know how you did it."

"It wasn't easy. But we managed."

"I want to thank you for rescuing my father. Even more importantly, Dad wanted me to see if you needed anything and if you did— "

"No," Katarina shook her head. She seemed to know what I was about to say before I asked. "I don't need anything, and there's no need for you to thank me. Your father did as much for us as we did for him. He not only saved my life and Adolph's too, but he gave us hope. And that's sometimes the best gift you can give anyone. The Americans made many sacrifices, and in return, we did what we could to help them."

"Still, you can't imagine how happy my father will be to know we've met, and I am too. A week ago, I never knew who you were. Then Sandor's letter arrived, and my father started telling me about you and Adolph and what you did. You were amazing. I'm in awe. "

"You needn't be. Others did as much and some much more."

"But you and Adolph, you saved my father's life. If you hadn't, he never would have come home, and my name wouldn't be Katarina Lawson."

"Katarina?"

"Yes. My father named me for you. I never knew why, and now that I do, I see I've got a lot to live up to."

"You give me too much credit. I'm flattered, but I only did what I felt needed to be done. It was a matter of survival for us all. In a sense, we saved each other."

Aanika interrupted. "But you risked your life. I've heard the stories. You were part of the underground. You made a difference. I don't know if I could have ever been so brave."

"One never knows how they'll react," Katarina said. "Sometimes, in a split second, things change, and you have to decide who you are. I wasn't always part of the resistance. Before the war, my husband Gyuri and I lived in Budapest. We were an ordinary couple, young and starting out. Our son, Adolph, was barely four-years-old. I worked as a nurse, and Gyuri worked as a pharmacist for Andor, Margit's husband. Back then, I had no idea the importance of that relationship or that I would ever be part of the underground."

"So, you knew Margit *before* the war?" The words slipped out of my mouth as I tried to understand Katarina's connection to Margit.

"I did. And neither of you ladies would be here if it weren't for that relationship. You see, Andor had done quite well. He had a pharmacy in Budapest and another in Keszthely, where he and his wife owned a small farmhouse near Lake Balaton. We became close friends, and they would frequently invite my husband and me to visit. Margit was a wonderful woman. I admired her. She was a patron of the arts and active in many charitable activities. But things were not good, the economy was in shatters, and they continued to deteriorate. Then, in 1941, Hungary aligned with Germany, the country was at war, and my husband was sent to fight against the Russians. And I never saw him again."

Katarina took a sip of her lemonade, and I noticed a slim gold band on her right ring finger. Like me, despite the years, she had never taken her wedding band off. I didn't need to look into her eyes to see the pain. I knew it as though it were my own. A loss like that never goes away.

"Our army suffered a terrible defeat." Katarina put her glass down. "We were all fearful of the Russians and convinced the Germans would do nothing to defend us. It was a very nervous time. The country was bankrupt, and anti-Semitism was rampant. Even so, like many Jews, Margit thought the stories they heard about what was happening in Germany couldn't possibly happen here. They believed they were Hungarian, and Hungary would protect them. That they had escaped the worst of the war."

Aanika pressed the pearls to her neck and looked away.

Katarina continued. "We soon learned how wrong they were. Jews were denied their rights to hold certain jobs or own land. Times were getting desperate. It was then that Andor forged the title on the lake property so that it appeared to be owned by my husband and me."

"He gave you Margit's home?" From the surprised look on Aanika's face, I could tell this for the first time she had heard any of this.

"On one condition," Katarina added, "when the time came for Margit and the girls to leave the city, I would agree to hide them. Which, of course, I promised to do. Then, in 1944, our Prime Minister Miklos Kallay signed a secret agreement with Britain that, in effect, allowed Hungary to switch sides. When Hitler learned of this, he ordered the occupation of Budapest. With their *Sieg Heil* salutes and black boots, the Germans arrived in their trucks and began their house-to-house search for our Jews. From within our midst, the Germans recruited young thugs for their Iron Cross movement. For the price of a shirt and a gun, they turned against their own countrymen and terrorized us all. Before it was all over, more than 434,000 Jews were sent by train to Auschwitz."

Aanika shook her head. "I can't imagine how awful it must have been. To see your neighbors pulled from their houses. Friends forced at gunpoint to leave."

"Until then, I had never thought about being part of the resistance. I had never handled a Molotov cocktail, but those of us in the underground learned quickly. We had to fight back. We blew up trucks. Sabotaged the German's communication equipment. And sometimes," Katarina paused, "I would do what I could to lure an unsuspecting German soldier into a trap. I had no problem with what I did. We were trying to survive. At one point, a group of us bombed a supply truck, and I was hurt. Some in our group were caught, but I escaped. Margit's husband was able to help me. A piece of exploding glass had sliced the side of my face, and I couldn't see out of my left eye. There was nothing we could do. I'd need surgery, but first, I had to get out of Budapest. Andor did what he could to help me and suggested I take Adolph and go to the lake. The property was now in my husband's name, and there was no reason I shouldn't be there."

"What about Margit and the girls?" Aanika asked.

"Margit refused to leave her husband. Andor thought they might be safe for a while longer. He had been trying to get papers from a young Swede named Raoul Wallenberg, who had arranged for a Schutz-pass or papers of protection. The papers would allow for them to go to a safe house that had been designated as Swedish property to shelter Jews."

"Safe houses?" I recalled reading about Raoul Wallenberg in my guidebook and his rescue of some of Budapest's Jews, but I had no idea about papers of protection or safe houses. "Am I understanding this correctly? In the middle of a war, there were safe houses?"

"It may seem odd, but yes. The Germans were very meticulous about paperwork and proper protocol. Initially, Raoul negotiated with the Germans for the safety of twelve-hundred Hungarian Jews. Later there were more documents, many of them forged. But it was a beginning."

"So if a Jew was lucky enough to have such papers and a German soldier stopped them, they would leave them alone?" I asked.

"Exactly. With papers, one would be exempt from wearing a yellow star and were treated as Swedish citizens."

"And the safe houses? Where were they?"

"Everywhere. In the city. The countryside. Raoul arranged for the Swedish legation to rent buildings for the Red Cross and put signs on them like The Swedish Library or Research Institute and a Swedish flag on the door."

I pointed over my shoulder to the home in front of the garden apartments and asked if it, too, had been a safe house. Katarina answered yes, and that there were many left. This property was still maintained by the Swedish Government and used as a retirement center. If I looked closely, I'd see places marked with a small yellow star or a Swedish flag.

"And was Andor able to get the papers for Margit and the girls?" I asked.

"No, but he was hopeful. He felt certain he would have them, so we agreed I would leave for the farmhouse, and if things didn't work out with the papers for Andor and his family, he would get word to me through the pharmacy in Keszthely. I was to go there and ask for amyl nitrite, a popular drug to treat angina and lower blood pressure. If the pharmacist told me they were out, I would assume everything was okay. That Andor, Margit, and the girls had made it to a safe house. But, if the pharmacist told me to come back, that he would have to get some, I would know I needed to find a way to get Margit and the girls here. We could only hope the Germans wouldn't cut the phone lines, and communication between Budapest and Keszthely would be working. If not, I was to assume the worst."

Chapter Twenty

"Szia, Anya." From the front porch, the sound of a man's voice echoed through the apartment, followed by a light tapping on the door.

"Adolph." Katarina held out her hand. "Come in, dear. We have company. You remember our Lieutenant Steve? This is his daughter, Kat, and her friend Aanika. Aanika is married to Margit's grandson, Sandor."

I stood up while Adolph went to his mother's side, kissed her lightly on the top of her head, then offered me his hand.

"You look like your father," he said. Then, turning to Aanika, he added, "And you look much younger than Margit." We all laughed. "I'm sorry I never met Sandor. He was here after I left, but I've heard stories. I hear he's done well for himself."

I didn't know what I expected Adolph to look like. In my mind, he was still a small boy in short pants. But standing in front of me was a tall, handsome gentleman with gray hair, several years my senior. And like me, in a mild state of shock.

"I can't believe this." Adolph put his hand on his mother's shoulder. "How did they find us?"

In Hungarian, Katarina quickly explained Sandor's letter to my father and how Aanika and I had come to Kezsethly searching for her.

Adolph took a straight-back chair from the kitchen and placed it next to his mother. "Your father had a big influence on me. I don't remember my own father. He died when I was young. But your father, he fell from the sky like a superhero, and when I grew up, I wanted to be just like him and learn to fly." Adolph reached for his mother's hand and squeezed it. "Lieutenant

Lawson was quite the man. He helped us through a very difficult time. How is he? Did he come with you?"

"No," I said. "My father couldn't come. He has cancer and can't travel. He wanted me to come instead. To thank you and your mother for rescuing him."

"It was your father who rescued us. Without him, we might have given up hope." Adolph looked up at the ceiling and pointed. "The first time I saw him, he was coming through the clouds. I thought he was Superman."

"Superman?" I laughed out loud. Of all the descriptions I expected from Adolph about my dad, the last was Superman. My father was more of a Clark Kent than Superman.

"I was a big fan. My mother had this Superman comic book hidden under the bed, and at night she would read it to me. We would laugh at the colorful pictures of Superman punching Hitler in the face. Pow!" Adolph made a fist and punched the air. "As a seven-year-old boy, I wanted to believe such a man existed. To us, the Americans were the good guys. That's what my mother said. And Superman was an American. They were going to help us win the war and beat the crap out of the Germans. So when I saw your dad in his parachute, I thought for sure he was Superman, come to save us."

"Aha!" Katarina laughed. "I'd forgotten all about that. The resistance had a few bootlegged copies of comic books with superheroes. Captain America. Batman. Superman. I believe your war department had a hand in distributing the books to GIs to boost their morale and may have even dropped some as propaganda to unsettle the Nazis. There was nothing like seeing a comic strip with Nazi bombers swept up into the hands of a superhero and destroyed. But, it was very dangerous to have such material, and if we'd been caught with them, we probably would have been shot. But the joy it brought to Adolph to see Hitler and his storm troopers destroyed by such superheroes made the risk worth it. Once your father and his men were hidden in the fortress, I hid the books in the tunnel, along with other valuables we didn't want the Germans to find."

"I remember your father reading to me," Adolph said. "My English wasn't so good back then, and my mother had to translate. That's how I first learned to speak, and it was a good thing I did. After the war, when the Russians came, my mother was sent off to a Russian camp, and I was sent to a school for orphaned kids. But because I spoke English, I was treated differently and was sent to better schools. Eventually, I was able to go to college, and later medical school."

"Adolph," Katarina tapped her son's arm, "there's something Kat might like to see. You remember the sketches Steve did."

"You have drawings?" I asked.

"We do," Katarina said. "After your father left, I found them. Adolph, they're in the dresser in the bedroom, bottom drawer. Could you bring them?"

Adolph excused himself and returned with a manilla folder, yellowed with age, and handed it to his mother.

"I've kept them all these years." Katarina opened the folder and took out three charcoal sketches.

"Here, let me help you." Adolph laid the sketches on the wooden coffee table between us.

"Your father was very talented. He tried to teach Adolph to draw, but he wasn't so good. These almost look like photographs."

I recognized my father's hand immediately, the bold lines and delicate shading. The first drawing was a scenic view from the fortress above Lake Balaton. The second, an illustration of Adolph with his mother, a handsome boy with his head tucked under his mother's arm—similar to the picture dad had put inside my backpack when I had left. And the third, three dark-haired women, a mother, and her two girls, huddled together, looking up at the night sky.

"Who's that?" I asked.

"You don't know?" Adolph looked at his mother. "You haven't told her?"

"That's Margit and her girls, Roza and Gizzy." Katarina folded her hands in her lap. "Margit was a warm and wonderful woman. And Roza, her oldest daughter, was very talented. Just nineteen. She loved to play the piano, and she had a beautiful voice. And Gizzy, she was younger than her sister by two years and a reader. I don't think I ever saw the girl when she didn't have her nose in a book."

Aanika picked up the sketch. "I've only seen photographs of Margit. She died before I met Sandor. But this…it captures what the camera couldn't. She looks like she must have been a very loving woman and a good mother."

The picture explained what Katarina hadn't, and suddenly I understood the importance of Margit and her daughters to Katarina and the risks she had taken all those years ago.

"You hid Margit and the girls as well?" I nudged Aanika. "Did you know?"Aanika shook her head. I wasn't sure if it was fear I saw in her eyes or if the pieces of the puzzle were just beginning to come together.

Katarina sighed. "It's a long story. After I left Budapest, I quickly realized how bad things had gotten. In the city, we had very little idea of what was happening around us. The Germans had done what they could to cut communication with the outside world. They had taken our radios, and many of the telephones had been destroyed. I worried that Andor couldn't call the pharmacy in Keszthely to send me a signal to come and that I was on my own. The German tanks had crossed the border. We were no longer partners. Hungary was now an occupied territory, and the Germans treated many of us as their enemy. I knew then if I were to survive, I had to befriend them. Because of my German-Hungarian roots and the fact that I spoke German, they assumed I was one of them—a German hausfrau waiting for her husband to return, and I let them think so. You have to understand I was a single woman with a small son and no means of defense."

"But my mother was a smart woman and an even better actress. One morning, shortly after we had arrived, a caravan of German soldiers stopped on the road outside the farmhouse. Several soldiers were in the garden stealing vegetables. My mother charged out of the house with a broom in her hand and threatened to hit them if they didn't stop. A soldier reached for his gun. I thought for sure he would shoot her, and I ran to her side and screamed, Bitte erschieß Meine Mama nicht. Please don't shoot my mother. Fortunately, the Commandant traveling with the caravan overheard my screams and stopped it before things got out of hand."

"After that," Katarina said, "the Commandant would stop by now and again.

He said they had been in the area for a while, and they thought my small farmhouse had been deserted. I think it was his way of apologizing for the soldiers raiding my garden." Katarina took another sip of her lemonade. "Of course, in truth, the house had been empty. But I told him I had been in hospital—surgery on my eye for an injury I incurred while coming to the aid of a German soldier who had been hurt when a bomb exploded. A neat little lie since the bomb that exploded was one I had set off. But the Commandant believed me and continued to stop by, and when he would, I'd make him something to drink, and we would talk. My relationship with him made me safe from any other German soldiers in the area. Which, in a way, was a blessing."

"Ironically, because of my mother's relationship with the Commandant, she was able to continue with her work with the resistance," Adolph said.

Katarina continued. "I was fortunate. The Commandant liked Adolph. He said Adolph reminded him of his son, who he missed very much back home in Bavaria. Ultimately, the Commandant asked Adolph to collect radios from the local farmers in the area. Of course, what he really wanted was time alone with me. But it was a safe job, and while Adolph collected radios, the Commandant and I would visit. You can interpret that as you like, but we all make sacrifices in times of war. Mine was very little compared to the information I learned, and as a result, what I came to know about what was happening around our small village and, more importantly, in Budapest."

"And that's how you knew that Margit's husband had been picked up and sent to a labor camp," Aanika asked. "From the Commandant?"

"I had no way of knowing for sure. But I knew if I had any chance at all of rescuing Margit and the girls, I needed to act fast. So I came up with a plan. Before I had left Budapest, I had worked as a nurse with the Countess Ilona Edelsheim-Gyulai. She was Regent Miklos Horthy's daughter-in-law. More importantly, she was part of the underground. She had recruited me, and I felt if I could get to her, she might be able to help me."

I leaned closer to Katarina. "And did she?"

"She did. But first, I made up a story and told the Commandant I needed to go back to the hospital in Budapest so that the surgeon could check my eye.

And while I was there, I suggested it might be good for the Commandant if I were to deliver a gift basket to Ferenc Szalasi, the leader of the Arrow Cross Party."

"The Commandant loved the idea, but the story gets better." Adolph sat back down in his chair.

"My own car was much too unreliable, and the roads were terribly torn up. So I asked the Commandant if I might borrow his car, a German jeep. At first, he insisted I have a driver–I think he might have liked to drive me himself, but he had too much to do here and, of course, couldn't leave. I insisted I wasn't an invalid and could drive myself. After all, the Commandant had assured me everything north of Lake Balaton and Budapest itself was in German hands. And we were on the north side, and the road I would be traveling on would be well protected. Nevertheless, we went back and forth on my driving myself several times, but finally, he agreed—provided I allowed for an escort. Which I did."

Listening to Katarina, I could understand why she had been such a successful spy.

"So you convinced the Commandant to have his troops escort you?" I loved it.

"The entire way. I drove the Commandant's jeep, with one of his troop's jeeps in front of me and the other in the rear. And while I wasn't able to meet with Ferenc Szálasi in person, I did drop off my gift basket at his headquarters, where I managed to lose my tail—or those two young German soldiers who had been assigned to escort me to and from Budapest."

"They didn't notice?" Aanika asked.

"Oh, I think I suggested they might like to get a smoke out back while I went in to see the Party Leader. Whatever, I scooted out from under them and went to the hospital."

Adolph bit his lips and smiled. Clearly, he was proud of his mother. Who wouldn't be? The woman was a hero.

"Word on the street was that even with Raoul Wallenberg's papers of protection, members of the Iron Cross were raiding some of the safe houses, and no one was safe. Jews were being pulled from inside the houses and shot on the banks of the Danube. I pleaded with the Countess and told her I needed help to get Andor, Margit, and the girls out of Budapest. I confessed to her I had a secret hiding place near the lake, but I couldn't just go and pick my friends up and take them there. If word got back to the Commandant that I was shuffling Jews around Budapest, I'd never see Adolph again. Adolph was the Commandant's guarantee I would return. But the Countess had a better idea and arranged for me to take an ambulance. Together with another member of our underground, we went to Margit's home."

"And were they all there?" I wondered how much of the story my father knew, and then I realized this was exactly why he hoped I'd find Katarina.

"No. Andor was gone. We were too late. A group from the Iron Cross had picked up Andor that morning. Margit believed he had been sent to a labor camp. They told Margit and the girls to pack a bag, and they would be back later that day to pick them up. As for the papers of protection, they never materialized. Margit was too frightened to move and had nowhere to go. I hustled the three of them into the ambulance, and we returned to the hospital.

When I got there, the Countess had loaded my jeep with enough medical equipment and blankets that we were able to hide Margit and the girls without notice. And so, with Margit and the girls hidden beneath blankets and medical supplies, I drove back to the lake and unpacked the Commandant's jeep in the barn. I then returned it to the Commandant with the much-needed medical supplies and picked up my son. The Commandant never questioned me, and for the next few days, I hid Margit and the girls in the cellar of the farmhouse and held my breath we wouldn't be caught."

"And then you moved them to the fortress?" I asked.

"It was the only place I felt was safe to hide them. The Germans had already checked it and decided it was of no use. The walls were crumbling, and they didn't know about the tunnels that ran through the mountains."

"Nobody did unless you were a particularly adventurous seven-year-old boy." Adolph winked at his mother. "There was a cave or grotto next to the river below the castle that, as a kid, I liked to explore. One day I found a tunnel inside and followed it. At first, I was afraid to go too far. But eventually, I went back with a flashlight, and I found my way from inside the cave and up into the mountain. To my surprise, after hiking through a maze of tunnels, I found an opening leading to the well inside of the fortress. The opening was maybe three feet below the lip of the well. I was pretty spry in those days, and I scrambled up the well's wall until I reached the courtyard. You can't imagine how excited I was. When I told my mother, she told me it was our secret and that I mustn't tell anyone. Later, when she explained we needed to hide Margit and the girls, I understood why. They couldn't stay hidden in the root cellar forever. It was too dangerous, and there was no fresh air or enough room for them to stand up. So one night, when my mother knew the Germans would be away from the area, we made our move."

"The Germans had stolen a pig from one of the farmers. They had prepared a slow roast, and the Commandant asked me to go with him to celebrate. I refused, saying I didn't want to leave Adolph alone and that the Commandant should go ahead. Then, we transferred Margit and the girls in Adolph's small wagon one by one. First to the cave and then up through the tunnel. Later, when we rescued your father and his men, we did it the same way. It was how we were able to take them up to the castle without being seen."

"Then you hid six people, my father, his men, and Margit and the girls, inside that old fortress, and the Germans never knew?"

"We hid a lot in those tunnels. Things I hope for my sake and those I love will remain forever buried. But yes, for a while, there were six souls hidden beneath the fortress. There is much more to it than I'm able to tell right now. Adolph can tell you the rest, but this excitement has exhausted me. I'm afraid I've had all I can handle for one day." Katarina stood up. "You'll have to excuse me. I need to lie down."

"Wait," I said. "May I take your picture? Both of you? My father's going to want to see it when I get home."

Adolph helped his mother to her feet, then stood with his arm around her shoulder while I snapped a quick photo.

"He's going to be so happy to see this," I said. "And to know you're both okay."

Katarina smiled. She looked tired. "Please, give him my love."

I watched as Adolph helped his mother to the bedroom.

Aanika whispered to me. "I had no idea. Her story's amazing."

"Can you imagine? Driving the Commandant's Jeep? She probably drove that same road we drove in on. What a story."

Adolph returned and picked the sketches up off the table. "You should take these. Give them to your father with my thanks."

I stared at the pictures, a glimpse into my father's past as he had seen it. The lake. Adolph and Katarina. And three women I didn't know about huddled together—the look in their eyes both of fear and hope. My father had captured it all. Carefully I slipped them back in the folder and held it against my chest.

"He'll treasure them," I said.

Adolph walked us to the door, and we said our goodbyes. He asked Aanika to give Sandor his best and hoped they might meet one day. Then he asked me how long I expected to be here.

"Not long," I said. "This is a quick trip. My flight home is Wednesday evening."

"Today's Saturday. I have a busy week. I'm a doctor and on staff at Saint John's, but if you're free for lunch Monday, perhaps we could meet then, and I can tell you the rest of the story about Margit and her girls. I'm sure your father will want to know."

Chapter Twenty-One

I couldn't wait to get back to the car to talk with Aanika. Her actions ever since we had arrived in Keszthely puzzled me. She had been so excited about going, and then once we got here, she seemed hesitant to look for Katarina. When we found her, I almost had to force Aanika to accompany me to Katarina's home.

"Tell me the truth, Aanika. Did you know Katarina had hidden Margit and the girls? Did Sandor ever mention it to you?"

"No." Aanika got in the car and slammed the door. "Sandor never said anything, and we never talk about what happened to his grandmother during the war. I don't think he knew."

"I don't believe you. I think you're lying."

"Sandor thought she was dead. Okay?" Aanika put both her hands on the wheel and hung her head.

I could see Aanika didn't want to talk, but I wasn't about to let it go.

"So, it was just luck then that we ran into Katarina today, right?"

"I don't know. Maybe." Aanika slammed her foot on the gas, and we surged forward.

I grabbed the dashboard.

"I didn't think we'd find Katarina. I'm as surprised as you are."

Aanika was rattled. By all appearances finding Katarina had been a big jolt. And if my instincts were correct, Aanika's frustration had everything to do with Sandor. Whether Sandor had known Katarina was alive or not, he didn't want us to find her. He had probably warned Aanika the night before that it wouldn't be a good idea if we were to actually discover my father's rescuer. It was the only possible explanation I could think of that explained why, from the moment Aanika and I arrived in Keszthely, that she had been so reluctant for us to look for Katarina. As for Aanika's conversations with the locals, they had all been in Hungarian. For all I knew, someone might have told Aanika they had just seen Katarina in the marketplace an hour earlier, and it spooked her. No wonder Aanika wanted to leave the market and go for ice cream. She didn't want to risk our running into Katarina. How could she possibly explain to Sandor if we did?

I rested my elbow on the car's open window and stared at the road ahead. If Sandor had been concerned we might find Katarina, Aanika would have some explaining to do—starting with the pearl necklace Katarina had given her.

"So, what will you tell Sandor?" I asked.

Aanika put her hand to her throat and covered the necklace. "What do you mean, what will I tell Sandor? I'll tell him we found Katarina. I'm sure he'll be pleased to know we were successful. "

I didn't think so, but I was hesitant to challenge Aanika while she was driving.

"Well, it was definitely a stroke of luck we found her. She's an amazing woman, isn't she?"

"Will you write about her?" Aanika glanced over at me.

"Yes, I think I will. Can you imagine Katarina driving on this road—in the Commandant's jeep? What a story she'd make. Maybe I'll even include something about you and Sandor and how you helped me to find her."

"What?" Aanika was lost in thought. I knew she wasn't listening from the way she was taking the curves on the road. Her mind was far away. I suspected she was focused on the conversation she would have with Sandor later that night.

"Nothing," I said. "I'm just thinking out loud." I looked at the pearls around Aanika's neck and thought back to Katarina's tiny apartment and the gypsy painting above the mantel. "If you don't mind, I think I'll close my eyes. I need to concentrate."

Aanika reached over the seat and grabbed the picnic blanket we had used the day before. "Here, cuddle up with this. It's getting cooler. You'll be comfy."

I curled up with the blanket and closed my eyes, my thoughts more on Sandor than on Katarina. Sandor had been surprised when I mentioned my father's request to find Katarina, and he had downplayed the likelihood I might find her from the start. But now that I had found her, I was beginning to think I understood why. If Margit had told Sandor about the cave and the things Katarina had hidden there, it might explain why he hadn't wanted me to find Katarina. After seeing the gypsy's painting above the mantel in her home, I wondered what other gifts Katarina might have accepted in exchange for her help. Was there more hidden in the cave? Things Sandor didn't want me to know about? I couldn't imagine Katarina visiting the cave in recent times. She couldn't have climbed up to the fortress, she was too old and feeble, and I doubted it would have been any easier for her to access her hiding place from within the grotto. But Sandor might have. And he might have worried my father had told me about the cave beneath the old fortress and the treasures Katarina had hidden there and feared I was on a mission to uncover her secret cache. But now that Aanika and I had found Katarina and Aanika was about to return home with Margit's pearls, I wondered what Sandor might do?

Chapter Twenty-Two

Miklos and Nora were in the kitchen when I returned. I didn't bother to stop and let them know I was back. Now that I had my own key, I didn't think it necessary to announce my return, and I was anxious to call home and share the news with my father that I had found Katarina and Adolph. I went quickly up the stairs, shut the door behind me, and dialed my folks' number.

While waiting for the call to go through, I crossed the room and opened the French doors. Nora had put fresh towels in the bath, another chocolate on my pillow, and—*dammit*—she had moved my journal. *Again!*

Before I had gone out, I had hidden the journal beneath the bedside table. And now, the pencil sketches my father had drawn of Adolph and Katarina were peeking out from beneath its cover—evidence Nora had been snooping through my things again.

I snatched my journal up off the bed and began to flip through the pages. I stopped on the page where I had taken notes about my father's last mission. Before I left home, dad had given me a ton of details about his plane. Everything he told me was exactly as Sandor had described when we had visited Bombshell Betty. Size. Wingspan. Bomb load. Even the crew positions. Right down to how freezing cold those bombing missions would have been. '*Colder than a witch's tit,*' Dad said. I had even underscored the quote, and now it stood out on the page like a flashing red light. Sandor said he had heard other airmen describe the plane and the frigid conditions inside, but the more I thought about it, the more certain I was Nora had been doing more than just searching my room—she had shared my journal with Sandor.

"Hello?" My mother answered the phone.

"Hi, Mom. I've got good news. Can you put Dad on the line? I found Adolph and Katarina. Can't wait to tell him." I slapped the journal shut, left it on the bed, and went to the balcony.

"Kat, honey, I need to warn you. Dad had a rough night. Don't exhaust him."

I wanted to ask more, but Dad got on the other line before I could ask.

"Hey there, Kat." Dad coughed, and I waited while he cleared his throat. "How are you, girl?"

"I'm fine. How are you doing?"

"Good as can be expected." Dad's voice was low and raspy. He sounded like he was struggling to talk. "Did you find Katarina and Adolph?"

"We did!" I explained how Aanika and I had gone back to Keszthely and found Katarina. I left out how difficult Katarina's life had been immediately after the war under the Russian occupation. I wanted this to be a good news call. The details I had uncovered, I would explain later. But for now, I wanted to share the news I knew my father had been waiting for. "She's not living in the farmhouse anymore. That's long since gone. After the war, she moved to Keszthely. It's nice there. Beautiful city, full of flowers, and she's living in a retirement home on her own. And Adolph? He's a doctor."

"A doctor, how about that."

"He lives in Budapest, but he was there today. He comes by once a week to visit his mother. They had so many good things to say about you. And you know what?"

"What?"

"Adolph said the first time he saw you, he thought you were Superman."

I wasn't sure if Dad was coughing or laughing at the same time. Either was a possibility. I waited until he stopped.

"They never knew if you made it back, Dad. But I got pictures and lots of stories."

My mother took the phone. Dad was still coughing in the background.

"Kat, this is terrific news. I know your dad wants to know more, but now's not the time. He needs his rest. The doctors have him on some new meds, which wears him out. When do you expect to be back?"

"Wednesday night late," I said, "but the earliest I can get to your house won't be 'til Thursday morning. Is everything okay?"

"For us, yes. But, there's something I need to tell you."

My stomach tightened. "Is it about, Dad?"

"No, it's not your father, Kat. It's Josh. He came by and—"

"He did what?"

When Josh had left, I was devastated and felt I was to blame for everything that had happened with my marriage. But now that I was more than six thousand miles away and had time to think, I wasn't feeling nearly as regretful. If anything, I felt more clear-headed about the situation. Perhaps if I had spoken up and insisted Josh and I sit down and really talk now and again, I might not have ended up in a pointless affair and lost my job. For that much, I could take responsibility. As for Josh's social distancing, the nights he spent locked in his study, and our empty bed, that much was on him.

"He came by to talk to your father. He said he's tried to call you several times and left messages but that you hadn't returned his calls."

"Yeah, well, it's a little hard from here."

"You need to call, Kat. He's your husband. He says you have an offer on the house, and he needs you to sign the papers."

"An offer on the house? What are you talking about?" I knew Josh was upset about the affair, but I couldn't believe he'd actually put the house on the market. Not without asking me, and certainly not without my signature.

"He said you agreed to sell—"

"I did no such thing. What are you talking about?"

"Kat, you're going to have to ask him. All I know is that he told your father there's an offer on the house, and he needs to talk to you."

"Yes, well, this all sounds a little fast." Until now, I had still thought we would be able to patch things up. Despite the affair, we could work things through, and I'd find another job, and somehow I'd put my life and us back together. I hated to admit failure.

"I thought so too, but according to your father, it shouldn't be much of a surprise. Josh told him he hadn't made payments for the last three months."

"Three months?" I had no idea.

"He's afraid the bank will foreclose if the two of you don't hurry up and sign the papers and get the house into escrow."

I couldn't believe what I was hearing.

"How can he not have made payments for the last three months? He has the money." Foolishly I had trusted Josh to handle the family bank account. As an investment banker with years more understanding of finance and accounting than I had, he had insisted he manage our finances. However, we split the bills, and I'd give him money for my share of the expenses every month. But lately, I had been too busy working and assumed that he had taken care of it like always. "What's he been doing with the money if he hasn't been paying the bills?"

I didn't expect an answer, but evidently, Josh had confided in my father, and my mother wasn't shy about telling me of his sudden desperation to find me.

"The race track. Online gambling. Vegas. Take your pick. Seems all those nights your father and I worried about you being alone, or working too hard, that Josh was gambling."

"Crap!" I wanted to throw the phone across the room. I knew Josh gambled now and then. He had promised me he knew what he was doing. He felt it gave him his edge and wasn't afraid to take a risk. "How much has he lost?"

"He didn't say. Only that you need to sign the papers, and quickly."

I didn't want to talk about Josh or our financial difficulties on an international call. I told my mother I'd call again tomorrow and hung up. Then I tried Josh's cell and got his voicemail. I wasn't about to leave a message. I'd call back when I knew he would be available, and hopefully, it wouldn't be a screaming match.

I threw the phone on the bed, Josh was a problem, but my more immediate issue, one I could no longer ignore, was Nora. If Nora had been showing my journal to Sandor, it was time I ran a test.

I opened the red notebook and sat down on the bed. Starting with today's date, I jotted down a few brief notes like I usually did at the end of each day. Only this time, I planned to seed a few ideas that I suspected might catch Nora's attention, and she would want to share with Miklos and Sandor.

I entered three short paragraphs—just enough bait to set the trap.

Saturday, July 20:

Nora's left chocolates for me again tonight. I wish she wouldn't. Sweets keep me up at night. But what a day. I doubt I'll sleep anyway. Went with Aanika to Keszthely and found Katarina! What stories she told, including about the tunnel where Dad hid. I need to go back and take pictures. Can't help but wonder what else she hid there? What a story it would make. Maybe tomorrow...???

Talked to Dad. He sounds worse. Docs have him on new meds. Mom said he needs to rest—and Josh is gambling, again! House in foreclosure. Need to arrange for a loan. ASAP.

Still need to find a few gifts to take home and a Curly pigs' wool sweater for mom. Can't find it anywhere.

Satisfied I had left enough clues, I closed my journal and put it back beneath the nightstand. If Nora was sharing my journal with Sandor, I'd know soon enough. Any mention about my wanting to go back to the old fortress and the grotto beneath it, or if Nora were to stop leaving chocolate on my pillow, would confirm my suspicion that I was being watched. Now all I had to do was wait and see.

I fingered the gold compass around my neck and went to the balcony. Dad always talked about finding his North Star. No matter how bad things got, he said if you knew where your North Star was, you could find your way home. The lights from the Buda side of the city twinkled back at me like a fairytale while riverboats, with their dinner cruises, sailed slowly up and down the waterway. I wondered about Aanika and what she would tell Sandor about our visit to Keszthely. And Sandor, how would he react to seeing his grandmother's pearl necklace around his wife's neck? Would he be surprised?

Whatever Sandor's response, I couldn't stop thinking about the cave and old fortress. I had to go back. Now that I knew the truth about where my father, his men, Margit, and the girls had hidden, I had to get pictures. I wanted to climb up through the tunnel and into the well, exactly as my father had done. But to do that, I was going to need help.

I needed Adrian.

I may not have believed in gypsy prophecies, but so far, Adrian was three for three—and the only person I felt I could trust. Adrian had predicted I'd find my father's plane. He knew about the tunnels beneath the fortress where my father had hidden. And I had found Katarina—precisely as he said I would. I didn't have a lot of time. In three days, I'd be back on a plane headed to the States. I grabbed my camera, my fanny pack with my wallet and headed out the door. I had a favor to ask.

* * *

A breeze had kicked up, and the hotter afternoon temperatures had given way to a much cooler evening, making for an almost celebratory mood with tourists and locals out for an evening stroll. I walked north along the riverwalk, toward Parliament with its huge central dome and tall spires, my eyes peeled for Adrian and his boat. When I got as far as the Elizabeth Bridge and still hadn't seen any sign of him, I turned around and headed back toward the apartment.

"Kat." I recognized Adrian's voice. Had he not called my name, I would not have spotted him. He was standing in an alcove in front of a tourist shack selling postcards. He folded an accordion stack of cards and put them inside his jacket. "I think you are looking for me. You want another ride on my boat? Or maybe you like I read for you."

"Neither," I said. "I have a favor to ask."

"Ahh, then this is no accident." Adrian brushed the hair from his eyes. "You have found Katarina and have returned with questions."

"I did, and I found your grandmother's picture, too. Exactly as you said I would."

"This is good news." Adrian smiled. The flash of his gold tooth caught the evening light. "You have found everything you came for."

I exhaled. I couldn't believe I was about to ask a gypsy for help, but what choice did I have? I certainly couldn't ask Sandor, and who else did I know? "Yes, but—"

"But you are not happy. I can tell. What is it?"

"I want to go back to Lake Balaton, to the caves beneath the fortress where my father hid. Can you go with me? Tomorrow?"

"Will you pay?"

"How much?" I rested my hand on my fanny pack.

"Fifty dollar, plus gas for car."

"Fifty dollars! I thought you said you owed me." After settling Adrian's dispute with the unhappy American tourist, I distinctly remembered him saying as much. But fifty dollars seemed like an exorbitant amount.

"That was before you say you want to go to Lake Balaton. Lake is all-day trip. And not so cheap." Adrian held his hand up and rubbed his thumb and index finger together, the international signal for money.

"Okay, then forty."

"Fifty, and I give you free reading. Tell you all bout romance and handsome man I see in your life."

"No, Adrian, I don't need a reading, and I'm not interested in romance. I've enough problems in that department. I'll pay you forty-five, and you can skip the reading." The thought of romance was the furthest thing from my mind. What would a gypsy boy, half my age, understand about my life?

"You lucky lady. I do for forty-five American dollar. Plus five dollar for gas. Deal?"

I looked up at the sky and shook my head. I didn't have time for further negotiation. "Deal," I said.

Adrian extended his hand, palm up. "You pay now."

"How about I pay you half now and the rest tomorrow?" I forked over five, five-dollar bills.

Adrian pocketed the money. "Meet me, Heroe's Square tomorrow. You know this place?" I nodded. Heroes' Square had been part of Sandor's nickel-dime tour when I first arrived. "Ten a.m. I have car. We take mine."

Chapter Twenty-Three

I f I thought Sandor's rusted, red beast was awful, Adrian's dilapidated, box-like, can-on-wheels was even worse. The car was so small I doubted it was possible for two people to actually sit in the front seat at the same time. But somehow, we managed to squeeze inside, shoulder to shoulder, with my knees beneath my chin. Adrian leaned out the window to check for traffic and adjusted the side mirror, which promptly fell off in his hand. Then with his foot on the gas, we pulled away from the curb, and the car groaned. The sound of metal scraping rusted metal, like that of a wounded elephant.

"You mind if I ask a question?" Adrian looked at me quickly, then back out the window with both hands on the wheel. "This guide you hire, what's his name?"

"Sandor," I said.

"So, why does this Sandor take you to where your father hides and not show you tunnel?"

"Good question." I hugged my backpack to my stomach. There was no room for it on the floor. "And the only answer I can come up with is that I think he's hiding something. And the people I'm staying with, I believe, are up to something as well. I'm not sure what, but right now, I don't trust anyone."

"Now *you* sound Hungarian. Suspicious of everyone."

"Yes, well, I have a good reason." I explained that Sandor had tried to convince me he didn't think Katarina was alive. But Aanika and I found Katarina and learned that she had hidden Sandor's grandmother in the fortress with my father. "Katarina had Sandor's grandmother's pearls, and she gave the necklace to Aanika."

"And now you think because Katarina has my grandmother's painting that she hides more valuables, maybe in the cave beneath the fortress?"

"Maybe. The truth is, I don't know what's going on, and I'm worried. I feel as though I've stumbled onto some secret I wasn't supposed to know about, and now that I have, I'm concerned I'm being watched. And I don't know why."

Adrian gripped the wheel and looked straight ahead.

"I think perhaps your guide may not be such a bad man—that maybe he protects Katarina."

"Really?" I hadn't thought of that. But after learning Margit and her girls had also hidden in the old fortress, my reporter's intuition told me there was more of a story there than I had been told, and I wasn't about to let the opportunity to discover what it might be, pass me by. This was a story I wanted.

Adrian reached into the glove box and pulled out a stack of postcards like those he had been selling the night before.

"Find card I give you, Caves of Tapolca, then read the back. I think this cave is very much like the cave where your father hide."

I sorted through the cards until I found the Caves of Tapolca. The cave was described as a winding three-hundred-meter limestone complex of caverns and tunnels, formed centuries ago by volcanic activity, much of which had yet to be explored. And much bigger than I imagined.

"Yes, but the cave I'm looking for is closer to Keszthely. This is much farther away—too far from the lake."

"It does not matter. There are many."

"If it helps, I know the fortress where my father hid is next to a river." I fingered the compass around my neck and glanced down at the directional needle. "But Sandor knew a way through the forest, and I doubt I could find the same path. It was overgrown and—"

"Is on top of mountain. Small fortress, above river."

"You know the area?"

147

Adrian plucked the cards from my hand and stuffed them above the visor. "For gypsies, the mountains and the rivers are our home."

"But you live in the city. You have a boat."

"It is where I sleep, but these hills, they are home. It is where I grow up and why I know of Katarina. You not worry, we will find cave. I promise."

I scanned the hillsides. Despite Adrian's old clunker, we had made relatively good time. I spotted the exit sign to Keszthely and told Adrian to slow down. We were getting close.

But Adrian ignored me, and we went another mile further and parked next to the lake. Unlike when Sandor had turned off the road and taken some unmarked road into the forest, Adrian appeared to know another way. We hiked from the lake towards the river's mouth, where we could see the tower of the old fortress in the hills above us. As we approached the river, I could see where it had once been deeper and far mightier. The river had cut into the rocks below its bank, creating narrow crevices and what looked like a cave further upstream.

I snapped a couple of pictures and ran ahead. This had to be the cave where Katarina and Adolph had brought my father and his men after they bailed out. And where Katarina had tossed Nick's chute into the river so the Germans would think they had drowned. I found a spot in the rock where I could climb down the river's embankment, then leaned over the steep ledge and peered inside.

"I think we've found it." Beneath me, I could make out a room-sized grotto that stretched far back into the dark crevasses of the mountain.

"Let's go." Adrian crawled around me and jumped down from the river's embankment and into the cave below. I could barely make out the water markings on the rocks. Still, it looked as though the water level had dropped considerably over the years and left enough of a ledge for Adrian to get a foothold without falling into the underground lake. He waved for me to join him. "Come. It's fine."

I gripped the rock's edge and stared at the turquoise waters beneath me, and froze. I couldn't jump. Caves frightened me. Tight spaces made me feel claustrophobic, and the grotto with its strangely seductive turquoise waters gave me pause. What if the water level rose and we were trapped? "I can't."

"Yes, you can. I catch you."

"What do you mean, catch me? I'll drown us both." I was at least half a foot taller than Adrian. Soaking wet, the boy probably didn't weigh more than a hundred and twenty-five pounds. I didn't imagine he could catch me, much less fish me out of the water, if I fell in.

"Just try. You can swim, yes?"

"Sure, I can swim. But—"

"Jump."

I took a deep breath. Did I really want to do this? Did my dad? My mind flashed on a vision of my father as he prepared to jump from his plane. His words echoed in my ears. *You don't know what you can do until you have to do it.*

I had to put my fear behind me. I couldn't write a story about my father's experience unless I had actually been inside the tunnel where he hid. I needed to take pictures. I had to experience it firsthand. There would be no excuse for my story if I didn't have all my facts in order.

I stood up, hugged my camera against my chest, and let go of the rock. *This is for you, Dad.*

I would have slipped into the pool if Adrian hadn't helped me to my feet. "You okay?"

"I'm fine." I looked around. Despite the translucent, turquoise water, the cave was dark, and I couldn't see beyond the limestone walls around me.

Adrian pointed a small flashlight attached to his key chain at the water. "You see that?"

"What?"

"The fish. Like little diamonds in the water. You make wish. They bring good luck."

I cupped my hand in the cool water and watched as several tiny, minnow-like fish spilled through my fingers, then stood up.

"What's that?" I pointed across the grotto to a long, narrow crevice beneath the cave's ceiling.

Adrian shined his light and shrugged. "Don't know. A blanket, maybe?"

"Whatever it is, I think it's covering something."

I inched toward the other side of the grotto, the water lapping the soles of my shoes as I felt along the limestone wall for the blanket. Or what I quickly realized wasn't just a blanket at all, but the moth-eaten remains of a bedroll covered with a calcified, chalky white limestone dust.

"Adrian, help me. There's something inside this blanket. I can feel it." Adrian refused to move, and I urged him one more time. "Come on, I need your help."

"Maybe we should just go," he said.

"No. I've come this far. Let's try to move this thing or at least unwrap it. I want to know what it is. Why's it hidden here?"

Adrian hesitated, then slipped along the water's narrow shelf until he was close enough to help me lift the blanket from its berth.

"Ready?" I waited until Adrian had hold of the blanket from one end while I had my hands on the other. "One. Two. Three."

On three, we lifted the blanket, and suddenly—it unrolled.

I jumped back against the wall. "Is that—"

"A body!" Adrian crossed himself with the sign of the cross.

I stared down at the skeletal remains of a German soldier still dressed in uniform as it started to sink slowly into the water.

"Quick, grab his leg. We need to put him back." I had no idea why I felt I needed to put the body back into its limestone grave. Only that it seemed wrong to just abandon it, and I wasn't about to leave any evidence I'd been there and risk being accused of grave robbing—or worse.

Fortunately, skeletons don't weigh much, and aside from the soldier's wet uniform, the body, or what remained of it, was more cumbersome than heavy. With Adrian's help, we rolled the body back into the blanket and managed to stuff the soldier's remains into the crevice.

I wiped my hands. Decided it best I not take a picture, then asked Adrian, "Can you give me your light?"

I focused Adrian's flashlight deeper into the cave and spotted a curious opening in the rock, a narrow tunnel big enough for a man to easily slip through.

"You see that?" I pointed the light in the direction of the tunnel, where the water had retreated, and a rock shelf was covered with limestone dust.

"Are those footprints?" Adrian asked.

"Somebody's been here," I said.

It might have been difficult for us to find our way were it not for the scuff marks on the cave's floor. There were several possible dark passages between the rocks that we might have taken. But because of the footprints, I chose to follow them and steeled my nerves to move forward.

The climb, combined with the warmth and humidity of the cave, caused me to sweat. Slowly, with my hands on the cave's crusty walls to steady myself, we crept between the rocks and followed the twisted hollow tunnel until we came to an alcove. I leaned back against the rocks and flashed the light, then stepped back and clung to the wall. Beyond the safety of the alcoves' shelf, a large cavernous opening stretched as far above our heads as it did below.

Like giant icicles, stalactites dripped from the top of the rocky cave, and from the floor below, massive stalagmites pushed upward. In the low light, they cast ghoulish shadows and together looked like the inside of a monster's mouth, with its giant teeth about to gnash down on us.

I focused my camera and took a couple shots. Then with the aid of Adrian's small flashlight, we crept forward until we came to another alcove where we stopped to catch our breath. I wiped the sweat from my brow, and when I removed my hand from my forehead, I blinked.

Ahead, sunlight streamed through a narrow opening. I pulled my compass locket from around my neck and checked the coordinates. If I was correct, our position showed precisely as it had when I stood in the center courtyard days before. We had to be directly below the fortress. I hurried in the direction of the light, anxious to find my way out, and then—

I tripped and fell to the ground.

"Are you okay?" Adrian rushed to me and put his hand on my shoulder.

"I'm fine. I twisted my ankle, that's all." I rotated my foot. Nothing was broken. "Is that a blanket?" I pointed to the mound over which I had tripped.

"Looks like it." Adrian picked up whatever was wrapped in the blanket and slowly began to unwrap it.

"Tell me there's not a body in it." I grabbed my knees to my chest. I didn't think I could take finding a second body.

"It's a portable radio. Look."

Adrian placed the small, brown box-shaped receiver on the blanket. It was in surprisingly good condition, roughly eleven inches wide and seven and a half inches tall. The batteries had long since died, but I could imagine my father sitting in the dark cave and listening to its scratchy signal.

I shined Adrian's light on the floor. Was there something else I might find? My eyes followed a trail of chalky dust to the wall, where it appeared to have been disturbed. I could see evidence something had dragged something across the cave's floor. A small trowel had been shoved between the rocks. Whoever had been here, we weren't the first to have visited the cave since the war ended, nor did I think we'd be the last. The question was, who was it? And why?

I wrapped the radio back in the blanket and pushed it back behind a rock. "So, how do we get out of here? I'm starting to feel claustrophobic."

"This way." Adrian titled his head to the cavern's far end, where a light was coming through a narrow opening.

I followed Adrian toward what looked like a chiseled hole in the wall and watched as he climbed up inside then disappeared. Moments passed, and the silence was so still that the only thing I could hear was the sound of my own breathing.

"Adrian?" I hollered into the hole. There was no answer, only the sound of my own voice as it echoed back to me. "You okay?"

Nothing.

Finally, I could hear the faint sound of movement from within the wall. Shoes scraping the limestone. Heavy breathing, and then Adrian popped his head out between the rocks.

"Can you climb?"

"What?"

"This leads to the well. We can climb up to the fortress from inside."

"You've got to be kidding? You want me to climb up inside a well?"

CHAPTER TWENTY-THREE

"It's not so bad. Less than two meters."

I calculated two meters to be about six feet. I wasn't much of a rock climber, but I wasn't about to risk going back through the tunnel and getting lost. I figured if Adrian could do it, I could too.

"Follow me." I watched as Adrian braced himself against the well's walls and began to climb up. "Just don't look down."

Chapter Twenty-Four

By the time Adrian and I got back to the city, I was starving. Adrian went to his boat while I went in search of food. I was hopeful I might find a quiet place to grab a quick bite to eat while I gathered my thoughts about the day. Dionysus, my handsome waiter friend, with his white apron tied about his waist, spotted me as I strolled the riverwalk.

"You like your table?" Dion pointed to the empty table where I had dined twice before. "Come, I have great wine for your tonight."

The familiarity of the wine master's greeting made me feel at home. I didn't need the menu. I knew what I wanted and asked Dion to bring me an order of fried flatbread, chicken, and a glass of red wine. The closest thing I could think of to comfort food.

While I waited for Dion to bring the wine, I replayed the day's events in my head. My trip to the grotto beneath the old fortress and the body Adrian and I had found hidden in the cave that I feared was that my father had killed. The old AM radio. The narrow window from inside the well that Adrian and I had used to climb up to the fortress. All of it, proof this was the cave Katarina had used. But it was the trowel and the scuff marks on the cave's floor that caused me to think the cave was still in use. And not for a moment did I think it was Katarina who had visited the cave. She wasn't in any kind of shape to hike up inside the mountain, much less attack the rugged mountain trail. And if it wasn't Katarina or Sandor, then who was it?

Adrian kept telling me he believed our mission to find my father's hiding place had been successful. That I was, as he had said many times before, a lucky lady. I had achieved everything I had set out to do. I had found my father's plane, his hiding place, as well as Katarina and Adolph.

"You should go home now and make your father happy. Before it is too late."

"Why, do you think my luck is about to run out?" I wasn't about to let any gypsy prophecy regarding my luck or lack of it dictate my plans to find out what was really hidden inside the cave.

"I can only tell you, Kat, you need to be careful. Someone close to you lies."

I didn't need a gypsy to tell me someone was lying. I could have told him as much. Everyone around me was lying about something. My husband had been lying about his gambling. Sandor was setting me up for something. I just hadn't figured out what, but I would have put money down if it had something to do with the cave. Nora, I didn't trust at all. And my father, I knew, wasn't being honest with me about his health. I didn't need a gypsy to tell me people around me weren't being honest.

* * *

I finished my meal, paid the bill then strolled back along the riverwalk to my apartment.

When I returned to my room, I found another chocolate on my pillow and my notepad exactly where I had left it beneath the nightstand. So much for my planted text that I had hoped would convince me of Nora's snooping.

I threw my fanny pack on the bed and was about to go into the bathroom when I heard a knock on my door.

"Miss Kat, I'm so sorry to disturb you so late. May I come in?" Nora entered my room carrying a large, brown leather suitcase.

"Nora? You speak English?" this was the first I had heard Nora speak more than a word of English. Up to now, our communication had been little more than a few nods and smiles.

"Some," she said very matter-of-factly. Then crossing the room, she placed the suitcase on a travel stand next to the dresser. "I want to make an apology. I wash your bag today. I think it's dirty, but the zipper broke. And now, it is no good. Please, you use this instead. It has key, and you need more room for gifts. No?" Nora placed a small gold key on top of the suitcase, patted it as though to confirm all was well. Then, with a curt nod, hurried to the door. "Oh, and one more thing. Sandor keeps calling. He asked me to tell you to call him. Good night, Miss Kat."

I was stunned. I stared at the bag like it was a coiled rattlesnake about to strike. Not for a second did I believe Nora had washed my bag. It was brand new, and despite the fact I had left it on the floor, hardly dirty. As for room for gifts, who was she kidding? She had read my journal, and we both knew it.

There could only be one reason anyone would want to switch my suitcase with one much larger. They needed somewhere to hide something and someone to carry it. And if that someone was me, I was going to find out why.

I moved the suitcase to the bed. It was smooth and subtle to the touch—an expensive gift to give to a traveler who one might never see again. It must have been at least thirty years old, an antique, with thin leather straps and brass buckles and locks. Not at all like the modern rollies so popular with travelers today.

I unlocked the case. Inside, the original lining had been removed. In its place, a soft blue patterned polyester material had been glued to the bottom, sides, and top of the case and trimmed with a thin royal blue velvet cord. I felt along the lining, hoping to find some hidden compartment, and then realized I was looking at it.

I pulled at the blue velvet cord until I removed the trim from the case's interior and then lifted the newly refurbished bottom from the case.

Hidden beneath the false bottom was a large manila envelope. I covered my mouth to prevent my silent scream from escaping. I had hoped I was wrong. Part of me wanted to believe I had imagined that Nora, Miklos, and Sandor were all part of some plan to scam me. But looking at the envelope, I knew it was no longer my imagination. This was real.

My heart raced as I picked up the envelope. I had no idea what was inside, but whatever it was, it couldn't be drugs. Dogs would have sniffed through the case and the envelope and immediately discovered any illegal substance.

I had to do something. I couldn't pretend whatever was inside wasn't there. If I were stopped at the airport and my luggage searched, I'd be arrested like the young woman whose photo I had seen in the newspaper. And if I let on to Nora that I knew anything about it, what might happen to me? I was an American woman alone in a foreign country. I didn't even want to think what trouble I might be in.

I had to open the envelope. I couldn't do anything until I knew what was inside. But first, I needed to make sure no one was watching. I pulled the curtains across the windowed French doors, then I went to the bedroom door and placed my ear softly against it. I twisted the bedroom door's small brass lock and prayed no one in the house heard it click shut. Downstairs was quiet. The baby was asleep, and Nora, Miklos, and the old man had retired to their rooms.

Satisfied no one heard me lock the door or could see me from the window, I took the envelope from the suitcase and carefully unsealed the flap. Inside was a single piece of woven paper, slightly bigger than a legal sheet. At first, I wasn't sure what I was looking at, and then I realized —it was an original Edgar Degas. One of his ballerina sketches. Signed and probably worth thousands, if not hundreds or thousands of dollars.

In college, my father encouraged me to take an art history class. I think he wanted to study art more than I did. I was surprised to find I enjoyed the course as much as I did and talking with him about it. While I'm not much of an artist, I found their stories and paintings fascinating. One of Dad's favorite artists was Edgar Degas, whose pencil sketches, with his dark bold strokes, reminded me a lot of my father's work. Dad was good, but he admitted he was no Degas. Degas was ahead of his time, more of a realist than an impressionist. His ballerina sketches were unique. The artist had developed a process of drawing on an inked plate, then running it through a press, and smearing a pastel paint overlay on top of the impression, giving his work an almost ghostly appearance. I also knew that the painting I held in my hand had been part of a collection owned by Baron Mor Lipot Herzog, a wealthy Hungarian art collector. One whose sad history we had studied in my class. Herzog had been one of the biggest art collectors in Europe, and his entire collection ultimately fell into the hands of the Nazis. Like the ballerinas' sketch, some had been lost during the war and never seen again.

I put the picture back inside the envelope, then placed the envelope back into the suitcase and replaced the false bottom on top of it.

Dammit. What had I got into? And what was I going to do about it?

I considered hiding the painting somewhere in the apartment and leaving it behind, but where? There was nowhere to hide it in the bedroom. I couldn't slip it under the mattress. Nora would find it as soon as she remade the bed. I couldn't hide it in the big bag my mother had insisted I bring with me. Like the suitcase, if I were caught with it when I went to the airport, I would have a hard time trying to prove I didn't know anything about an original Degas in my bag. I had to find a place to hide it. And then I remembered the attic, just outside my bedroom door.

I was going to need a flashlight if I hoped to see anything at all. I turned the light off in my room and waited in the dark until it was almost midnight, then reached for my journal and pen. The pen I kept with my journal was a promotional item the newspaper had passed out a year ago: a small battery-operated penlight, ideal for journaling at night or in places with little light. A handy device I wished I had thought to bring with me earlier that day when Adrian and I had gone to the cave.

When I was sure everyone in the house was asleep, I tiptoed barefoot to the bedroom door, quietly turned the lock, then slipped outside to the open alcove that made up the attic.

Stacked against the wall were furnishings; wooden chairs, a loveseat, several lamps, clocks, and some type of art deco statue of a woman from another era. An antique dealer might have found them a wise investment. They were partially covered with a tarp, and judging from the thin film of dust that had settled on everything, hadn't seen the light of day in years. I crouched down and quietly snuck beneath the attic's eaves, where several frames were leaning against the outside wall. One, a large, life-sized canvas had been turned sideways to accommodate the low ceiling, and in front of it, several smaller framed oils. Using my penlight, I examined each work as best I could. I hoped I might recognize it or at least a signature. But in the low light, it was impossible. I would have to move them away from their grouping and risk being heard.

But I didn't dare.

Directly below me, I heard Miklos in the hallway. I clicked off my penlight and crouched further into the corner of the attic, afraid to breathe. I could hear my heart pounding in my ears. I prayed Miklos hadn't heard me and wasn't about to come upstairs. *What would I say? What could I do?* There was nowhere I could hide. He would find me, and then what? Minutes passed, and then I realized Miklos wasn't coming upstairs. He was pacing the hallway on the second floor with the baby, cooing his young son back to sleep. I must have waited an hour, my legs cramping until I heard Miklos put Márkó down and the door to the baby's room shut. Finally, when I felt it was safe enough to sneak to the top of the stairway, I looked down to make sure Miklos had returned to the master bedroom.

I flashed my penlight back into the attic. I could hide the Degas here among the other antiques and paintings in the attic. And then, just as I was about to turn off my light and return to my room, I noticed footprints in the dust on the floor. A few of the prints I knew had to be mine, and to the others, might have been Nora's. But a set of larger, man-sized footprints looked to be the size of those I had seen in the cave. I couldn't be sure if they were the same, but the coincidence made me think there had to be a connection. Miklos and Sandor must have moved things from the cave to the apartment's attic and then, like the Degas, to my suitcase.

I clicked my penlight off, then slipped silently back into my room and closed the door behind me.

At last, I understood what Sandor's plan was. What his little side business was all about, and how I was to fit into that plan. I was to be his mule. The unsuspecting tourist. Exactly what Sandor and Miklos needed to secret those treasures in the attic and from beneath the old fortress out of the country. It wasn't just for convenience's sake that Sandor had arranged for me to stay with Miklos and Nora. It was all part of what they needed for their smuggling operation. And Nosey-Nora hadn't just been looking through my things. Her job had been to spy on me, read my journal, and report back to Sandor on my every move. If all worked as they hoped, I would go home, happy to have seen those places I wanted to see, and—unbeknownst to me—with a priceless piece of stolen artwork hidden inside my bag. Not that I'd ever see it or know about it. My guess was that somewhere, while en route back to the United States, a black marketer would steal my suitcase, and I'd be none the wiser.

Unless I came up with a plan of my own.

Chapter Twenty-Five

I couldn't sleep. My mind was racing. Every time I tried to close my eyes, I kept seeing the stolen Degas in the bottom of my bag and the other paintings stacked against the wall in the attic. I had to do something. The Degas wasn't going to disappear, and I couldn't ignore it and just hope for the best. If I didn't do something, I could be arrested for smuggling stolen art at the airport. It might be days or even weeks before I could get an attorney and be released. I didn't have that kind of time, not with my father's failing health and my need to get home and share what I had learned.

On the other hand, if I were to hide the Degas in the attic, I might make it home before it was discovered, but I would never be able to prove anything. Eventually, whoever the Degas had been intended for would make it known the painting hadn't been in the suitcase, and Nora and Miklos would search the house and find the Degas in the attic. Any hope I had about writing some exposé and saving my career as a journalist would vanish.

I stared at the clock. It was nearly two a.m. If things were going to change, it had to start with me.

I picked up my phone.

I hadn't said goodbye to Josh before I left Phoenix. I figured Josh needed time and space before we hashed things out. I didn't dare tell him I was traveling to Budapest and looking for Adolph and Katarina. Or working on a story that I thought might resurrect my career. I would have never heard the end of it. Josh thought most of what I did as a reporter was just an excuse for newspapers to sell advertising. But waiting and hoping for the best with Josh because I didn't want to admit failure wasn't going to work for me anymore. Katarina never would have waited for things to happen. She would have taken control like she did when she drove the commandant's jeep into Budapest to rescue Margit and the girls. Maybe that's what my dad hoped I might learn. Or at least remember. Before Josh, or before I was fired from the paper, the old me wouldn't have waited for Josh to decide what was next.

I needed to get her back.

I dialed Josh's number, and while I waited for the call to go through, I thought about Josh and the things I thought I loved about him. Like the element of surprise Josh brought to our marriage and how he would make me laugh. Whether it was a new dance step or some new fusion recipe he had found and wanted to try, Josh was always up on the latest trend, and I never knew what to expect when I walked in the door at the end of the day. I remember being so excited about us when we first met. Back then, Josh was unpredictable in a fun sort of way. He was like the Energizer Bunny until he wasn't and ran out of juice. I'd come home, and Josh wouldn't be there, or I'd find him sitting in a darkened room, the drapes drawn, and wearing dark glasses. If I tried to pull him out of his funk or ask him what was wrong or where he had been, he'd get mad and retreat to the study and lock the doors. Then the next day, everything would be fine. He'd be apologetic and blame his black mood on business or something I had said. I tried reasoning with him. I suggested we try therapy, but Josh wouldn't go. Eventually, I found it easier to spend more time at the paper and less time at home.

"Hello?" Josh answered. It was five p.m. Phoenix time, and he sounded rushed, as though he was just leaving his office—probably on the way to the track.

"Hi, it's me—"

"Kat? Where the hell are you?"

Lately, I couldn't remember a time that Josh didn't address me as though he were angry.

"I'm in Hungary."

"What the—"

"I'm here for my father." I didn't bother with further explanation. "What's going on, Josh?"

"What do you mean what's going on? I haven't been able to find you. I assume your father told you I put the house on the market. We got an offer—"

"Why, Josh. Why would you do that? Dad said the house was about to go into foreclosure."

It was no wonder I thought everyone was lying to me. Josh had been fooling me for so long, I didn't know who I could trust. I had begun to doubt everyone, including myself.

"Not anymore."

"What's that mean—not anymore?"

"I signed your name—"

"You what?" I couldn't believe what I was hearing.

"Forged your signature, Kat. The house is sold. We sold short, but we avoided being foreclosed on or filing for bankruptcy. End of story."

"Wait a minute." I sat up in bed. How could this be happening? "Why didn't you tell me?"

"Wasn't anything to tell. I made some bad investments, and I paid them off."

"You mean gambling debts." I ran my fingers through my hair.

"Look, Kat, I needed the cash. So I borrowed against the house. Most of it was my money anyway. You paid for a few improvements, but you know how the market's been. It's bad. What, did you have your head in the sand?"

Evidently, I did. After we were married, I had given Josh money from my account to pay for a few improvements and reimburse some of what he had put down on the house. It seemed only fitting since we were a couple. But now that Josh had sold the house to pay off his gambling debts, any money I had in the house was gone as well.

"You might have said something. That was my money, too."

"Well, I didn't, okay? Just like you didn't tell me about your affair."

That stung. And there was nothing I could say that I hadn't already said to try to explain it.

Leo had been a mistake. I never intended my relationship with him to be more than a friendship. It just kind of happened. Leo wasn't a predator or anyone I would have thought of having an affair with. He was a geek with thick black glasses. But what Leo had was a good ear. He listened to me, and he was there those late nights when I was alone and had no one to go home to. He made me laugh, and right or wrong, he filled the void in my life when I needed a friend. It was a coworker who reported us. I was going to end it, but she had gone to management and convinced them I had used Leo to cherry-pick assignments. And management, whether they agreed with her or not, dismissed me. Despite the fact, both Leo and I had worked at the paper for an equal amount of time. Evidently, Leo they needed. Me? Not so much.

"Life's not fair, Kat."

"You're right, Josh. Life's not fair." I thought about Katarina and how the war had destroyed her young life. If I took one thing from meeting her, it was that it's not what happens to us, but what we make of what happens that defines us. Katarina was a hero, like a Phoenix, she had risen from the ashes of her pain and lit the way for others and herself. Without her, I wouldn't be here. My own disappointments, my own failures, they weren't going to hold me back. "We don't always get the pretty picture we want."

"Well, I'm glad you see it that way. Maybe there's hope for us after all. I did what I had to do and acted quickly. If we lost the house, we'd have to declare bankruptcy, which wouldn't reflect well on my business. But, hey, the house didn't get repoed, and you and I, no reason we can't put this all behind us. We both made our mistakes, right?"

"Wha—!" My voice caught in my throat. It was so Josh to flip back and forth emotionally. Did he really expect me to come running home? "I don't think so, Josh."

"What's that supposed to mean?"

"It means we're finished." I held the phone away from my ear, and looked at the screen, then punched the disconnect button. I was done. It was over. It was time to rebuild my life and move on. "Goodbye, Josh."

Chapter Twenty-Six

I don't know how long it was after I got off the phone with Josh that I finally fell asleep. But I slept late the next morning and felt refreshed when I woke. As though I had shed an enormous burden, and the only obstacle ahead of me was the story I wanted to chase, and I couldn't wait to get started.

I made myself a cup of coffee and opened the French doors. It was a beautiful day, the river as close to blue as I had seen, and there were wispy white clouds in the sky. In a few hours, I was going to have lunch with Adolph. And, much as I wanted to believe Adolph couldn't possibly have anything to do with whatever Sandor, Miklos, and Nora were involved in, I didn't dare trust anyone. I had a growing list of questions. And depending upon how Adolph answered, my lunch would either be enjoyable and today mark the beginning of a new friendship, or I'd have my eyes opened and would need to proceed cautiously.

Despite the fact I had packed light, I must have changed clothes at least three times before deciding on the simple black summer shift I had worn my first evening in Budapest. I'm usually more of a dress and dash type of gal and not much for primping. But knowing I was meeting Adolph, I paid particular attention to how I looked. I checked myself in the mirror and added a pair of gold hoop earrings and a touch of lip gloss. Along with the glow of a Hungarian tan I had picked up the last couple of days, I liked the look. I felt smart, and while slightly anxious about our meeting—confident.

I debated whether I should take the larger leather bag my mother insisted I bring with me. It was definitely more chic than my fanny pack, and more importantly, it had room for my passport, airline ticket, travel guide, and the sketches Katarina had given me that my father had drawn. Things I would need to keep on my person in case I wanted to leave the country in a hurry. Plus, I had enough space to stuff a pair of strappy sandals inside to wear for lunch. My plan was to don my tennis shoes and walk as far as the Chain Bridge. From there, I'd hail a cab to the hospital, where I'd meet Adolph for lunch.

Without giving it further thought, I grabbed the leather bag, double-checked to make sure I had what I would need, and hurried down the circular staircase. I was almost to the first floor when one of the stairs beneath my foot gave way.

Whoops!" I grabbed the railing. My knees buckled beneath me as I collapsed in a near-curtsy at the base of the staircase while my bag tumbled to the floor ahead of me.

Miklos was sitting on the couch reading the paper and looked up. "Are you okay?"

"I...I must have missed the step," I said.

Miklos folded his paper and stood up. "You need be more careful, Miss Kat. It's a narrow stairway, and it can be quite tricky."

Like his wife, Miklos' English suddenly sounded much better. His accent, not nearly so indecipherable. I sat on the bottom step, my legs stretched out in front of me, and rotated my left foot. The same ankle as I had twisted in the cave the day before.

Miklos put his hand beneath my elbow and helped me to my feet. "You sure you're okay?"

"Yes, I'm a bit of a klutz. I'll be fine, I'm sure."

Miklos let go of my arm. "It's best you be careful and remember to watch your step. You wouldn't want to fall and hurt yourself. Accidents do happen."

I laughed nervously and tested my weight on my foot. My foot was fine, but Miklos' comment felt less so, more like a warning than a concern for my safety.

Miklos handed me my bag. "Have you been enjoying your stay?"

"Yes," I said, "very much."

"Lots of sightseeing, I assume?" Miklos returned to the couch and picked up the newspaper.

I wasn't sure if Miklos was asking or probing. I was confident both he and Nora knew about the Degas hidden in the suitcase Nora had given me. Was this a test to see if I had gotten curious and found the stolen painting? Was he sitting on the couch on Monday morning because he didn't have to go to work or because he wanted to see me before I went out the door and was looking for a sign I might be on to them? And the loose step on the stairway, could it have been a warning? As often as I had been up and down the stairs, I could have sworn it wasn't loose before. Had Miklos loosened it to unsettle me?

I smiled innocently. "I want to see as much as I can before I return home. You know what they say, so much to see, and so little time." I surrendered the palms of my hands to the air above my head.

"And where are you off to today?" Miklos looked down at the newspaper as though he weren't really interested in my answer.

I suspected differently. In fact, I felt as though he were weighing my words.

"Nowhere special," I said. "I thought I'd take a walk along the river, then lunch on the Buda side. I'd like to get a few more pictures of Pest and the Parliament building from that side of the river before I leave."

"I hope you plan to do a little shopping as well. A few souvenirs, maybe? You've plenty of room now with the new suitcase."

My stomach knotted. I was face to face with a man who, if for any reason thought I was on to him, might have me disappear. I had to play it smart. I might not get a second chance.

"You're right. I have plenty of room, and I've loads of shopping to do. I've put it off until now. I was worried about getting all those souvenirs home that I wanted to buy. It was nice of you to give the suitcase to me. You didn't need to."

Miklos stood up and walked to the door. "It's nothing. We've enjoyed having you. Perhaps, when you come back, you might bring it with you."

"Come back?"

"The door's always open. It's a beautiful country. Certainly, there's more you'd like to see and do here? And for friends, we have a special rate. Perhaps you'll come back this winter for the holidays."

So that's how it was. Whether Miklos thought I was on to him or not, he'd make every effort to see me return. After all, I was his mule. He needed me to come back. Better to appear flattered and agreeable than suspicious.

"Of course," I said. "I'd be happy to."

Miklos opened the door and stood back. "You have a nice day now."

Chapter Twenty-Seven

Adolph was waiting on the steps when I arrived at the hospital. He was dressed in his white doctor's coat with his stethoscope wrapped casually around his neck. He spotted my cab and waved, then skipped down the stairs and took care of the cabbie's fee.

Offering me his hand, he helped me out of the car. "You know, you're much prettier than your father."

I squelched a smile and dropped my head. If I had dared to look into those pale blue eyes, I feared I might have melted. I was here to investigate, and flattery, no matter how attractive I thought Adolph was, wasn't going to deter my mission. But as Adrian, my newly-trusted gypsy guide, had said, romance finds us when least expected, and this was most unexpected.

I shook off what I determined had to be no more than anxiety and, from beneath my brow, looked up at him, all six feet of charm and grace.

"Are you flirting with me? Or is this just a Hungarian thing to make me feel welcome?"

"Is that not okay?" Adolph held my hand for a moment longer than necessary and nodded to my empty ring finger. "Unless, of course, there is a reason I shouldn't?"

I withdrew my hand. "Not at all," I said,

"Good, then, in the spirit of advancing our international relationship and getting to know one another better, I've made reservations at a favorite restaurant of mine down the street. I hope you like spicy Hungarian food."

"Is there any other kind?" I asked.

"Not for this Hungarian."

Adolph slipped his hand beneath my arm, and we strolled down the street to a charming, old-world café with small windows and light that seemed to dance on the glazed glass. The maître d' stood outside, and spotting Adolph as one of his regulars, led us to a small solo table inside that had been reserved.

A waiter arrived with menus, and Adolph placed them aside.

"I have a surprise for you."

"Me?"

Adolph winked. "Yes. Something I think you should have." Then reaching beneath his white coat, he produced a small silk handkerchief and handed it to me.

"What's this?"

"It's a map." Adolph took the scarf from my hands and laid it on the table between us. "On one side is Europe—the areas your father bombed. Northern Italy. Germany. Austria. Hungary. Romania." He pointed to each and then turned the scarf over. "The other side here is more detailed with roads and riverways in Hungary and Romania. All of them leading to the Black Sea. It marks a safe escape route. During the war, the airmen were all given a scarf like this to assist them should they be shot down and, like your father, trapped behind enemy lines."

"How did you get this?"

"Your father gave it to me. He used it to show me where we were, and the Germans and the Russians, too. After you and Aanika left my mother the other day, I remembered I had hidden it in the tunnel beneath the fortress. Back then, if I had been caught with it, it would have been certain death. So my mother and I hid it, along with some other things, and—"

"And then you went back into the cave?"

"Not to the cave. At least not entirely. I'd probably get lost these days if I tried. There's quite a maze of tunnels down there." Adolph smoothed his napkin on his lap as he explained how he had climbed down through the well to gain access to the cave. "I'm not as spry as I once was, but the entrance is just a couple of feet beneath the well's foundation. It wasn't terribly difficult. Your father told you about it, right?"

"Yes, he did."

I held the scarf to my face. It smelled moldy and felt scratchy against my cheek. Happy as I was to have something of my father's from the war, the fact Adolph had it worried me. If Adolph had gone back to the tunnel after Aanika and I had left his mother, it could only mean one thing. The footprints on the cave floor had to have been Adolph's.

I proceeded carefully.

"What other things?" I wrinkled my nose and hoped my question sounded innocent enough. "You said your mother hid other things. Like what?"

Adolph leaned forward and whispered. "If you were a Russian spy, I'd have to kill you. But, if you must know, I went back for my Superman comic books."

"What?" I laughed out loud. I couldn't help myself. Whether it was Adolph's charm or he was really as transparent as he projected, I could only hope he wasn't involved with whatever side business Sandor and company had gotten themselves into. "They were still there?"

"Hidden in the wall, exactly where I left them. It would have been impossible for anyone to have found them unless they knew where to look."

"And nothing else?"

"Why do you ask?" Adolph tilted his head.

"Just curious. One hears about things hidden in caves. Particularly caves in Europe. I just wondered."

Adolph paused. His eyes swept the room before he spoke. "There were other things. My mother, as you know, was a member of a group of partisans. They did favors and hid things. People and valuables from the Nazis. It was a scary time. I remember a priest from the local church came to my mother. He needed to hide several paintings and a statue, and my mother risked her life to hide them. But those things, they're long gone from there now. After the war, they were returned. Anything else inside that cave, best remain forever hidden."

"But the war was fifty-plus years ago. There can't be anything there that would be a problem today."

Before Adolph could answer, the waiter returned to our table, obviously anxious that we order. Adolph tapped his index finger to his lips and looked down at the menu. I interpreted the action as either a signal that Adolph didn't want the waiter to hear our conversation or was thinking about what to order.

A moment passed, and Adolph raised a finger.

"It's warm outside. Might I recommend the cherry soup? It's slightly sour, and if you haven't had it, quite good and cold. And with an order of lángos very filling." Lángos, I had learned from wanderings through the marketplace, was a deep-fried circular dough, similar to a thick crust pizza but lighter and topped with grated cheese and sour cream.

"Sounds good," I said.

But the truth was, I had little interest in eating. I was focused more on Adolph and why he had suddenly stopped talking about the cave in front of the waiter. Was he trying to protect his mother, or what other treasures might be hidden in the cave?

Adolph told the waiter to bring the cherry soup for two, an order of lángos, and two white wines.

Once the waiter disappeared, Adolph leaned across the table. "You have to understand, Kat, for partisans like my mother, the war didn't end her involvement with the movement. Some of those same partisans who raged against the Germans also opposed the Soviet occupation. They wanted independence, and when the Soviets marched in and rid the country of the Germans, we were once again an occupied territory. Then, in 1956, there was a revolt. Twenty-five hundred Hungarians were killed. The lucky ones fled the country. And I believe my mother may have helped hide some of those on the run. But she never told me."

"And you think there may be evidence of her involvement with the partisans hidden in the cave?"

"I wouldn't be at all surprised. Times may have changed, Kat. The Russians are gone, but there are still those around who watch and listen. There are ears everywhere." Adolph nodded to the waiter. "Perhaps it is cultural. We've had a history of occupation. Trust does not come easily to us."

I believed Adolph. He couldn't possibly have known I would show up at his mother's house. And seeing how protective he was of her, I couldn't imagine he would use the cave to hide anything that might risk bringing attention to her.

"But the tunnels around that area are no secret. Certainly, others have discovered them."

"Even if someone were to find the cave beneath the fortress, it's doubtful they would find anything. Most of the caves in the area are uncharted. Some of the tunnels are quite long and can be treacherous. It would be difficult to find something unless you knew where and what you were looking for."

"What about Sandor?"

"Margit's grandson?"

"Yes, did he know about the caves?" It was a leading question. I knew the answer, but still, it was one I needed to ask. If Adolph was aware Sandor knew about the caves, then maybe the two of them and Miklos were involved. But Adolph didn't flinch.

"I don't know. I've never met Sandor. By the time Margit returned to Keszthely with him, I was gone. She might have shown Sandor the old fortress, but I'd be surprised if he ever went down inside the well or into the cave."

The waiter returned with our wine, and Adolph waited until he was gone before he began to speak.

"After the war, we all agreed we would never come back. Although, I suspect my mother did during the revolution. But, far as I know, no one ever returned to the cave."

I wasn't convinced. Someone had been in the cave. I had seen footprints and scuff marks leading from the grotto inside the tunnel beneath the fortress. If I had to guess, it was either Sandor or Miklos.

"And you don't think Sandor ever did a little exploring, maybe with his cousin Miklos?"

I waited to see if I saw some sign of recognition on Adolph's face. Some small tell or clue that he might know more than he projected. But I saw nothing.

Instead, Adolph shook his head. "When Margit and the girls went back to

Budapest—before they left for Israel—she may have shared with her family about where she hid. But I doubt any of them went exploring. People didn't move around easily under Soviet rule."

I took a sip of my wine. "My father never mentioned anything about the caves or his hiding place. Not until I called him the other day and told him I'd been to the fortress. It was the first he had ever mentioned anything about it."

"It was a difficult time. Not many pleasant memories."

"I suppose not. And until Sandor contacted him about his plane, I had no idea about you or your mother or the fortress where he hid. And to be honest, I'm not so sure what I should tell him when I go back."

"You're afraid you might say something to upset him?"

My eyes started to fill with tears. Adolph handed me his napkin.

"Kat, I'm not a psychologist. I'm a cardiologist. But I think, if your father sent you here to find my mother and me, you could talk to him about the good things we remember about him and what he did for us."

"Like what?" I wiped the corner of my eyes.

"It was your father who taught me to find the North Star. One night, after my mother and I had brought food up to them, we went up to the courtyard to look at the stars. It was so peaceful. Then I remember we heard bombers like your father flew, and the German cannons began firing as they approached. There wasn't time for us to climb back into the tunnel. We could feel the heat from the plane's lights as they flew directly above us, with their bomb doors open. The sound and the sight so frightening I thought we'd melt to the rocky ground beneath us."

I looked at the map and traced the area of Lake Balaton with the tips of my fingers.

"Your father told us the bombers weren't aiming for us. He said the air force wouldn't bomb some old ruined fortress. Even so, soon as we could, he helped us back down into the well and into the tunnel."

"But how? With Margit, the girls, and Nick, it couldn't have been easy."

"The same way the Romans did. We made a rope swing on a pulley and used it to help Margit and the girls get in and out of the well. Centuries ago, the Romans had stored all their grain in a cavern beneath the fortress and used it as a hiding place. It's a pretty good-sized cavern, and we jokingly called it the living room. It was big enough that everyone had their private space. Margit, and the girls in one area, your dad, Bill, and Nick in another. The girls never went much beyond the living room. And Nick, with his broken leg, didn't move around a lot. At night, your dad and Bill frequently went up to the courtyard. And when things got scary, and the bombers would come, that tunnel was a pretty good bomb shelter."

I crushed the silk map in my hand. "And that's where you hid this? In the living room?"

"Right next to my comic books."

"And when you went back, you didn't go any further than to the living room? You didn't go down to the grotto?"

"I didn't have time. It was getting late, and I had everything I wanted. Like I said, anything else buried in that cave had best stay that way."

I was happy with Adolph's answer. Convinced it was his trowel I had seen in the living room beneath the fortress and someone else's footprints in the grotto. Sandor or Miklos' prints, maybe.

"Tell me more." I wanted to know everything. "What did you do? How did you all survive?"

"There wasn't much we could do. We visited and told stories. Your dad's stories, though, they were always the best."

I wiped my eyes with the back of my hand. "Dad always has a story."

When I was a little girl, I was afraid of the dark, and my dad would come and sit on the edge of my bed and show me how to make shadow puppets on the wall. He told me they would protect me from the imaginary ghosts I believed lived in my closet.

"You have to understand much of what your dad said had to be translated. Margit didn't speak English. Roza, Margit's oldest daughter, and her little sister Gizella spoke some. Nick spoke a little Hungarian, and my mother was fluent in at least three languages—Hungarian, German, English, and a little Romanian. Somehow we figured out what the story was about. Although to this day, I'm really not so sure about that."

I laughed

"Plus, your father had a few voices he made up to make the story more fun. I don't know what language he used—something nonsensical, I think.

"Pig Latin, probably. He still uses it. Drives my mother nuts."

"Well, it was very entertaining. One night, after he finished telling us a story, we heard the bombers overhead. The girls were frightened, and your father started to tell us how when the Germans bombed England, the English went to parties and danced."

"I've heard those stories. People would get dressed up and go out as though nothing were wrong. I can't imagine being that brave. Knowing you could be bombed while attending a party."

"People wanted some sense of normal. Roza, Margit's daughter, she was just nineteen. I had a kind of crush on her back then. She was beautiful with long, dark wavy hair and these big brown eyes. She was so frightened that night. She was trembling, her eyes like a trapped deer. The ground was shaking, and I remember she grabbed your father's hand. She was crying and said she was tired of living in fear, and she wanted to dance like they did in London. She was afraid she'd never get a chance to go to a party or dance with a man. Your father told her that it wasn't true. The war would end, and there would be plenty of parties, dances, and pretty dresses for her to wear. But Roza didn't believe him, and Nick told them they should dance while they could because life didn't have any guarantees. So your father took Roza by the hand, and they went up to the courtyard, and one by one, we followed. It's hard to imagine, but there, beneath the moonlight, with the bombers flying so close overhead, I thought I could touch them, they danced. Your father was an excellent dancer. I'll never forget how beautiful it was. The two of them, dancing beneath a full moon, in the middle of that medieval courtyard while the bombers flew overhead with the sound of German guns firing. There were clouds of white and black smoke in the air, but still, your father and Roza danced, and for that moment, there was no war."

Listening to Adolph tell the story, I could almost see it. Dad loved to dance. Often I would see him in the kitchen dancing with my mother. He would come in from work and waltz her around the room like he couldn't wait to get home to her.

The waiter arrived with our food, and Adolph tore off a piece of his cheesy-fried bread and offered me a piece.

"And after the war, what happened to them?"

"Margit and the girls returned to the city soon as it was safe. Things were chaotic. There were a lot of displaced persons there, but Margit surprised us. She found her husband."

"I thought he'd been sent to a concentration camp and died."

"So did Margit, but turned out that some of the men the Germans rounded up were forced into military labor camps. A factory on a small island in the middle of the Danube made ammunition for the German army, and Margit's husband and brother were sent there. And because they were never deported to a concentration camp, they survived. Later, Margit and the family all emigrated to Israel. Roza married a survivor she met there, and Gizzy went on to school. Unfortunately, Roza and her husband were killed in an auto accident shortly after Sandor was born. A couple of years later, Margit and her husband, along with their grandson, returned to Hungary."

"But why come back? I don't think I'd ever come back, not after everything that happened to the Jews here."

"Margit felt like she never fit in with the Israelis. Some of them blamed the survivors for not fighting hard enough and standing up to the Nazis. Others felt the European Jews had become secular and that God had punished them for leaving the faith."

"And my dad, and Bill and Nick, how did they escape?"

"Your dad had a good idea about where the Russians were. We all did. I had smuggled a small portable radio up to the fortress, and we'd listen whenever he felt it was safe. Between what we could hear on the air and what the Commandant had shared with my mother about the state of the war, we felt confident that if my mother could find a boat, your father and his men could row across Lake Balaton, and they'd be safe. The Russians had taken Budapest. There was still street-to-street fighting, but the Germans were in retreat, and most of Eastern Hungary was in Russian hands. Lake Balaton is nine miles wide at its widest point, but it was maybe only three miles across from where we were, and we knew if your dad and Bill could get Nick in the boat and to the other side of the lake, they'd be okay. At least we hoped so. My mother found a small rowboat. We hid it inside the grotto beneath the fortress. The idea was to wait for nightfall, and once the fog came in, your father and his men would leave." Adolph paused and dunked his bread into his soup. "Then, one night when everything was in place, and we thought the time right, my mother and I went up with some supplies and said our goodbyes."

Adolph took a bite of his bread, and I got the feeling he intended for the story to end right there.

I prompted him. "But there's more to it than that. Sandor told me about the soldier my father killed."

"It happened after we said goodbye. My mother and I were on the way home, and we were stopped by a German soldier. Your father must have seen it from the watchtower, climbed over the fortress wall, and killed him. It was pretty horrendous. I wouldn't ask your father to try and remember. But if your father hadn't killed the soldier, he would have revealed our hiding place, and a lot of innocent people would have died."

I looked down at my food. I had scarcely touched my soup. "And the body?"

"We buried it deep inside the grotto."

Adolph's pager went off.

"I'm sorry, it's the hospital. I need to get back. It's an emergency. Can I call you a cab?"

"No, I'll be fine." I pointed to my shoulder bag. "I brought my walking shoes. I planned to do a self-guided tour of Buda after lunch anyway."

Adolph counted out several bills and placed them on the table. "Please, stay and finish your lunch. Perhaps, if you've time, we might see each other again before you go?"

"That would be nice," I said.

"I have surgery tomorrow, and there's still so much I'd like to know about your father and you. You haven't begun to tell me anything about yourself, and selfishly there's more I'd like to know. Can I see you again?"

CHAPTER TWENTY-SEVEN

"I leave Wednesday," I said. "But my flight doesn't leave until four p.m."

"Lunch then. I'll pick you up in the morning." Adolph asked for my cell number, entered it into his phone, then leaned down and kissed me lightly on the cheek. "I'll make reservations at Szazaves, the oldest restaurant in Budapest. And you can plan on me dropping you at the airport afterward. Unless, of course, I can convince you to stay."

Chapter Twenty-Eight

U*nless, of course, I can convince you to stay.* What an impossible thought. I might have been tempted to extend my stay any other time, but I needed to get back to Phoenix. Dad wasn't getting any better, and should the worst happen, I wanted to be at his bedside. And after my tumble on the staircase that morning, I was growing anxious about the Degas hidden in my bag. Spending another two nights with Nora and Miklos was more than I felt I could handle.

I finished my soup and replayed my conversation with Adolph in my head. After listening to him talk about the cave, I was convinced that whatever remained hidden inside needed to stay that way, for his mother's sake. The footprints I had seen in the grotto couldn't possibly be his. Adolph had been inside the tunnel beneath the fortress alright, but he hadn't entered through the river's grotto entrance. If he had, he would have noticed the body of a German soldier crudely stuffed into a crevice in the grotto's far corner. He would have seen the scuff marks on the cave's floor and realized someone had been searching for something and found a body instead. Then moved it and continued to search until they found what they were looking for—the Degas, maybe?

I finished my lunch and went outside, and laced up my tennis shoes. I needed a brisk walk to center my thoughts while I planned my next move. I considered going to the police and telling them my story. But I didn't see that as a quick fix. If I were to tell the police that I suspected my Hungarian friends of trafficking stolen art, the three of them, Sandor, Miklos, and Nora, would likely turn the tables on me. And then where would I be? If none of them had a record of thievery or worse, I'd be hours if not days explaining why I had come to Hungary and gone back into the caves. How would I explain a gypsy? Or that I believed the cave Katarina had used to hide my father during the war was now a cache for lost art. If I were to tell the police about her hidden hiding place, I might expose Katarina and her past partisan activities, which even today, Adolph feared might land her in jail. And how would I explain the Degas hidden in my suitcase? I didn't see how any of this could be resolved quickly, nor did I see a scenario that involved me going to the police and still ending up on a plane home in thirty-six hours.

I had seen firsthand how the police dealt with suspected smugglers. I remembered the headlines in the newspapers and a black-and-white photo of a very shocked-looking young woman who had been caught with drugs in her baggage. Thinking about the similarity to my own circumstances sent goosebumps up and down my arms. I decided my best move, one that would allow me to achieve my objective while remaining within the law's confines, was to remove the canvass from my bag and hide it somewhere safe. Then, once I was home, I'd report to the authorities what I knew.

But until then I needed to maintain a low profile, collect as many facts as I could about who I thought might be involved, and pretend as though nothing were amiss. Which meant, if I were being watched, that I do exactly as I had said I would do that morning and proceed with my own self-guided tour of Buda.

I checked my guidebook for the Buda Castle. I wanted to see the hospital that had been built in the rock beneath the castle, where Katarina had gone the day she went to rescue Margit and the girls. The castle was an easy downhill walk from the restaurant, and I was within several blocks when my phone rang.

"Kat, it's Sandor. We need to talk. Aanika told me you found Katarina."

"Yes, what a surprise." I held the phone tight to my ear and tried to keep my voice light and friendly. I could imagine the shocked look on Sandor's face when Aanika showed him Margit's pearls and told him we had found Katarina.

"There's more you need to know. There's an outdoor café across from St.

Stephen's Basilica. The one with all the colorful umbrellas. We passed it the first day you were here. You remember?"

"Yes," I said. I remembered the smell of coffee. Sandor had said it was the best in the city, but we didn't stop because we had so much to see.

"Good. I'll meet you there in an hour."

* * *

I spotted Sandor and Aanika in front of the café across from St. Stephen's. They were seated at an outdoor table. Sandor was smoking—the butts of two cigarettes lay crumpled in the ashtray in front of him—and Aanika hugged her coffee cup with both hands, her head bowed. She looked up at me as I approached and smiled wistfully. I took the empty seat opposite them and asked the waiter to bring me a beer.

"So, what is it you wanted to tell me?" I asked.

Sandor squashed the last of his cigarette in the ashtray, "First, congratulations on finding Katarina. I had no idea she was still alive. This is a big surprise to me." Sandor paused and rubbed the back of his neck. "After my grandmother died, Aanika and I went to Keszthely for our honeymoon. I looked for Katarina everywhere. I think maybe I can find her, but no. She is nowhere, and I believe for sure she has passed. When Aanika says she wants to go back to Keszthely with you, I begin to think, what if I am wrong? What if you find Katarina and learn my story."

The waiter brought my beer, and I waited for him to leave.

"And just what is your story, Sandor?" I forced a grin. "I'm a little confused. I didn't realize Katarina hid your grandmother and your mother and your aunt in the same fortress where my father and his men hid. Or did you forget to tell me that because you didn't want me to know?"

"Please," Sandor raised his hands. "I never intend for you to know any of this."

"Any of what?" I asked.

"This." Sandor took a piece of paper from inside his jacket pocket and placed it on the table between us. "Does it look familiar?"

I stared at a sketch of Bombshell Betty, my father's demolished plane in the field where she had crashed. "Did you draw this?"

"I did."

"It's very nice," I said. "But what has it got to do with me?"

"I was hoping you might give it to your father in exchange for the sketch Katarina gave you yesterday. "

"You mean the one my father drew of your grandmother and her daughters?"

"Yes," Sandor said. "I thought we might make a trade. It would mean a great deal to me."

"Of course," I said. "I probably should have offered it to Aanika yesterday when Katarina told me who the women were." I reached into my bag, took out the manila folder with the sketches, and placed the three women's picture on the table. "Is that your grandmother?" I pointed to the older of the women in the sketch.

Sandor nodded.

"And this?" I moved my finger to the head of the older daughter. "Is she your mother?"

"Yes," Sandor said. "Her name was Roza Zsabo. I have nothing left of her, and when Aanika told me about the sketch, I hoped you might be willing to give it to me."

I looked closer at the drawing. There was no doubt Sandor was her son. He had the same round face and broad smile.

"You look like her," I said.

"My grandmother used to tell me so, too. My mother and father died in a traffic accident when I was three. I never really knew them."

"I'm sorry," I said.

"My father's name was Izsak Zselnegeller. He was a concentration camp survivor. My mother married him after she immigrated to Israel, where they met. My grandmother said he was an older man and never well. After my parents die, my grandmother brings me here to Hungary. But I never think this man is my father. You understand?"

"I'm not sure I do. What are you trying to tell me?"

183

"You don't see it?"

"What?" I asked.

"Look. The sketches," Sandor gestured to the drawings of Margit and girls and Bombshell Betty on the table, "they could have been done by the same artist or an artist with a very similar style."

I had no doubt my father had drawn the picture of Margit and the girls. I knew his hand. I had grown up watching him sketch. The quick, broad strokes, the subtle charcoal shading he created with the tips of his fingers. Granted, there was a similarity in style between the two, but I didn't dare let on.

I feared this might be some type of test. I knew Nora had searched my room and read my journal. It didn't take much to think she had shared what she had read or that she had given the sketch my father had drawn of Katarina and Adolph to her husband. Miklos could easily have copied it and given it to Sandor to study.

This had to be a trap. I paused and thought carefully about how to respond. I didn't want to sound at all suspicious.

"I'm really not much of a critic. But I'm sure my father will appreciate it, and I want to thank you for your time and the tour." And then, for effect's sake, I gushed and added, "You and Aanika have been wonderful hosts. But I probably should get going. It's getting late, and I've some souvenir shopping I need to get done."

I started to get up from the table, but Sandor grabbed my wrist.

"Wait. Sit down, please. Just listen to me. You need to know what I am about to tell you. It's important. Kat."

I sat back down.

"My birthday is November 30. The war in Europe ended on May 8, 1945. In June, my mother immigrated to Israel, and she married my father on August 4, 1945."

"What are you saying?"

"I'm saying Izsak Zselnegeller couldn't possibly be my father."

I blinked. "Are you saying what I think you're saying?" I couldn't believe the words about to come out of my mouth."You think my father might be your father?"

"My grandmother said Izsak was a good man. He married my mother just like I was his."

"No, I don't believe it."

"It was wartime, Kat. Bombs were falling from the sky. The Germans were everywhere."

"What is this, one of your small jokes? Because, if it is, it's not funny." I took the sketches off the table and put them back in my bag. My instincts had been correct all along. This was a scam. "What do you want, money? Is that what this is all about? Entertain the tourists, then try to blackmail them with some made-up story about some illicit affair?"

"Stop." Aanika put her hands on top of Sandor's. "What Sandor's trying to say is things happened back then. He never intended to tell you. He only wanted a chance to see if maybe, after all these years, he might find out about Lieutenant Steve and what happened to him."

I stood up and threw my napkin on the table. I had heard enough.

* * *

Sandor's scam was low, even for a con artist. I didn't believe any of it. What I did think was that he was surprised I had found Katarina. And now that I had, he was afraid I might be on to him and know something about the cave and the valuables Katarina had hidden there. In an attempt to intimidate me and hide the greater scam, Sandor proposed the crazy idea he was my brother.

Sandor didn't need to say anything about the cave or the Degas Nora had hidden in my suitcase. It didn't matter to him if I knew about the Degas or not. What did matter was that he knew I had found Katarina and had knowledge of the cave and its contents. And that should I be tempted to write or say anything about it, along with his little side-business that included selling lost art on the black market, that he was prepared to blackmail me. All he had to do was suggest my father wasn't the saint I believed him to be. He knew I'd do whatever it took to keep such news from my mother.

185

He had our home address. He knew how protective I was of my father's memory and that I'd do anything not to upset him. I wondered how many other American airmen Sandor had used to traffic his black-market art and threatened with similar scams.

It was too early for me to return to the apartment, and I didn't want to hang out there any longer than necessary. I needed a plan, and as I walked back toward the riverfront, I began to formulate an idea.

Step one would require I find someone who could help me and who wasn't involved in any way with what I was beginning to think of as Sandor and Company. And the only two persons who came to mind were Dion, my friendly sommelier, or Adrian.

I decided on Adrian and returned to where he had last tied his small boat.

Upon seeing me, Adrian stood up and hollered. "Are you stalking *me* now?"

I laughed and climbed aboard. "I may be. I'm in need of your services. What are you doing tomorrow morning?"

"You want another tour?"

"No, but I do need your help. Can you meet me in front of the copy center across from St. Stephen's tomorrow morning? Ten o'clock sharp?"

"How much?" Adrian held out his hand.

"Fifty dollars," I said.

Adrian whistled. "Is a lot of money. Is legal?"

"Yes, Adrian, it's legal. I wouldn't ask you to do something that wasn't."

I could see in Adrian's eyes he was calculating the odds I wasn't telling the truth.

"It's important, Adrian. At least it is to me."

"You pay me now?"

"No," I said. "I'll pay you ten now and forty when I see you tomorrow." Much as I had grown to like Adrian, I didn't trust he'd show up on time, and I needed a guarantee he'd be there when I needed him.

"Is fine. You pay me tomorrow. Sixty dollars."

"Sixty? I thought we agreed on fifty?"

"Interest," Adrian said.

"Fine. Sixty dollars. Tomorrow morning, ten o'clock." I climbed off the boat.

"What you do rest of the day? You want more river tour?"

"No," I said. "I'm going shopping."

Step two would have made my mother happy. She was a big proponent that when the going gets tough, the tough go shopping. And I had a suitcase to fill with souvenirs and gifts to take home from my trip—just as I had promised Miklos I would.

My guidebook suggested the best area for shopping was along the Vaci Utca, which wasn't far from my apartment and sounded like the perfect place for a late afternoon stroll. From Vörösmarty Square to Vámház körút, the promenade was considered to be the Champs-Elysees of Budapest, famous for its majestic old homes built above cafes and art studios. Despite the war, many of the buildings along Vaci Utca had all been restored with their sculptured facades and small French balconies overlooking the busy pedestrian walkway. Just looking at the architecture was like a trip back in time.

The first shop I wandered into was a small knit boutique with a friendly owner who knew exactly what I was looking for when I asked for pig's wool, or as she called, it Magtalitsa. I bought several skeins or enough for what the owner suggested would make a nice sweater, then continued down the street where I stopped at a bank for some cash and American dollars, enough to pay Adrian for his help tomorrow and for the trip home. I then continued on until I came to a gift store where I decided it was time I purchased some typical tourist souvenirs. The store was packed with gifty ideas, embroidered pillows, porcelain coffee mugs with pictures of the Parliament buildings, aprons, honey, and all types of bottled paprika. I bought three different varieties—sweet, smoked, and hot—each of which I was beginning to appreciate and a poster of the Parliament Building that came wrapped in a round cardboard mailing tube. Perfect!

Chapter Twenty-Nine

I stopped for a cup of coffee at a sidewalk café along Vaci Utca's promenade before returning to the apartment. It was still early, the sun hadn't set, and the clouds in the sky cast a hazy orange glow on the river. My plan was to go directly to my room. Nora would be busy feeding the baby, the old man napping in his rocker, and Miklos yet to return from work. I wanted to avoid any chance for idle chit-chat.

Unfortunately, things didn't go as I had hoped.

When I started up the stairs to the apartment's front door, I noticed the baby's buggy was gone and the stairwell unusually silent. At first, I thought how lucky. Nora had probably taken the baby for a walk, allowing me to quietly tiptoe up the stairs without disruption. But I was surprised. When I opened the front door, the old man wasn't napping in his rocker as I had expected. Instead, sitting on the couch—exactly as he had been that morning—was Miklos. He appeared to be waiting.

"Where've you been?" Upon seeing me, Miklos stood up and closed the door behind me.

No escape. "Sightseeing," I said. "Why? Is there a problem?" A chill ran down my back. "Where's Nora?"

"She took the baby for a walk. I thought you and I should talk. Sandor's been calling. He thinks you're upset. He and Aanika want to come by tomorrow afternoon before you leave. And now that you're here, you and I have a little business to discuss as well."

I figured my best defense was to play it cool. The less Miklos thought I knew, the better.

188

"You mean the bill for the room?" I squeezed my bag beneath my arm and clutched my shopping bags close to me. "I was going to put cash in an envelope and give it to Nora later tonight. But I can give it to you now if you like. I just went to the bank."

"That's not the conversation we need to have. I know you went back to Keszthely yesterday. Nora showed me your journal. I followed you and your gypsy guide." Miklos took my bags and nodded to the stairway. "Shall we?"

I felt as though I was being led up the steps to the gallows, and seeing no escape, proceeded up the stairs with Miklos behind me. When we reached the top of the staircase, I noticed the door to my room was ajar, and on the bed—not where I had left it—was the suitcase Nora had given me. It, too, was open.

"I see you find the Degas." Miklos put my bags on the floor and kicked the door shut behind him.

I didn't answer. The Degas lay on the bed next to the suitcase's false bottom. The evidence was obvious.

"Why don't you take a seat on the end of the bed? I have an offer for you that I think you'll find quite attractive. But first, I believe a little history lesson is in order."

I sat down on the bed.

Miklos went to the French doors and looked out at the river. "You ever wonder how a clerk who works at a copy center has an apartment like this?"

"No," I said.

"Strange, as a writer, I'd think you'd be curious. An apartment like this is quite expensive. It used to belong to my grandmother's family. Back then, of course, before the war, it was much larger. They owned the bakery below, and they were quite well off. My grandfather, the old man you see downstairs? He and Margit's husband were brothers. Together, they ran a pharmacy, and my father, who was a very young man, did deliveries for them. My grandmother's family maintained the bakery until things changed, and Jews were not allowed to own certain businesses. They were rounded up and sent to live in ghettos and then off onto trains for concentration camps. Most of this, I imagine, Sandor's told you, or you've figured out by now."

"It wasn't that difficult," I said.

"What you don't know is that my grandmother escaped a concentration camp because of a man named Raoul Wallenberg. You ever hear of him?"

I nodded.

"One day, this man comes into the bakery. He speaks to my grandmother and says his name is Raoul Wallenberg. He is a Swede and has arranged with the Germans to rent this very building in the Swedish government's name. The building is to be a safe house, and he arranges for a Swedish flag to be hung from the door. He gives my grandmother a Shutz-Pass, papers of protection that keep her safe from the Nazis. He says he has only one pass left to give and no more. Soon there are maybe one hundred people in her home. So many there is not enough room for anyone to lay down, but they are safe."

"But your father, and grandfather, and Margit's husband aren't so lucky."

"So, you have heard this story."

"Some," I said. What I knew was what Aanika had told me, but I didn't know the whole story.

"The Germans go to the pharmacy where my father, grandfather, and uncle work. They are sent to a labor camp and forced to make ammunition for the Germans. When the war ends, my father and grandfather return. They come to look for my grandmother, but she is dead. All that remains are a few items from their home and things my grandmother has hidden in the attic. Paintings and valuables, things many brought with them to hide. Most, I'm sure, hoped they might retrieve them later, or if necessary, use them to barter for their lives. But it was of no use. Toward the end of the war, the Germans raided the safe houses. Many were forced onto trains and sent to concentration camps or marched to the river, where the Germans shot them. After the war, the Russians allow my father and grandfather to move into the apartment they once owned. But now it subdivided into smaller apartments to accommodate all the displaced persons."

Miklos paced the room, then adjusted the Van Gogh poster above the bed.

"For years, my grandfather hoped to return some of what people brought with them to hide from the Nazis. My grandfather is a good man. But no one comes back. My first wife, she tells me to sell these things. She says, 'Miklos, you could make a lot of money from these things in the attic.' But my grandfather forbids me to sell, and I don't listen to her. And then, my wife leaves me for a Russian soldier, and I start to think about these things again. I am broke, both my heart and my wallet. Sandor tells me he is worried about me, that I need to get out and back in shape. Back then, I am fat like Sandor. But no more." Miklos patted his flat stomach and glanced out the window. "I exercise and take long walks in hills. It is then I remember the story Margit has told us."

"She told you about the cave?"

"After Margit returned from Israel, she comes to visit my father and grandfather here. She has many stories, some about Katarina and how she rescued her and my aunts. How Katarina comes in an ambulance, Margit and the girls hide inside, and later in Commandant's car to Katarina's home near the lake. Margit says she takes with her several small Degas paintings and sews money and jewels into her clothes. She hides them with her in the cave. One day Margit says when Katarina returns from Russian prison, they will go and bring it home. But it does not happen. They are both very old, and I think they do not want to go back to the cave. And Margit says all that is left should go to Katarina for what she did."

"But you didn't think so." By now, it didn't matter what I said. Miklos knew I had been to the cave. He knew I was on to him.

"It was many years ago. My father and I think maybe we will go and find it, but then Hungary has a revolution. My father goes to fight against the Soviets, and he disappears. Years pass, and I don't think about the cave again. After my first wife leaves me, I wonder, maybe those things Margit hid are still in cave, and if I find them, I could sell and make money. I will not sell what is in attic because of my promise to my grandfather. But I don't make so much at the copy center, and I need money. Sandor works for his wife's uncle as truck driver when not doing tours, and he is doing fine. But me? I am broke, and I must support my grandfather."

"Are you saying you did this alone? That no one else knows anything about it? Not Sandor? Or Adolph?" I was pretty sure after having lunch with Adolph that he had no idea that anything of value remained in the cave, but the journalist in me required I check and verify. After Josh, I wasn't about to be taken in by another pretty face.

"The fewer people who know what I do, the better. Sandor had no idea. As for Adolph, he was just a boy. I doubt Katarina tells him all she has done or what she has hidden in the cave. And after the war, the Russians send both Adolph and his mother away—so the cave is empty. Katarina, they send to prison and Adolph to an orphanage. I am sure Katarina thinks if Russians find the cave that they will take everything. Just like they did when they left Hungary. Back then, I build a wall in the attic to hide what you see today. If not, the Russians steal it, too. As for Adolph, I doubt he ever goes back to the cave. But I knew where it was. Margit's description had been good, and it was easy to find. So I go to the cave and explore. I make many trips, and I find those things Margit had taken with her to hide, and others, too—small statues, jewelry, and furs. Things one might easily smuggle so that they do not fall into the hands of the Nazis. Do you know about the Gold Trains?"

Miklos explained that between boxcars filled with Jews, the Germans ran Gold Trains, trainloads full of artwork seized from the homes and galleries of those Jews sent to death camps. The Hungarian government had enacted a law requiring all Jews to hand over their art for safekeeping.

"The Jews who had seen their friends and neighbors rounded up and the Nazis invade their homes wanted to hide as many of their personal belongings as possible. Some hoped to use them to barter for their lives or hide somewhere safe and maybe come back later. But, of course, few did."

"So you moved what you found in the cave to the attic?"

"Not all." Miklos pointed to the picture above the bed. "Some like this Van Gogh is already here—hidden in the attic. When I found it, I researched and learned it is one of several Van Gogh had sent to his brother, an art dealer in Paris. It ends up here in Hungary in Baron Herzog's collection. But under Hungarian law, because Herzog is Jewish, the Nazis take many paintings and sculptures. Herzog is able to hide some and asks my grandmother to take this and several more paintings."

CHAPTER TWENTY-NINE

"Then it's real?" I looked over my shoulder.

"You wouldn't know, would you? Framed like it is with such heavy glass. Who'd believe I would have an original Van Gogh?"

I stood up and looked closely at what I had thought was a poorly framed print. Despite the heavy glass, the colors were vibrant. "If it is real, it's one of several self-portraits Van Gogh did toward the end of his life. I studied him in college. Van Gogh was a prolific artist. He painted and sketched more than two-thousand pieces of work in his lifetime."

"I see you know something of the art world. That could be useful."

"What do you mean?"

"I'm waiting for the right buyer. My grandfather no longer knows what is in the attic. I believe he has forgotten. And now that Hungary is no longer behind the Iron Curtain, it is possible to make contact with the Western world and those with money. But is not easy. After all, it is not like I can advertise."

"So, how do you find the right buyer?"

"At first, it was difficult. I started with one of the Degas I found in the cave. Because it was small, I could go to the copy center late at night after it was closed, and I copied one of Degas' sketches. There were several. Margit had a small collection. She had taken them out of their frames and slipped them beneath her clothes in her suitcase. Like I have with you."

"How convenient," I said.

"I didn't know much about Degas. But I knew just looking at the sketches of the ballerinas they were valuable. I did a little research and learned Degas had made a series of ballerinas sketches and that they were missing. I hung the copy in the store. Some people saw it and came in. I explained I am a big fan and made copies from an art book. But it was a subtle signal to anyone interested in such art. You'd be surprised how many people know someone willing to pay to own an original for their private gallery. I sell the sketch, and soon I make enough money to fix up my apartment, and I meet Nora. Women like Nora like money, and she thinks I am a rich man. She knows nothing, but it is her idea we make a guest room. She thinks it is a good business opportunity, and I think she is right."

"And you convince her to spy on me?"

Miklos shrugged.

"Sandor needed her help. When he tells me you are coming to Hungary to see your father's plane, he is worried he cannot find a hotel. And I think this is the perfect opportunity. I can help him, and he can help me. I have a buyer in America who wants the Degas and will give it a good home in his private gallery. All I need is a way to get it there."

"Who's the buyer?" I asked.

"Is better you not know." Miklos picked the Degas up off the bed and placed it back inside the envelope. "I tell Sandor if he likes, my guest room is finished, and I can make you a nice offer."

"Yeah, twenty dollars a day with breakfast. Very nice." I should have trusted my instincts.

"Sandor is a good man. All he wants is to know about you and Lieutenant Lawson. He thinks perhaps you are his sister."

"Right," I laughed sarcastically. "So he used Nora to read my journal. To learn about my father and me." I nodded to the red spiral notebook beneath the nightstand. "Her English is better than she lets on—as is yours, by the way."

"Nora used to work in a hotel for the concierge. She's quite proficient."

I should have known. The chocolates on my pillow at night, the fresh flowers in my room, the way Nora straightened up the room each day. Of course, she had worked in the hotel industry.

"And she shared with Sandor everything I wrote in my journal. And you, too, obviously."

"We all do what we have to do. And, if it helps to know, I am sorry to learn that your father's sick. I would have liked to meet him. But now I think, maybe I can help you, and you can help me."

"By smuggling art out of the country?"

"You need money. Your husband gambles, and you're about to lose your house. I have access to money, and there is very little risk. And all you need do is take the suitcase through customs, then check it, and it will disappear. The tags on the bag with your ID will be destroyed, and when you arrive home, you'll be told that your bag has been lost. You, of course, will fill out a description of the bag, and the airline will try to find it. Several days later, you'll get a call from the airline telling you a bag similar to that you filed a report on has been found and will be delivered to your residence. Meanwhile, I will have wired money into your account. It will be enough to hold off your creditors, and when you come back to Hungary, we can do it again."

"Again? You expect me to do this again?"

"Why not?" Miklos put the envelope with the Dega inside back into the bottom of the suitcase. Then secured the false bottom on top of it. "You have the perfect excuse. You've discovered you have family here and want to establish a relationship with them. Of course, if you decide differently, I could arrange for a DNA test that might convince you of your relationship with Sandor. We have an excellent lab here in Budapest. I could take your DNA and Sandor's to the lab and have the results mailed to you and your mother—"

"How dare you!"

"I'm afraid you don't have much choice. If you hadn't been so curious, you might never have suspected any of this. Unfortunately, you have, and I have no other options. You either go along, or I'm afraid you'll just disappear—tourists do you know. A young woman who travels alone and is too trusting of strangers, gypsies in particular." Miklos closed the suitcase and snapped the locks shut, then placed it back on the suitcase stand. "I'll leave you to think about it."

Chapter Thirty

Miklos shut the door behind him, and moments later, I heard Nora return with the baby. I opened the bedroom door a crack and listened as their muffled voices traveled up the staircase. Their conversation sounded strained, and I heard Nora mention Sandor's name several times.

Quietly, I shut the door and turned the lock. I had a lot of work to do and less than twenty-four hours to put my plan into action. I began by unpacking the souvenirs I had bought that afternoon while I sorted through my thoughts about Sandor.

The idea that Sandor and I could be related was absurd. My father had been married to my mother for fifty-five years. They had just celebrated their anniversary. My folks still had their wedding picture above the mantel in the living room. To my knowledge, my father had never done anything that might have caused my mother to doubt his fidelity. In my opinion, they were as close and happy as any two married people can be, and I envied them. I only wished I could have had such a match. They had their arguments, and I'm sure there had been some innocent flirtations along the way. Women found my dad attractive, but I never had a hint of any action on his part. Whereas my mother loved getting all dolled up, and men adored her. The only argument I ever remember their having was when my mother danced with Nick at a squadron reunion party at the Air Force Academy. Dad was upset about it. He felt Nick had been out of line and a little too flirtatious.

No. None of what Sandor said made any sense. If anyone was Sandor's father, it was Nick. Nick was the party boy, the womanizer. The one left inside the cave with the women who liked to flirt. It had to have been Nick. In my father's defense, Nora had searched my room and read my diary. Between what she had shared with Miklos and Sandor, they had fabricated a story to blackmail me. As for Sandor's birth date? It may have been November 4, 1945, but what proof did I have what he told me was the truth? Sandor didn't look like my father—and yet—there were similarities. He liked to draw and tell stories, and just like Dad and me, he was claustrophobic. But that didn't make us related. Even so, I didn't want to think about what a forged DNA report, like Miklos had threatened to send my mother, would do to my parents and the pain it would cause.

As for Sandor and Nora? If what Miklos told me was true, and they had no idea about what he was up to, then I'd deal with them later. But for now, I had work to do.

I started with the suitcase and removed the false bottom and the envelope with the Degas inside. I then exchanged the Degas with the picture of parliament I had bought that afternoon. I was about to put the envelope back inside the suitcase when I had a second idea and tore a piece of paper from my journal.

I scribbled a quick note. *Missing something? Call 602-555-0101.*

The number was for an automated answering service I had used while working undercover on stories for the newspaper. While the paper may have fired me, the service was good through the end of July. With any luck at all, the thief who found the poster would call the number—irate at finding the Degas had been removed and make all kinds of threats. I would then have their voice on tape to turn over to investigators and proof that Miklos had intended to use me as his mule. Which was exactly what I wanted.

I then put the envelope back inside the suitcase and sealed the false bottom. Satisfied it looked undisturbed, I slipped the Degas inside the roll-tube the picture of parliament had come in and tossed it on the bed for later use. Finally, I packed up most of my clothes, sans those I would wear for the next couple of days, and stuffed the souvenirs I had purchased on top, and closed the bag. Miklos may have spelled out his terms tonight, but tomorrow, I planned to surprise him with a few ideas of my own.

* * *

I woke up to the smell of muffins and showered quickly. I never considered myself much of an actress. I had taken several drama classes in high school, and while I never had anything beyond a supporting role, I did learn one thing. Acting is all about attitude. If you want the part, you have to sell it. And that was precisely what I intended to do that morning.

I bounded down the stairs with a big smile on my face. I wanted to appear at peace with my decision to do what I could to help Miklos, and I went directly to the kitchen. Miklos and Nora were quietly seated at the table, the old man at one end and the baby in his high chair next to his mother, quietly playing with a few loose blueberries on his tray. When Márkó saw me, he squealed and clenched his pudgy hands.

I patted the baby on his head and took an empty seat at the table.

Miklos looked up from the paper. "You look well, Kat."

"Thank you," I said. "I slept well. And this is for you." I took an envelope I had stuffed with American twenty-dollar bills from my jeans pocket and laid it on the table. "American, right?"

Miklos glanced inside, then folded the envelope over and slipped it in his pocket. "Thank you."

"You're welcome," I said. "Hopefully, this won't be my last visit. I've really enjoyed my stay, and I hope I can come back again. You've made me feel very at home."

"That would be nice," Miklos said. "I'm sure we can arrange that."

"Would you like a muffin?" Nora filled the coffee cup in front of me.

"Yes, please." Then looking at Miklos, I said, "I wonder if I might ask a favor? I've been thinking about Sandor, and I feel bad about how I left things yesterday. I know he's planning to come by with Aanika later this afternoon, and I wanted to get a copy of the sketch my father had done of Margit and the girls. I'd leave the original, but I'd like to get a copy for myself to show my dad. I think he might enjoy seeing it. I was wondering if we might visit the copy store where you work this morning?"

Miklos checked his watch. It wasn't yet nine. "I don't see why not. Store opens at ten. We can go first thing."

"Fabulous. Soon as I finish my breakfast, I'll run upstairs and get the sketch."

Miklos was easier to manipulate than I anticipated. We took a cab to Saint Stephen's, just across the street from the Copy Center where Miklos worked.

When we got there, I handed him the rolled tube with the Degas inside. He thought the tube contained the sketch of Margit and girls, and what he didn't know was about to surprise him.

"You mind if I don't go in with you? I didn't get any shots of St. Stephen's when I was here the other day. If it's okay with you, I'd really like to go in and take a few photos. I won't be long. I'll meet you inside the copy center in five."

"Take your time." Miklos took the tube, and I crossed the street, where I found Adrian waiting.

I crushed fifty dollars into his hand and told him to follow Miklos.

"When he opens the tube, you'll see an original Degas. Miklos will probably panic, and you'll have to act fast. Do something to draw attention to the painting. Miklos may try to leave, but don't let him. Grab the painting and—"

"And what? Run?"

"No. Holler for the police. There's a policeman standing guard outside Saint Stephen's. Once I know you've cornered Miklos, I'll alert him that I think something strange is going on inside the copy center. Any luck at all, he'll come running, see the Degas, and call for backup. When the police come, tell them when you saw the painting, and you got suspicious. If you play it right, they may even reward you."

Adrian laughed. "I doubt they reward gypsy. But, no worry, I know my way around. I see you again next trip."

Adrian was more confident about my return than I was. All I could think about was getting home. I dashed inside Saint Stephen's and waited until I felt certain Adrian would have approached Miklos and seen the Degas. Then, just as I had told Adrian I would, I ran back across the street and looked inside the copy center's window. I could see a small crowd had begun to surround Miklos and Adrian, and I screamed.

The policeman stationed outside the church looked at me. I pointed in the direction of the copy center, and the policeman pushed me aside. While the police ran into the copy center, I slipped casually into a café chair in front of Saint Stephens and sat back and prepared to watch as the action unfolded.

Within minutes I could hear the sound of sirens blaring, followed by the arrival of two police cars. I ordered a black coffee, and before the waiter appeared, the police had handcuffed Miklos and escorted him out of the copy center to a waiting car. Miklos saw me just as the waiter returned with my coffee. I took my camera from my bag, snapped a quick shot, and waved.

Chapter Thirty-One

I had one more errand to complete before I returned to the apartment. I wanted to get a copy of the sketch my father had made of Margit and the girls and give it to Sandor. Despite his lying to me, I felt he needed the picture. It would have some meaning to him, and I still needed to pay him for his time. I figured I could do both when he came by the apartment that afternoon and be done with him. I wasn't interested in hearing anything more about how he thought we might be related. His trick hadn't worked on me, and the sooner I paid him and bid him goodbye, the better.

I finished my coffee and waited until all the excitement inside the Copy Center had quieted down. Then walked across the street to the center. I made a single copy of the sketch, put it and the original back in my bag, and then hailed a cab to the riverfront. I wanted to take one final stroll along the river and paused long enough to take a few more pictures before returning to the apartment.

I decided not to mention anything to Nora about the arrest. Instead, I would tell her that I had left Miklos at the Copy Center and then done a little more sightseeing. If Miklos had been allowed to call Nora and told her otherwise, I'd play it by ear.

Soon as I entered the front door, I felt as though I had walked into an intervention.

Five people, Nora with the baby on her hip, Miklos' grandfather, Sandor, and Aanika, stared at me. All appeared to be in a state of shock. Hungary's legal system, like our own, allows an arrestee one phone call, and Miklos had called Nora. Like the old telephone game of gossip, Nora had called

Sandor, and Sandor called Aanika, and suddenly the house was full. And not just with family, but the police as well, who were in the middle of a search. They had turned over furnishings, opened drawers, and removed everything from the attic, plus taken several small framed oil paintings off the walls and the Van Gogh poster from above the bed in the guest room.

Upon seeing me, Nora threw herself into my arms. "They've arrested Miklos."

Obviously, Miklos had not explained the details of his arrest or my involvement.

"What?" I feigned surprise. Clearly, I was the only person in the room who knew what Miklos had been up to. Neither Nora nor Sandor had a clue. Nora was simply the wife Miklos wanted to impress, and Sandor had been nothing more than a convenient pawn for Miklos' black market venture.

"You didn't know?" Sandor took the baby from Nora's arms. "Weren't you with him? Nora said you had gone to the Copy Center together."

"I did," I said. I gently broke from Nora's embrace. "But I left Miklos outside so I could go across the street to Saint Stephen's. I wanted to get a few interior shots. I told him I'd meet him inside the Copy Center when I finished. But he was nowhere to be found when I came out. I figured he had probably been called away on business."

One of the policemen shoved a clipboard in front of Nora with a list of items they had taken and insisted she sign. Without checking, she scribbled her signature then took the baby back from Sandor.

"I don't know what's going on," she said. "I knew Miklos was up to something, but I thought it might have something to do with work. I can't imagine why the cops would arrest Miklos or what they think they'll find here?"

"Nora, please, sit down." Sandor put his arm around Nora and helped her to the couch. He and Aanika sat down on either side of her. "I don't know what Miklos is up to, but we're family. Whatever it is, you'll be okay. I promise."

The old man toddled back to his rocker, and everybody looked at me standing in the center of the room with nowhere to go.

I knew none of them had been aware of what Miklos had been up to. But I felt awkward standing in the middle of the room as though they were waiting for me to say or do something.

"What?" I asked. "What's the matter?"

It was Sandor who spoke first. "Kat, we need to finish the conversation we started the other day."

"Oh, stop." I held my hand up. "If you're trying to convince me you're my brother, I've heard all I want to hear. I don't mean to be rude, particularly after all that's just happened here with Miklos. But the truth is, Sandor, I've thought you've been up to something from the beginning. I had no idea what it was, but you and me," I pointed to him, then back to myself, "We are *not* related." I started to turn my back and was about to go upstairs. I didn't need to hear any more lies.

Sandor stood up. "Kat, wait, please. I know you think what I tell you is a lie. But your father, he is my father, too. I never wanted for you to find out about me. There was no need. All I wanted was to know about you and your father. I know this must be hard. When my grandmother tells me, I was surprised too. But somehow, I think I always knew. And then, before she dies... my grandmother gives this to me." Sandor took a metal chain with a soldier's dog tag from his pocket and handed it to me. "It was your father's."

Embedded on the plate was my father's full name, Steve Leslie Lawson, a middle name Sandor wouldn't have known. His blood type: O. Next of Kin: My mother's name, Lynn Ann Lawson. And religion: Protestant.

"The truth is, after the Russians leave, I make contact with your DOD. Before then, it is not possible. I ask DOD for information about your father's plane that I find near Tamasi. They give me the historian for your father's group, and she helps me make contact with Lieutenant Lawson. I write to him, and when he says he can not come but that you will come in his place, I am excited to meet you. And I arrange for you to stay here."

"So that Nora could spy on me?"

"Yes." Sandor bowed his head. "I not proud, but I want to know something about Lieutenant Lawson and what had happened after the war. And when I meet you, I am excited to know I have a sister, and I want to know all about you."

"And are you happy with what you've learned?" I fisted my father's ID in my hand.

"Most happy," he said.

I couldn't speak, and I closed my eyes. Maybe I should be happy too. I had always wanted a sibling. Perhaps this wasn't such bad news, just news I needed to digest slowly. After all, none of my suspicions about Sandor were true. He had been hiding something, but nothing as terrible as I had thought. He was just a man trying to find his past, and I was just a woman trying to find my future. And somehow, maybe we were going to help each other do that.

I opened my eyes and put the chain with my father's dog tag around my neck, then took the sketch my father had done of Margit and the girls from my bag.

"I should have left this with you yesterday. You're right, this is difficult for me. I'm still not sure what I should do with the news."

"Please, you don't need to tell anyone. I don't want anything from you or your father or to upset your mother."

I took several small pictures of my dad from my wallet. One, after he had graduated flight school and gotten his wings. The other, of him sitting in his easy chair, taken just weeks before I had left. I handed the first to Sandor.

"You look more like your mother," I said. "But you have a lot of my father's traits, your smile for one. It's slightly crooked. And like dad, you do love to tell stories."

"And I'm an artist, like he is."

"And a salesman, who never knows when to stop selling," I said.

Aanika laughed. "You mean you can't walk out of a room without him following you and trying to convince you of his idea."

"That's dad," I said.

We all laughed.

Sandor took the second photo from my hand. "And this is him now?"

"It is. Not quite so handsome, but still the same wonderful guy. Full of ideas and positive energy. There isn't anything he doesn't think I can do."

CHAPTER THIRTY-ONE

"I can see why," Sandor said.

"He always makes you believe in yourself." My cell phone rang before I could say anymore. "Excuse me, I need to take this."

Chapter Thirty-Two

"Kat, it's mom. You need to come home." I was standing by the stairs, my hand on the railing, when I heard my mother's voice on my cell. I knew before she could tell me the call was bad news. "Your father's taken a turn for the worse. The doctor wants him to go to the hospital, but he refuses. I'm worried, Kat. How soon can you get here?"

My hand slipped from the railing, and I sank to a sitting position on the bottom step.

"What's the matter?" Sandor helped me to my feet.

I clutched the phone to my chest. "I need to get home. Dad's taken a turn for the worse. How soon can I get a flight back?"

Sandor looked at his watch. "It's almost two. There's a flight from here to Frankfort at four-thirty. If you're lucky, you can book something from Frankfort and on to New York without much of a problem. But we need to leave now."

I told my mother I'd call her from the airport and to give Dad my love. I hung up and looked back at Sandor. "It won't take me but a minute to pack, and I'll be ready to go."

I took the stairs two at a time, grabbed the suitcase Nora had given me, and threw the few cosmetics I had left on the bathroom counter into my backpack. Minutes later, I was downstairs and said goodbye to my newfound family—viszontlátásra.

Sandor hurried me out the door, shoved the suitcase into the trunk of the red beast, and lit a cigarette as he got in the car.

I reached across the seat, took the cigarette from between his lips, then threw it out the window. "Promise me something,"

"What?"

"Stop smoking. Cigarettes and anything else, okay?" I didn't think I needed to expand. Weed wasn't legal, and tobacco wasn't healthy. "I'd like to think we might have a future together...and smoking's not good for you."

"Is this is how it's going to be to have a sister, eh?"

"Yeah. This is how it's going to be. Get used to it."

Sandor took the pack of cigarettes from his pocket and threw it out the window. "Alright, then. Let's get you to the airport."

Despite the beast's rusted rattle, we made it to the airport in record time. Rather than search for parking, Sandor hollered to one of the curbside police, stuffed several Hungarian forints into his hands, and said something I figured must be the equivalent of an emergency. Suddenly people parted ways in front of us, and we zipped through passport control and baggage check without a problem and then on to the airline window. The check-in person handed me a boarding pass, and the large leather bag Nora had given me was loaded onto the carousel for the flight home. Before I even knew what was happening, Sandor had exchanged my ticket for the last seat available on the next flight to Frankfort.

"Come on, we don't have a lot of time." Sandor grabbed my hand. "We need to hurry. The plane's loading now."

We raced, hand in hand, through the terminal to the gate, then stopped—both of us out of breath.

Sandor turned to me, panting and nearly doubled over with his hands on his knees. "I hope you'll be back, Kat. I'm sorry we met like this, but I'm not sorry about the way it turned out."

"Please," I put my hands on his shoulders. "I'm glad I know. I think that's why my Dad wanted me to come. He never said anything, but I think he must have known."

Sandor stood up, and I felt tears well in my eyes.

"You're family now," he said. "That is if that's what you want. You're welcome anytime."

The ticket agent announced the last boarding call.

Sandor hugged me. "Will you tell him about me?"

"I don't know yet." I stepped out from under his arm. "But I'll call, I promise."

I waved goodbye and hurried down the boarding gate and onto the plane. By the time I found my seat and sat down, I wondered what I would tell my father? Was it best to leave everything behind me, never say a word and spare a lot of awkward feelings and explanations for which I knew there were no easy answers?

I fastened my seatbelt, and I was about to turn off my phone when I realized I hadn't called Adolph to cancel our lunch.

The cabin steward hadn't finished securing the cabin, and I dialed his number. I felt lucky my call hadn't gone to his answering service. I didn't want my last message to him to be a voicemail. I smiled when I heard his voice.

"Adolph. Hi, it's Kat. I'm sorry. I'm not going to be able to have lunch with you tomorrow. I'm on a plane. I need to leave early, and there was no time—"

"You're leaving? So soon?" Adolph chuckled, "You Lawsons, you're always rushing out without a proper goodbye."

"It's my father. My mother called. I need to get back."

"Then I am sorry, too, Kat. Please, give him my best. And your mother as well. I know this isn't an easy time for you, but I hope you'll return. And when you do, maybe you won't be so quick to leave again."

My eyes started to well up. "Thank you."

Chapter Thirty-Three

Wednesday, July 24, 1996

Phoenix, Arizona

T he flight home was impossibly long. From Budapest, through Frankfort to New York and on to Phoenix, was nearly twenty-four hours. By the time the jet pulled up to Sky Harbor's gateway, it was Wednesday morning, seven a.m.

I didn't even bother to go by baggage claim. I knew without checking, my bag wouldn't be there.

I took a taxi from the airport and went directly to my folk's condo. I didn't know what to expect. Outside, things looked like they always did. The cactus gardens, with their gravel beds surrounding the pathways leading to my folk's small duplex, were all neatly combed. The Palo Verde trees, with their leaves like yellow gold, stood still in the heat. It was hot. A hundred and ten in the shade, and my mother's plastic wreath on the front door was dusty from the desert air.

I knocked on the door and walked in. It was freezing cold inside. Mom had cranked the air conditioning down, and the temperature difference was chilling.

"Mom, hi. It's me. I'm back. How's Dad?"

My mother appeared from the kitchen. She was wearing a red apron and had a spatula in her hand. Seeing me, she opened her arms wide, embraced me like she wasn't going to let go, and kissed me on the cheek.

"He's in the guest bedroom, Sweetie. Hospice has been here. They've been in and out all morning. I'm making snickerdoodles. I thought I'd make something nice for when they return. How are you, dear? How was your flight?"

"I'm fine. What's happened? Dad was doing fine before I left. I thought we had time."

"He didn't want you to know. I told you his doctor had started him on a new drug, but it wasn't working. After you left, your dad told the doctor he didn't want to keep trying. I thought he'd hold his own. You know how he is. Never complained or wanted anyone to know if he was sick. But he just started going downhill. And when we saw the doctor again, the doctor said it was time we called hospice. They brought a hospital bed in, and we decided it was best if he was in the guestroom. He's more comfortable there."

"Is he awake?"

"He should be. Go ahead. He'll be glad to see you. My cookies have a few more minutes. I'll bring some in when they're out of the oven."

I tip-toed to the guestroom door and knocked lightly. Dad was laid out on the hospital bed, the head raised slightly. A bible on his chest.

"Dad?"

"Kat? That you girl?"

I went to the edge of the bed, sat down, and took his hand. It felt cold.

"I'm back, Dad. How're you feeling?"

"I'm in good hands." He patted the bible on his chest. "Don't you worry about me. How was the trip?"

"I'm glad I went. Adolph and Katarina? They're fantastic." I reached into my bag and took out the picture Dad had sketched of Lake Balaton from the castle tower. "You recognize this? Katarina gave it to me. She wanted you to have it."

Dad reached for the sketch, his thin, frail hands shaking.

"Did I do this?" he asked.

"You did. It's the view from the fortress tower. Do you remember?"

He nodded.

"Katarina kept it all these years, along with another sketch you did of her with Adolph."

"How are they?"

"They're good. Really good. Adolph says he still remembers the stories you used to tell."

"He probably has a few of his own now."

"He does. And he told me some about Katarina. She was remarkable. I'm glad I met her. She's living by herself in a small apartment now. She walks with a cane, but her memory's intact, and she remembers you fondly."

I glanced over my shoulder, in the direction of the kitchen, where I could smell the cinnamon from mom's cookies in the oven. I had a few moments before I knew she would join us.

"Dad, there's something else Katarina gave me." I took the third sketch of Margit and the girls from my bag and held it up for him to see. "Do you remember drawing this?"

Dad's hands shook as he took the drawing from me. "That's Margit. And Roza. And Gizzy. Did Katarina tell you about them?"

"Adolph did," I said. "And after the war ended, they went back to Budapest. They found Margit's husband. He had been sent to a work camp, and they all went to Israel as soon as they could. Roza married a man she met there. He was a concentration camp survivor, and they had a son, and Gizzy went on to college."

"So they made it," Dad said.

"Yes." I paused to make sure my mother wasn't within earshot. What I had to say, I needed to share with Dad alone. "But that's not the end of the story. Several years later, Margit, her husband, and her grandson Sandor left Israel and returned to Hungary."

Dad stared at the sketch of the three women. "Not Roza?"

"No, Dad. Roza died, and her husband died as well. After Margit returned, she went back to Keszthely to see Katarina. Margit used to bring her grandson with her, and they kept in touch until Margit died several years ago. It was Margit's grandson who drew this."

I unfolded the final sketch I had in my bag and showed it to my father.

"What's this?"

"It's a drawing of your plane, Dad. Sandor drew it."

"Sandor? The tour guide?"

"Remarkable, isn't it? The style. The shading. If I didn't know better, I would have thought you drew it."

Dad paused and traced the lines of the drawing with his finger.

"Sandor was Roza's son, Dad. He was born in Israel six months after the war in Europe ended."

Dad put the sketch of the plane down and picked up the drawing of Margit and the girls. His eyes focused on Roza. "She was pregnant, then."

"She was." I touched my father's shoulder.

"And I must be—"

"His father. But he doesn't want anything. They don't need money. Sandor just needed to know who you were, and when he learned you were alive, he wanted to find out about you."

"It was so long ago, Kat. I never meant it to happen. It just did. Things happen during a war. Things you can't talk about. Some you want to forget, some you can't, and others you can't do anything about. In the end, when we left, it was so sudden. There was never time to look back, and I never told your mother. I could only hope they would be alright. For years I wondered, and when I never heard, I thought maybe the worst had happened."

"Sandor didn't want me to tell you. He begged me not to, but I thought you should know. He's a good man, Dad. A lot like you. He's an artist and a great storyteller. You'd be proud of him."

Dad closed his eyes. "You can't tell your mother."

"It's not my story to tell, Dad."

"What story are you two talking about now?" Mom stood in the doorway with a plate of freshly baked cookies. The sweet smell of cinnamon wafted into the room.

"Dad was just about to tell me what happened after he got across Lake Balaton," I said.

"The important thing was your father came home," Mom said, "and he wasn't hurt."

I tapped the end of the bed and nodded for my mother to sit down. "Maybe he wants to tell it again. I don't think I ever heard what happened."

"Your mom's right. What's important is that the war ended. I never wanted to dwell on it, and life here had its own demands."

"All right, I get it," I said. "You don't want to talk about how you escaped or got across Lake Balaton. That's probably classified information anyway. Right, Dad?" I winked.

"I'm not sure how classified any of that would be anymore, but getting across that lake was damn scary."

"I'd love to hear," I said.

Dad asked me to raise the head of the bed so he could sit up. Mom protested, but then when he asked for one of her cookies, she relented. He may have been weak, but he still loved to tell a story, and he wasn't going to be denied the opportunity.

"We had to row across the lake at night. Fortunately, from where we started on the north shore to the south side, the lake's not that wide. Nick was in bad shape with a broken leg, so the rowing was up to Bill and me. We all knew our lives depended upon our getting across that lake, so we probably set a rowing record."

I took a cookie from mom's plate. It was sweet and good to be home.

"Fortunately, the Russians picked us up once we got to the south side of the lake. I don't think they really trusted who we were at first. They thought we might have been Germans, and they took our guns. I had a 45 on me, and since I was the ranking officer, they took me to a schoolhouse in Dombovar, where I was questioned by a Russian with a big picture of Stalin behind him. The interpreter looked like he was a WW1 survivor who had been gassed, and he spoke English through a hole in his throat. My answers must have been okay because we went by truck to an area outside Pecs the next day. From there, we drove east toward the Danube and crossed over to a town called Baja, where we spent the night. The mayor of that town wanted to introduce me to his daughter. I think he was hoping to marry her off to an American."

"Steve," my mother scolded. "Don't tease."

Dad coughed, and I adjusted the pillow behind his back.

"Mom, don't be silly. We all know you've always been the only woman in Dad's life."

Dad finished the story. From Baja, the Russians loaded them onto a train to Timosar in Romania, and they stayed there for a couple of days. Then it was on to Bucharest, where they met up with the rest of their crew. It must have been a happy reunion from the way he talked about it. Seeing one another again. Knowing they had all survived. Bob, the pilot, and his co-pilot Mark and the rest of the crew didn't bail out as fast as Nick, Bill, and my dad had. Dad called them lucky stiffs. They had landed on the south side of Lake Balaton. Those couple of miles made all the difference. For almost two weeks, they holed up in private homes and schoolhouses until they all met up, and along with several other surviving crews that had also been shot down, they were then flown in a C-47 back to Bari, Italy. Once back to the base, they each got a week off, and then it was right back up in the air. They flew thirteen more missions before heading home.

"Excuse me." One of the hospice workers poked her head into the room. "We're back. How's our patient doing?"

"Thirsty," Dad said.

"Well, that's something we can fix," she said.

"Let me." Mom got up. "I made snickerdoodles. There's more on the counter. Help yourself."

Dad rested his head back against the pillow. "We're going to be fine, Kat. Death isn't so bad. Not when you've had a good life."

"Dad, please." I took his hand in mine. "Don't talk like that."

"Your mom's got all she'll need. You don't need to worry. And you've given me the answers I wanted. All but one."

"What's that, Dad?"

"What are you going to do now, Kat? And don't tell me you're going to try to patch things up with that jerk of a husband of yours."

"Not a chance. Turns out my affair probably did both Josh and me a favor. Gave him an excuse to leave and me space to think."

"And what is it you're thinking about?"

"I'm not quite sure. But you were right, the trip did me good. It opened my eyes to possibilities I didn't know I had."

"Like what, Kat?

"To start with, I have a brother I didn't know about, and maybe an opportunity. Probably more than I have here anyway. That is unless the only remaining paper in town plans to offer me a job, and I doubt that."

"You never know, Kat."

"Maybe not, but I've been thinking about something both you and Katarina said about never knowing what you can do until you have to do it. Seems to me both of you refused to let the war define you. Katarina not only lost a husband and her country, but she also lost her youth and her innocence. And you, you grew up quick. One moment you were a skinny kid in college, and the next thing you know, you're in the middle of a warzone, and a bunch of crazy Germans are trying to shoot you out of the sky, and you get saved by some little boy and his mother who you never would have known."

"And I named you after her."

"Yeah, you did." I wiped a tear from my eye.

"Bad things happen every day, Kat. Wars, natural catastrophes, financial difficulties, divorce. They can knock you down, but you don't have to stay there. It's not what happens to you. It's what you determine to make of it that matters. That's what makes you a stronger person."

"I see that now. And, I think you'll like what I've got in mind."

"Tell me."

"I've been playing around with going back to Hungary and writing travel features or maybe even a book."

"A book? My story, maybe?"

I laughed. Dad and Sandor both wanted me to write a book.

"Yours and maybe a few others. But don't worry, I'll change the names and places. Nobody will know it's your story."

"I think you'll do really well with that."

"And, I promised Adolph I'd give him a call when I return."

"Adolph, huh?" Dad smiled. "I like that idea. I always thought that boy would grow up to be a good man."

* * *

A few days later, the airline called. They had found my bag, exactly as Miklos said they would. I called the automated answering service, the same number I had included on the note I had hidden with the picture of parliament in the bottom of the suitcase. Sure enough, I had a call from an unknown caller who said he wanted to talk and left his number. He didn't need to say why he wanted to speak to me. But from the angst in his voice, I knew he wasn't happy. And since the bag didn't have any identification on it, I wasn't worried about him coming after me. I notified the FBI, they handle stolen art and cultural property crimes, and I told them about my experience in Hungary. They asked me to meet with them at their offices, and after explaining everything I knew and why I had gone to Hungary, they made me an attractive offer. They wanted me to return to Hungary to write travel features. Or at least that was to be my cover. It was a new beginning. One I never would have predicted.

A Note from the Author

When my father died, I was named executor of his affairs. As such, I spent a lot of time lost in a file cabinet full of important documents, and some, like the aging yellow sheets of a World War 2 flight log, were the inspiration to the book you have just read.

Dad was a WWII navigator/bombardier with a crew of ten aboard a B-24 stationed in Bari, Italy. He flew thirteen missions before being shot down over Linz, Austria, and Missing-In-Action for three weeks. Growing up, I heard bits and pieces of this story, but not all. Men of my father's generation seldom spoke of the war and returned to make a new and better life.

But in 1996, my dad received a letter from the Department of Defense informing him a young man in Hungary had written to them. He had found the remains of a B-24, included the tail numbers, and wished to contact the crew. The DOD did their homework and matched the plane's tail numbers to my father's fateful flight. And to my father's surprise, several weeks later, a letter appeared in his mailbox with a piece of the plane's thin skin.

Thus, my inspiration for *The Navigator's Daughter,* and the end of what was my father's story, and the beginning of the fictional story you have just read.

The day my father was shot down, March 2, 1945, the Germans had amassed their troops to retake Hungary. Hungary had changed sides and aligned herself with the Allied Powers. The Russian ground troops took a terrible toll in their efforts to drive out the German invaders. Fortunately, my father had bailed out south of Lake Balaton, within earshot of the battlefield, and safely behind the Russian lines.

But as I stared at the yellowed flight log in my hands, I thought…what if things had been different? What if my father had bailed out north of Lake

Balaton, where Hitler's troops stood at the ready? How different might his experience have been?

In March 1944, Hitler invaded Hungary. German forces occupied Budapest, and hundreds of thousands of Jews who thought they had evaded the worst of the war were rounded up, sent on trains to concentration camps.

And that's what fiction is. A novelist's leap into the unknown. A blend of history, fact, and imagination meld a story that might have been. While I've paid particular attention to important dates and historical facts, aside from German and Hungarian officials' names, the principal characters in this work are all fictional, a combination of those partisans and Jews who suffered under unbearable conditions.

Many thanks to the brave young men of the 15th Air Force, the 465th Bomb Group, and the 781st Squadron. You were my father's brothers.

781st Squadron. Left to right (top row) Bill Brigs, Engineer. Frank Donahue, Ball Gunner. Fred Wagner, Radio Engineer. Denny Horton, Nose Gunner.

Fran Quagon, Top Gunner. Leman Wood, Tail Gunner.

Bottom Row (Left to right) Dave Bowman, Navigator. Nick Schaps, Bombardier. Bob Frend, Pilot. Ken Parkhurst, co-Pilot.

Acknowledgements

No matter how many tormenting hours, weeks, or years it takes for an author to pull together their ideas and research for a book or as isolating as that process can be, it's never totally solitary. There are times when I know it feels so, but without the support and help of family, friends, readers, and editors, the letters on the page just wouldn't happen. And for that, I'm thankful to so many people who have supported me with a helpful ear, a cup of coffee, or a pat on the back.

The Navigator's Daughter is a work of fiction based on my father's experiences in the Second World War, but it never would have become a book without my father's guidance. I'm thankful to him, David Leslie Bowman, an outstanding father and role model, and the notes he left that inspired this book. I also want to thank the Pantanella News, the 781st Bomb Squadron's Newsletter, which still exists today and helped me research so much about the squadron and those last missions they flew toward the end of the war.

Most of all I want to thank my dad's crew and the outstanding men and women who made the ultimate sacrifice to help bring peace to a world in turmoil.

I would also like to thank the Pima Air and Space Museum in Tucson, Arizona, which still maintains a shining silver B24 Liberator and where I was able to actually walk beneath its wings.

As always, I'd like to thank my friend and first reader of anything I write, Rhona Robbie, who patiently listens to me as we hike together every week. I call Rhona, my walking therapist. She helps keep me on track—literally—and is the pat on the back I so often need.

My thanks to the Dames of Destruction at Level Best Books, Shawn Reilly

Simmons, who said yes to the idea of this book, and to my editors Verena Rose, and Harriette Sackler, who have been more than supportive.

To my kids, who I know scratch their heads every time I pitch a new idea. To Ali, my standard poodle companion who sits by my side and reminds me when it's time to take a break, and most importantly to my husband, Bruce Silverman, whose support and belief in me make this all possible.

781st Squadron. Left to right (top row) Bill Brigs, Engineer. Frank Donahue, Ball Gunner. Fred Wagner, Radio Engineer. Denny Horton, Nose Gunner. Fran Quagon, Top Gunner. Leman Wood, Tail Gunner.

Bottom Row (Left to right) Dave Bowman, Navigator. Nick Schaps, Bombardier. Bob Frend, Pilot. Ken Parkhurst, co-Pilot.

About the Author

Nancy Cole Silverman spent nearly twenty-five years in news and talk radio, beginning her career in college on the talent side as one of the first female voices on the air. Later on the business side in Los Angeles, she retired as one of two female general managers in the nation's second-largest radio market. After a successful career in the radio industry, Silverman retired to write fiction. Her short stories and crime-focused novels—the Carol Childs and Misty Dawn Mysteries,(Henery Press)—are both Los Angeles-based. Her newest series, *The Navigator's Daughter* (Level Best Books), takes a more international approach. Silverman lives in Los Angeles with her husband and a thoroughly pampered standard poodle.

SOCIAL MEDIA HANDLES:
  FACEBOOK: https://www.facebook.com/nancy.silverman.90/
  Twitter: @nancycolesilver
  EMAIL: Nancy@NancyColeSilverman.com

AUTHOR WEBSITE:
  www.nancycolesilverman.com

Also by Nancy Cole Silverman

The Carol Childs Mysteries

The Misty Dawn Mysteries

Numerous short stories

9 781685 120900